D1447138

Anticipations

Anticipations

edited by

CHRISTOPHER PRIEST

Charles Scribner's Sons

NEW YORK

823.0876
Anticipations...

Printed in Great Britain
Library of Congress Card Number 78–52223
ISBN 0 684 15634 2

Contents

Introduction

All the stories in this book are brand-new, and in almost every case have been written especially for it. What I believe is more important, though, is that this is not just a collection of short stories, but is more accurately described as a book of writers. Everyone in this book was invited to contribute because of my own very high regard for his work. The result is that here we have several of the best science fiction writers working today; each one has a reputation and a following of his own, and it's unnecessary for me to make extravagant claims for the stories. The publication of this book is the first occasion on which all these writers have been brought together under one roof, so to speak.

(I should mention in passing that there are other writers I should like to have included, but restrictions of space make it necessary for this to be a partial selection. I'm also sorry that there are no women writers here, as I should have liked to include some; there is nothing sinisterly anti-feminist about what could seem by intent to be an all-male preserve.)

I'm emphasizing the writerly nature of this book because I feel this has been an area of neglect in science fiction.

The friends of science fiction (of whom there are many) point with justification to the stimulating ideas it produces, and to its immediacy and its relevance to the modern world.

Those who dislike science fiction or ignore it (of whom there are many more) point with some justification to its sensationalist past or to its more blatant examples of hackneyed writing.

Both friend and foe (if that is the word) speak thus of science fiction in the abstract ... and it is perfectly possible to treat science fiction as something that can be identified and separated and discussed. One can say to a certain extent what it can do and what it can't, or what it is, and what it isn't. There's a general consensus on these matters, with enough marginal material to provide consternation and contention to those prepared to bend their minds around the problem. But whatever anyone says, science fiction does not have an actual existence, as a mountain, for instance, can be said to have an existence. It is much more like the name of a city: one can walk through a place collectively known as, say, "London", but no one building or street or person can be said to represent the distilled essence of Londonness.

(Probably the only concrete existence that science fiction enjoys is the labelling employed by publishers and booksellers to identify the category ... but isn't this similar to the signposts on city limits?)

It is also misleading to talk about the "rules" of science fiction, although a lot of breath is expended on this, particularly regarding the scientific content of sf. I once had the cheek to set one of my novels in the nineteenth century ("Is this the way science fiction should be going?" thundered a few of the critics, as if I was driving a train into the wrong tunnel), and at least two of the stories in this collection do not have strict scientific rationalizations. The rules of science fiction seem to me rather like the rules of grammar applied to literature: good writing is usually grammatical, but grammar alone does not make for good writing.

Literature and cultural evolution are the shapers and changers of what is considered grammatical, and so it is that our understanding of the abstract nature of science fiction should be shaped and changed by what is written.

Anyway, as Brian Aldiss said many years ago, all good sf hovers on the verge of being something other than sf.

If all this sounds slightly defensive, it is because the *abstract* nature of sf often comes in for dismissal from those who feel there are better things to do in life than read science fiction. (I remember watching a trendy academic on television dismiss science fiction as trashy popular culture, then excuse *The War of the Worlds*, *Nineteen Eighty-Four* and a handful of other titles, because they were, after all, by good writers.) It is sometimes said or implied, for instance, that the *genre* nature of science fiction entitles it to the same sort of literary dismiss-iveness one would accord to a Western or a romance, and thus the point is missed that the label is a publishing expedient and not a literary judgement. The good writers of science fiction have about as much in common with each other as do good writers of any other fiction (a fact which I hope will be clear from this book).

The readers, too, of science fiction are not what one would expect to find clustered around a category of fiction. Regular readers of romances take comfort from the reassuring famili-arity they find; Western readers are quickly disappointed if the writer does not supply them with the expected ritual of bar-room brawls, ranchers, six-guns and frontier violence. Most *genre*-writing is pitched at the same sort of intellectual level as television light-entertainment or series-drama, present-ing as its only innovations plot-twists or character-orientation. The audience for science fiction expects, and usually gets, fic-tion that presents narrative intrigue, emotional involvement, cerebral stimulation and a considerable element of surprise. There is also a large audience for writers who are ambitious with style and language, and who are as much concerned with literary values as they are with innovative concepts.

Of course, all this is equally true of the best general fiction ... but that isn't published with computer-typeface on the cover, and colourful renderings of exotic landscapes.

This is why I prefer to place the emphasis of this book on the contributors as individual writers, rather than on the "kind" of fiction they might be said to be writing. I hope you will therefore read and enjoy these stories in the same way as I did when they were sent to me: as the latest and newest work from some of the best science fiction writers of today.

A few words about the authors and their stories:

Ian Watson. Ian Watson and I often find ourselves at friendly odds with each other (he's unlikely to agree with much of what I have so far said in this Introduction, for instance), and our individual approaches to writing could hardly be more different. Nevertheless, I find myself in great admiration of most of his work. It is only a relatively short time since his first novel, the rightly acclaimed *The Embedding*, was published.

However, few authors have established themselves quite so quickly; by the time this book is published at least four of Watson's novels will be in print. His books have a Wagnerian quality to them, with immense clashings of intellectual bravura and cosmic event. (*The Jonah Kit*, for example, takes as a *secondary* proposition the idea that the Universe is illusory.) "The Very Slow Time Machine" seems at first sight, and perhaps on the strength of its title, to be one of those novelty-ideas that pop up from time to time, but before many pages have been turned it quickly becomes clear that the eponymous machine carries with it some awesome significance. I think it's a tremendously good story.

Robert Sheckley. It seems an extraordinary thing to say, but Robert Sheckley is one of the most seriously underrated writers in science fiction. The sf world is inordinately fond of giving prizes to its writers, and yet Sheckley, in more than a quarter-century of professional writing, has managed to achieve the paradoxical position of never having won a single major award, while at the same time being one of the most consistently popular and widely read authors. I suspect this is because his work accurately reflects the mood of the day, so that his virtues are appreciated only after the qualifying period for the Hugo or Nebula, or whatever, is long past. Sheckley writes with a deft combination of wit, cynicism and paranoia, thus evoking the unusual simultaneous response of laughter and nervous twitch. His collection *The Same to you Doubled* contains some of his best work. The story in this book, "Is *That* What People Do?", is Sheckley slightly to the left of centre, lighter on the satire than usual, but with his observation of the human animal as sharply focused as ever, and the paranoia standing by, ready to pounce on the reader on the way out.

Bob Shaw. Bob Shaw is the master of the telling detail and the evocative metaphor, by which I mean he has the enviable talent of persuading his readers of the most outrageous cosmic concepts by first persuading them of the truth of his characters, and later by writing about those characters and their adventures in unadorned and succinct prose that stimulates, but does not belabour, the imagination. This kind of writing has honourable precedents in science fiction—notably in the work of John Wyndham and Arthur C. Clarke—but for my money Shaw has a better imagination than one of them, and is a better writer than the other. Of his novels, I like *Orbitsville* and *A Wreath of Stars* the best; his collections of short stories are also worth finding. Writing about "Amphitheatre", the story in this book, Shaw says: "This story is one of the most personal I've ever written, one which tries to express an emotion rather than an intellectual concept." Hearing this, some will be surprised to discover that this story, of all those here, is the one that lies closest to the traditional heart of science fiction: adventure on an alien planet. It is typical of Shaw that he should treat his subject-matter in such a way.

Christopher Priest. I can't pretend that my story in this book does not exist, so allow me to enjoy the indulgence of writing about myself. My first novel was published in 1970, and since then there have been four others. Perhaps my best-known book is *Inverted World* (for which one critic adroitly labelled me "hyperbolist without exaggeration"), but the one I like best myself—though probably for the wrong reasons—is *The Space Machine* (the one where I took the train into the wrong tunnel). My most recent novel is *A Dream of Wessex*. I wrote "The Negation" especially for this book (because I'm the boss), and it's part of a series I'm presently working through, about a world where the islands known as the Dream Archipelago are the dominant physical feature.

Harry Harrison. There are two literary manifestations of Harry Harrison: one as an anarchically funny writer, and one deeply serious. His serious work, though, does not have the po-faced solemnity of the clown playing Hamlet, for he always writes with pace and flair, and a crispness of image; his novel *A Transatlantic Tunnel, Hurrah!* is one of his best. He has written one of the most compelling novels on overpopulation, *Make Room! Make Room!* (later filmed, with passing fidelity to the text, as *Soylent Green*), and, more recently, a long novel about an Apollo/Soyuz disaster, *Skyfall*. His humorous writing includes *Bill, the Galactic Hero*, his novels about the Stainless Steel Rat and *Star Smashers of the Galaxy Rangers* (which last sends up just about every cliché of the space-adventure, a type of story not short on clichés). "The Greening of the Green" falls somewhere between the two: the jokes are fired from the hip, but beneath the hail is a straightforward science fiction idea. The fact that Harrison is now a resident of Ireland is not coincidental to the story.

Thomas M. Disch. Tom Disch is a writer of such extreme precision and delicacy that it is entirely possible to enjoy his work for the qualities of the prose alone (a statement partly supported by the fact that a book-length structuralist critical study by Samuel R. Delany of one of Disch's short stories, "Angouleme", will be published in the United States soon). Disch is also a poet, and a volume of his poetry, *The Right Way to Figure Plumbing*, has been published in the States. Like many science fiction writers, Disch is intrigued by the possibilities of the subject-matter, and his extant body of work constitutes a remarkable achievement. His first novel, *The Genocides*, was an utterly bleak and pessimistic story about the destruction of the human species, relieved by astonishing passages of mordant wit; other novels have included the philosophically complex *Camp Concentration* and perhaps his best novel so far, *334* (of which "Angouleme" was a part). "Mutability", included here, is not a short story as such (although it can certainly be read as one) but is an extract from *The Pressure of Time*, one of two science fiction novels he is writing at the moment.

J. G. Ballard. My first awareness of J. G. Ballard's fiction was when he was a regular contributor to the British sf magazine *New Worlds* in the early 1960s. His haunting stories—a blend of the naggingly familiar and the bizarrely surreal—were, in their day, outstanding, and time has not diminished them; most of them are still in print in his many story-collections. Ballard first drew critical attention, notably from Kingsley Amis, for his three "disaster" novels, *The Drowned World, The Drought* and *The Crystal World*, but for me his later novels are more successful. One of them—*Crash*, published in 1973— strikes me as one of the most extraordinary and original novels of any kind published in the last five years or so. Ballard's work is remarkable for the intensity and uniqueness of vision: his obsessed protagonists, moving towards a kind of psychic fulfilment through a landscape cluttered with the rusting technology and abandoned arte- facts of a corrupt society, are archetypal modern men. Ballard's fiction will one day be seen as a most accurate literary reflection of the late twentieth century. "One Afternoon at Utah Beach", which I am delighted to publish here, has a pleasing hardness at its core that is as memorable as the starkness of the author's images.

Brian W. Aldiss. Brian Aldiss has had a great influence on science fiction (which he would probably try to deny), both in terms of the approach to the writing of it, and in the way sf writers address themselves to the world at large. He was, for instance, one of the first writers of real literary ability to stand up and say, in no uncertain terms, that he was a *science fiction* writer. Although he has published general fiction (*The Hand- Reared Boy* was a famous success) and has written on art, travel and drama, and published a long history of science fiction, it is probably his sf that will be seen as his major work. From the beginning, Aldiss has been a stylist, and his best work celebrates the English language with an infectious joy. The novels of his I have particularly enjoyed, and continue to admire, are *Non-Stop, Greybeard, A Soldier Erect* and the glorious *Frankenstein Unbound.* His short stories too have been exceptional; a good selection can be found in *The Best SF Stories of Brian W. Aldiss.* Recently, Aldiss has been writing novella-length stories, and "A Chinese Perspective" is the latest. I believe this is amongst the best of his recent work: a wry and humorous story, which, in spite of apparent whim- sicalities, leads to a serious and complex philosophical dilemma.

I'd like to close by expressing gratitude and respect to my publisher, Charles Monteith, whose help and friendly co- operation with the preparation of the book made this whole enterprise possible.

IAN WATSON

■■■

The Very Slow Time Machine

(1990)

The Very Slow Time Machine—for convenience: the VSTM*
—made its first appearance at exactly midday 1 December 1985
in an unoccupied space at the National Physical Laboratory. It
signalled its arrival with a loud bang and a squall of expelled
air. Dr. Kelvin, who happened to be looking in its direction,
reported that the VSTM did not exactly *spring* into existence
instantly, but rather expanded very rapidly from a point source,
presumably explaining the absence of a more devastating explo-
sion as the VSTM jostled with the air already present in the
room. Later, Kelvin declared that what he had actually seen
was the *implosion* of the VSTM. Doors were sucked shut by the
rush of air, instead of bursting open, after all. However it was a
most confused moment—and the confusion persisted, since the
occupant of the VSTM (who alone could shed light on its
nature) was not only time-reversed with regard to us, but also
quite crazy.

One infuriating thing is that the occupant visibly grows saner
and more presentable (in his reversed way) the more that time
passes. We feel that all the hard work and thought devoted to
the enigma of the VSTM is so much energy poured down the
entropy sink—because the answer is going to come from him,
from inside, not from us; so that we may as well just have bided
our time until his condition improved (or, from his point of
view, began to degenerate). And in the meantime his arrival
distorted and perverted essential research at our laboratory from
its course without providing any tangible return for it.

The VSTM was the size of a small caravan; but it had the

* *The term VSTM is introduced retrospectively in view of our subsequent understanding of the problem (2019).*

shape of a huge lead sulphide, or galena, crystal—which is, in crystallographers' jargon, an octahedron-with-cube formation consisting of eight large hexagonal faces with six smaller square faces filling in the gaps. It perched precariously—but immovably—on the base square, the four lower hexagons bellying up and out towards its waist where four more squares (oblique, vertically) connected with the mirror-image upper hemisphere, rising to a square north pole. Indeed it looked like a kind of world globe, lopped and sheered into flat planes: and has remained very much a separate, private world to this day, along with its passenger.

All faces were blank metal except for one equatorial square facing southwards into the main body of the laboratory. This was a window—of glass as thick as that of a deep-ocean diving bell—which could apparently be opened from inside, and only from inside.

The passenger within looked as ragged and tattered as a tramp; as crazy, dirty, woe-begone and tangle-haired as any lunatic in an ancient Bedlam cell. He was apparently very old; or at any rate long solitary confinement in that cell made him seem so. He was pallid, crookbacked, skinny and rotten-toothed. He raved and mumbled soundlessly at our spotlights. Or maybe he only mouthed his ravings and mumbles, since we could hear nothing whatever through the thick glass. When we obtained the services of a lipreader two days later the mad old man seemed to be mouthing mere garbage, a mishmash of sounds. Or was he? Obviously no one could be expected to lipread backwards; already Dr. Yang had suggested from his actions and gestures that the man was time-reversed. So we videotaped the passenger's mouthings and played the tape backwards for our lipreader. Well, it was still garbage. Backwards, or forwards, the unfortunate passenger had visibly cracked up. Indeed, one proof of his insanity was that he should be trying to talk to us at all at this late stage of his journey rather than communicate by holding up written messages—as he has now begun to do. (But more of these messages later; they only begin—or, from his point of view, *cease* as he descends further into madness—in the summer of 1989.)

Abandoning hope of enlightenment from him, we set out on

the track of scientific explanations. (Fruitlessly. Ruining our other, more important work. Overturning our laboratory projects—and the whole of physics in the process.)

To indicate the way in which we wasted our time, I might record that the first "clue" came from the shape of the VSTM which, as I said, was that of a lead sulphide or galena crystal. Yang emphasized that galena is used as a semiconductor in crystal rectifiers: devices for transforming alternating current into direct current. They set up a much higher resistance to an electric current flowing in one direction than another. Was there an analogy with the current of time? Could the geometry of the VSTM—or the geometry of energies circulating in its metal walls, presumably interlaid with printed circuits—effectively impede the forward flow of time, and reverse it? We had no way to break into the VSTM. Attempts to cut into it proved quite ineffective and were soon discontinued; while X-raying it was foiled, conceivably by lead alloyed in the walls. Sonic scanning provided rough pictures of internal shapes, but nothing as intricate as circuitry; so we had to rely on what we could see of the outward shape, or through the window—and on pure theory.

Yang also stressed that galena rectifiers operate in the same manner as diode valves. Besides transforming the flow of an electric current they can also *demodulate*. They separate information out from a modulated carrier wave—as in a radio or TV set. Were we witnessing, in the VSTM, a machine for separating out "information"—in the form of the physical vehicle itself, with its passenger—from a carrier wave stretching back through time? Was the VSTM a solid, tangible analogy of a three-dimensional TV picture, played backwards?

We made many models of VSTMs based on these ideas and tried to send them off into the past, or the future—or anywhere for that matter! They all stayed monotonously present in the laboratory, stubbornly locked to our space and time.

Kelvin, recalling his impression that the VSTM had seemed to expand outward from a point, remarked that this was how three-dimensional beings such as ourselves might well perceive a four-dimensional object first impinging on us. Thus a 4-D sphere would appear as a point and swell into a full sphere then contract again to a point. But a 4-D octahedron-and-cube? According to our maths this shape couldn't have a regular analogue in 4-space, only a simple octahedron could. Besides, what would be the use of a 4-D time machine which shrank to a point at precisely the moment when the passenger needed to mount it? No, the VSTM wasn't a genuine four-dimensional body; though we wasted many weeks running computer programs to describe it as one, and arguing that its passenger was a normal 3-space man imprisoned within a 4-space structure— the discrepancy of one dimension between him and his vehicle effectively isolating him from the rest of the universe so that he could travel hindwards.

That he was indeed travelling hindwards was by now absolutely clear from his feeding habits (i.e. he regurgitated) though his extreme furtiveness about bodily functions coupled with his filthy condition meant that it took several months before we were positive, on these grounds.

All this, in turn, raised another unanswerable question: if the VSTM was indeed travelling backwards through time, precisely where did it *disappear* to, in that instant of its arrival on 1 December 1985? The passenger was hardly on an archeological jaunt, or he would have tried to climb out.

At long last, on midsummer day 1989, our passenger held up a notice printed on a big plastic eraser slate.

CRAWLING DOWNHILL, SLIDING UPHILL!

He held this up for ten minutes, against the window. The printing was spidery and ragged; so was he.

This could well have been his last lucid moment before the final descent into madness, in despair at the pointlessness of trying to communicate with us. Thereafter it would be *downhill all the way*, we interpreted. Seeing us with all our still eager, still baffled faces, he could only gibber incoherently thenceforth like an enraged monkey at our sheer stupidity.

He didn't communicate for another three months.

When he held up his next (i.e. penultimate) sign, he looked slightly sprucer, a little less crazy (though only comparatively so, having regard to his final mumbling squalor).

THE LONELINESS! BUT LEAVE ME ALONE!
IGNORE ME TILL 1995!

We held up signs (to which, we soon realized, his sign was a response):

ARE YOU TRAVELLING BACK THROUGH TIME? HOW? WHY?

We would have also dearly loved to ask: WHERE DO YOU DISAPPEAR TO ON DEC 1 1985? But we judged it unwise to ask this most pertinent of all questions in case his disappearance was some sort of disaster; so that we would in effect be foredooming him, accelerating his mental breakdown. Dr. Franklin insisted that this was nonsense; he broke down *anyway*. Still, if we *had* held up that sign, what remorse we would have felt: because we *might* have caused his breakdown and ruined some magnificent scientific undertaking. . . . We were certain that it had to be a magnificent undertaking to involve such personal sacrifice, such abnegation, such a cutting off of oneself from the rest of the human race. This is about all we were certain of.

(1995)

No progress with our enigma. All our research is dedicated to solving it; but we keep this out of sight of him. While rotas of postgraduate students observe him round the clock, our best brains get on with the real thinking elsewhere in the building. He sits inside his vehicle, less dirty and dishevelled now, but monumentally taciturn: a trappist monk under a vow of silence. He spends most of his time re-reading the same dog-eared books, which have fallen to pieces back in our past: Defoe's *Journal of the Plague Year* and *Robinson Crusoe* and Jules Verne's *Journey to the Centre of the Earth;* and listening to what is presumably taped music—which he shreds from the cassettes back in 1989, flinging streamers around his tiny living quarters in a brief mad fiesta (which of course we see as a sudden frenzy of disentangling and repackaging, with maniacal speed and neatness, of tapes which have lain around, trodden underfoot, for years).

Superficially we have ignored him (and he, us) until 1995: assuming that his last sign had some significance. Having got nowhere ourselves, we expect something from him now.

Since he is cleaner, tidier and saner now, in this year 1995 (not to mention ten years younger) we have a better idea of how old he actually is; thus some clue as to when he might have started his journey.

He must be in his late forties or early fifties—though he aged dreadfully in the last ten years, looking more like seventy or eighty when he reached 1985. Assuming that the future does not hold in store any longevity drugs (in which case he might be a century old, or more!) he should have entered the VSTM sometime between 2010 and 2025. The later date, putting him in his very early twenties if not teens, does rather suggest a "suicide volunteer" who is merely a passenger in the vehicle. The earlier date suggests a more mature researcher who played a major role in the development of the VSTM and was only prepared to test it on his own person. Certainly, now that his madness has abated into a tight, meditative fixity of posture, accompanied by normal activities such as reading, we incline to think him a man of moral stature rather than a time-kamikaze; so we put the date of commencement of the journey around 2010 to 2015 (only fifteen to twenty years ahead) when he will be in his thirties.

Besides theoretical physics, basic space science has by now been hugely sidetracked by his presence.

The lead hope of getting man to the stars was the development of some deep-sleep or refrigeration system. Plainly this does not exist by 2015 or so—or our passenger would be using it. Only a lunatic would voluntarily sit in a tiny compartment for decades on end, ageing and rotting, if he could sleep the time away just as well, and awake as young as the day he set off. On the other hand, his life-support systems seem so impeccable that he can exist for decades within the narrow confines of that vehicle using recycled air, water and solid matter to 100 per cent efficiency. This represents no inconsiderable outlay in research and development—which must have been borrowed from another field; obviously the space sciences. Therefore the astronauts of 2015 or thereabouts require very long-term life support systems capable of sustaining them for years and decades, up and awake. What kind of space travel must they be engaged in, to need these? Well, they can only be going to the stars—the slow way; though not a *very* slow way. Not hundreds of years; but decades. Highly dedicated men must be spending many years cooped up alone in tiny spacecraft to reach Alpha Centaurus, Tau Ceti, Epislon Eridani or wherever. If their surroundings are so tiny, then any extra payload costs prohibitively. Now who would contemplate such a journey merely out of curiosity? No one. The notion is ridiculous—*unless* these heroes are carrying something to their destination which will then link it inexorably and instantaneously with Earth. A tachyon descrambler is the only obvious explanation. They are carrying with them the other end of a tachyon-transmission system for beaming material objects, and even living human beings, out to the stars!

So, while one half of physics nowadays grapples with the problems of reverse-time, the other half, funded by most of the money from the space vote, pre-empting the whole previously extant space programme, is trying to work out ways to harness and modulate tachyons.

These faster-than-light particles certainly *seem* to exist; we're fairly certain of that now. The main problem is that the technology for harnessing them is needed *beforehand*, to prove that they do exist and so to work out exactly *how* to harness them.

All these reorientations of science—because of *him* sitting in his enigmatic vehicle in deliberate alienation from us, reading *Robinson Crusoe*, a strained expression on his face as he slowly approaches his own personal crack-up.

(1996)

If you were locked up in a VSTM for X years, would you want a calendar on permanent display—or not? Would it be consoling or taunting? Obviously his instruments are calibrated—unless it was completely fortuitous that his journey ended on 1 December 1985 at precisely midday! But can he see the calibrations? Or would he prefer to be overtaken suddenly by the end of his journey, rather than have the slow grind of years unwind itself? You see, we are trying to explain why he did not communicate with us in 1995.

Convicts in solitary confinement keep their sanity by scratching five-barred gates of days on the walls with their fingernails;

the sense of time passing keeps their spirits up. But on the other hand, tests of time perception carried out on potholers who volunteered to stay below ground for several months on end show that the internal clock lags grossly—by as much as two weeks in a three month period. Our VSTM passenger might gain a reprieve of a year—or five years!—on his total subjective journey time, by ignoring the passing of time. The potholers had no clue to night and day; but then, neither does he! Ever since his arrival, lights have been burning constantly in the laboratory; he has been under constant observation. . . .

He isn't a convict, or he would surely protest, beg to be let out, throw himself on our mercy, give us some clue to the nature of his predicament. Is he the carrier of some fatal disease—a disease so incredibly infectious that it must affect the whole human race, unless he were isolated? Which can only be isolated by a time capsule? Which even isolation on the Moon or Mars would not keep from spreading to the human race? He hardly appears to be. . . .

Suppose that he had to be isolated for some very good reason, and suppose that he concurs in his own isolation (which he visibly does, sitting there reading Defoe for the *n*th time), what demands this unique dissection of one man from the whole continuum of human life and from his own time and space? Medicine, psychiatry, sociology, all the human sciences are being drawn in to the problem in the wake of physics and space science. Sitting there doing nothing, he has become a kind of funnel for all the physical and social sciences: a human black hole into which vast energy pours, for a very slight increase in our radius of understanding. That single individual has accumulated as much disruptive potential as a single atom accelerated to the speed of light—which requires all the available energy in the universe to sustain it in its impermissible state.

Meanwhile the orbiting tachyon laboratories report that they are just on the point of uniting quantum mechanics, gravitational theory and relativity; whereupon they will at last "jump" the first high-speed particle packages over the C-barrier into a faster-than-light mode, and back again into our space. But they reported *that* last year—only to have their particle packages "jump back" as antimatter, annihilating five billion dollars' worth of equipment and taking thirty lives. They hadn't jumped into a tachyon mode at all, but had "möbiused" themselves through wormholes in the space-time fabric.

Nevertheless, prisoner of conscience (his own conscience, surely!) or whatever he is, our VSTM passenger seems nobler year by year. As we move away from his terminal madness, increasingly what strikes us is his dedication, his self-sacrifice (for a cause still beyond our comprehension), his Wittgensteinian spirituality. "Take him for all in all, he is a Man. We shall not look upon his like. . . ." Again? We shall look upon his like. Upon the man himself, gaining stature every year! That's the wonderful thing. It's as though Christ, fully exonerated as Son of God, is uncrucified and his whole life re-enacted before our eyes in full and certain knowledge of his true role. (Except . . . that this man's role is silence.)

(1997)

Undoubtedly he is a holy man who will suffer mental crucifixion for the sake of some great human project. Now he re-reads Defoe's *Plague Year*, that classic of collective incarceration and the resistance of the human spirit and human organizing ability. Surely the "plague" hint in the title is irrelevant. It's the sheer force of spirit which beat the Great Plague of London, that is the real keynote of the book.

Our passenger is the object of popular cults by now—a focus for finer feelings. In this way his mere presence has drawn the world's peoples closer together, cultivating respect and dignity, pulling us back from the brink of war, liberating tens of thousands from their concentration camps. These cults extend from purely fashionable manifestations—shirts printed with his face, now neatly shaven in a Vandyke style; rings and worry-beads made from galena crystals—through the architectural (octahedron-and-cube meditation modules) to life-styles themselves: a Zen-like "sitting quietly, doing nothing".

He's Rodin's *Thinker*, the *Belvedere Apollo*, and Michelangelo's *David* rolled into one for our world as the millennium draws to its close. Never have so many copies of Defoe's two books and the Jules Verne been in print before. People memorize them as meditation exercises and recite them as the supremely lucid, rational Western mantras.

The National Physical Laboratory has become a place of pilgrimage, our lawns and grounds a vast camping site— Woodstock and Avalon, Rome and Arlington all in one. About the sheer tattered degradation of his final days less is said; though that has its cultists too, its late twentieth-century anchorites, its Saint Anthonies pole-squatting or cave—immuring themselves in the midst of the urban desert, bringing austere spirituality back to a world which appeared to have lost its soul—though this latter is a fringe phenomenon; the general keynote is nobility, restraint, quiet consideration for others.

And now he holds up a notice.

I IMPLY NOTHING. PAY NO ATTENTION TO MY PRESENCE. KINDLY GET ON DOING YOUR OWN THINGS. I CANNOT EXPLAIN TILL 2000.

He holds it up for a whole day, looking not exactly angry, but slightly pained. The whole world, hearing of it, sighs with joy at his modesty, his self-containment, his reticence, his humility. This must be the promised 1995 message, two years late (or two years early; obviously he still has a long way to come). Now he is Oracle; he is the Millennium. This place is Delphi.

The orbiting laboratories run into more difficulties with their tachyon research; but still funds pour into them, private donations too on an unprecedented scale. The world strips itself of excess wealth to strip matter and propel it over the interface between sub-light and trans-light.

The development of closed-cycle living-pods for the carriers of those tachyon receivers to the stars is coming along well; a fact which naturally raises the paradoxical question of whether his presence has in fact stimulated the development of the technology by which he himself survives. We at the National Physical Laboratory and at all other such laboratories around the world are convinced that we shall soon make a breakthrough in our understanding of time-reversal—which, intuitively, should connect with that other universal interface in the realm of matter, between our world and the tachyon world—and we feel too, paradoxically, that our current research must surely lead to the development of the VSTM which will then become so opportunely necessary to us, for reasons yet unknown. No one feels they are wasting their time. He is the Future. His presence here vindicates our every effort—even the blindest of blind alleys.

What kind of Messiah must he be, by the time he enters the VSTM? How much charisma, respect, adoration and wonder must he have accrued by his starting point? Why, the whole world will send him off! He will be the focus of so much collective hope and worship that we even start to investigate *Psi* phenomena seriously: the concept of group mental thrust as a hypothesis for his mode of travel—as though he is vectored not through time or 4-space at all but down the waveguide of human will-power and desire.

(2001)

The millennium comes and goes without any revelation. Of course that is predictable; he is lagging by a year or eighteen months. (Obviously he can't see the calibrations on his instruments; it was his choice—that was his way to keep sane on the long haul.)

But finally, now in the autumn of 2001, he holds up a sign, with a certain quiet jubilation:

WILL I LEAVE 1985 SOUND IN WIND & LIMB?

Quiet jubilation, because we have already (from his point of view) held up the sign in answer:

YES! YES!

We're all rooting for him passionately. It isn't really a lie that we tell him. He did leave relatively sound in wind and limb. It was just his mind that was in tatters. . . . Maybe that is inessential, irrelevant, or he wouldn't have phrased his question to refer merely to his physical body.

He must be approaching his take-off point. He's having a mild fit of tenth-year blues, first decade anxiety, self-doubt; which we clear up for him. . . .

Why doesn't he know what shape he arrived in? Surely that

must be a matter of record before he sets off. . . . . *No!* Time
can not be invariable, determined. Not even the Past. Time
is probabilistic. He has refrained from comment for all these
years so as not to unpluck the strands of time past and reweave
them in another, undesirable way. A tower of strength he has
been. *Ein' feste Burg ist unser Zeitgänger!* Well, back to the
drawing board, and to probabilistic equations for (a) tachyon-
scatter out of normal space (b) time-reversal.

A few weeks later he holds up another sign, which must be
his promised Delphic revelation:

I AM THE MATRIX OF MAN.

Of course! Of course! He has made himself that over the
years. What else?

A matrix is a mould for shaping a cast. And indeed, out of
him have men been moulded increasingly since the late 1990s,
such has been his influence.

Was he sent hindwards to save the world from self-slaughter
by presenting such a perfect paradigm—which only frayed and
tattered in the Eighties when it did not matter any more; when
he had already succeeded?

But a matrix is also an array of components for translating
from one code into another. So Yang's demodulation of information hypothesis is revived, coupled now with the idea that
the VSTM is perhaps a matrix for transmitting the "information" contained in a man across space and time (and the man-
transmitter experiments in orbit redouble their efforts); with
the corollary (though this could hardly be voiced to the enraptured world at large) that perhaps the passenger was *not
there* at all in any real sense; and he had never been; that we
merely were witnessing an experiment in the possibility of
transmitting a man across the galaxy, performed on a future
Earth by future science to test out the degradation factor: the
decay of information—mapped from space on to time so that
it could be observed by us, their predecessors! Thus the onset
of madness (i.e. information decay) in our passenger, timed in
years from his starting point, might set a physical limit in
light-years to the distance to which man could be beamed
(tachyonically?). And this was at once a terrible kick in the teeth

to space science—and a great boost. A kick in the teeth, as this suggested that physical travel through interstellar space must be impossible, perhaps because of Man's frailty in face of cosmic ray bombardment; and thus the whole development of intensive closed-cycle life-pods for single astronaut couriers must be deemed irrelevant. Yet a great boost too, since the possibility of a receiverless transmitter loomed. The now elderly Yang suggested that 1 December 1985 was actually a moment of lift-off to the stars. Where our passenger went then, in all his madness, was to a point in space thirty or forty light-years distant. The VSTM was thus the testing to destruction of a future man-beaming system and practical future models would only deal in distances (in times) of the order of seven or eight years. (Hence no other VSTMs had imploded into existence, hitherto.)

(2010)
I am tired with a lifetime's fruitless work; however the human race at large is at once calmly loving—and frenetic with hope. For we must be nearing our goal. Our passenger is in his thirties now (whether a live individual, or only an epiphenomenon of a system for transmitting the information present in a human being: literally a "ghost in the machine"). This sets a limit. It sets a limit. He couldn't have set off with such strength of mind much earlier than his twenties or (I sincerely hope not) his late teens. Although the teens *are* a prime time for taking vows of chastity, for entering monasteries, for pledging one's life to a cause. . . .

(2015)
Boosted out of my weariness by the general euphoria, I have successfully put off my retirement for another four years. Our passenger is now in his middle twenties and a curious inversion in his "worship" is taking place, representing (I think) a subconscious groundswell of anxiety as well as joy. Joy, obviously, that the moment is coming when he makes his choice and steps into the VSTM, as Christ gave up carpentry and stepped out from Nazareth. Anxiety, though, at the possibility that he may pass beyond this critical point, towards infancy; ridiculous as

this seems! He knows how to read books; he couldn't have taught himself to read. Nor could he have taught himself how to speak *in vitro*—and he has certainly delivered lucid, if mysterious, messages to us from time to time. The hit song of the whole world, nevertheless, this year is William Blake's "*The Mental Traveller*" set to sitar and gongs and glockenspiel . . .

> *For as he eats and drinks he grows*
> *Younger and younger every day;*
> *And on the desert wild they both*
> *Wander in terror and dismay . . .*

The unvoiced fear represented by this song's sweeping of the world being that he may yet evade us; that he may slide down towards infancy, and at the moment of his birth (whatever life-support mechanisms extrude to keep him alive till then!) the VSTM will implode back whence it came: sick joke of some alien superconsciousness, intervening in human affairs with a scientific "miracle" to make all human striving meaningless and pointless. Not many people feel this way openly. It isn't a popular view. A man could be torn limb from limb for espousing it in public. The human mind will never accept it; and purges this fear in a long song of joy which at once mocks and copies and adores the mystery of the VSTM.

Men put this supreme *man* into the machine. Even so, Madonna and Child does haunt the world's mind. . . . and a soft femininity prevails—men's skirts are the new soft gracious mode of dress in the West. Yet he is now so noble, so handsome in his youth, so glowing and strong; such a Zarathustra, locked up in there.

(2018)

He can only be 21 or 22. The world adores him, mothers him, across the unbridgeable gulf of reversed time. No progress in the Solar System, let alone on the interstellar front. Why should we travel out and away, even as far as Mars, let alone Pluto, when a revelation is at hand; when all the secrets will be unlocked here on Earth? No progress on the tachyon or negative-time fronts, either. Nor any further messages from him. But he *is* his own message. His presence alone is sufficient to express Mankind: hopes, courage, holiness, determination.

(2019)

I am called back from retirement, for he is holding up signs again: the athlete holding up the Olympic Flame.

He holds them up for half an hour at a stretch—as though we are not all eyes agog, filming every moment in case we miss something, anything.

When I arrive, the signs that he has already held up have announced:

(*Sign One*) THIS IS A VERY SLOW TIME MACHINE. (And I amend accordingly, crossing out all the other titles we had bestowed on it successively, over the years. For a few seconds I wonder whether he was really naming the machine— defining it—or complaining about it! As though he'd been fooled into being its passenger on the assumption that a time machine should proceed to its destination *instanter* instead of at a snail's pace. But no. He was naming it.) TO TRAVEL INTO THE FUTURE, YOU MUST FIRST TRAVEL INTO THE PAST, ACCUMULATING HINDWARD POTENTIAL. (THIS IS CRAWLING DOWNHILL.)

(*Sign Two*) AS SOON AS YOU ACCUMULATE ONE LARGE QUANTUM OF TIME, YOU LEAP FORWARD BY THE SAME TIMESPAN *AHEAD* OF YOUR STARTING POINT. (THIS IS SLIDING UPHILL.)

(*Sign Three*) YOUR JOURNEY INTO THE FUTURE TAKES THE SAME TIME AS IT WOULD TAKE TO LIVE THROUGH THE YEARS IN REAL-TIME; YET YOU ALSO *OMIT* THE INTERVENING YEARS, ARRIVING AHEAD INSTANTLY. (PRINCIPLE OF CON- SERVATION OF TIME.)

(*Sign Four*) SO, TO LEAP THE GAP, YOU MUST CRAWL THE OTHER WAY.

(*Sign Five*) TIME DIVIDES INTO ELEMENTARY QUANTA. NO MEASURING ROD CAN BE SMALLER THAN THE INDI- VISIBLE ELEMENTARY ELECTRON; THIS IS ONE "ELEMENTARY

LENGTH" (*EL*). THE TIME TAKEN FOR LIGHT TO TRAVEL ONE *EL* IS "ELEMENTARY TIME" (*ET*): I.E. 10^{-23} SECONDS; THIS IS ONE ELEMENTARY QUANTUM OF TIME. TIME CONSTANTLY LEAPS AHEAD BY THESE TINY QUANTA FOR EVERY PARTICLE; BUT, NOT BEING SYNCHRONIZED, THESE FORM A CONTINUOUS TIME-OCEAN RATHER THAN SUCCESSIVE DISCRETE "MOMENTS", OR WE WOULD HAVE NO CONNECTED UNIVERSE.

(*Sign Six*) TIME REVERSAL OCCURS NORMALLY IN STRONG NUCLEAR INTERACTIONS I.E. IN EVENTS OF ORDER 10^{-23} SECS. THIS REPRESENTS THE "FROZEN GHOST" OF THE FIRST MOMENT OF UNIVERSE WHEN AN "ARROW OF TIME" WAS FIRST STOCHASTICALLY DETERMINED.

(*Sign Seven*) (And this is when I arrived, to be shown Polaroid photographs of the first seven signs. Remarkably, he is holding up each sign in a linear sequence from *our* point of view; a considerable feat of forethought and memory, though no less then we expect of him.) NOW, THE "BIG NUMBERS" OF UNIVERSE ARE ALL RELATED; THUS PRESENT SIZE OF UNIVERSE IS 10^{40} *EL*, THE PRESENT AGE IS 10^{40} *ET*. *ET* IS INVARIABLE & FROZEN IN; YET UNIVERSE AGES. AT ANY POINT IN TIME IT IS *X* TIMES *ET* OLD. ($T = X \times ET$.) *X* EQUALS *ET* TIMES THE RADIUS OF UNIVERSE (*R*) DIVIDED BY RATE OF EXPANSION $\left(X = \frac{ET \times R}{r} \right) = 35$ YEARS, AT PRESENT.

(*Sign Eight*) CONSTRUCT AN "ELECTRON SHELL" BY SYNCHRONIZING ELECTRON REVERSAL. THE LOCAL SYSTEM WILL THEN FORM A TIME-REVERSED MINI-COSMOS & PROCEED HINDWARDS TILL *X* ELAPSES WHEN TIME CONSERVATION OF THE TOTAL UNIVERSE WILL PULL THE MINI-COSMOS (OF THE VSTM) FORWARD INTO MESH WITH UNIVERSE AGAIN I.E. BY 35 PLUS 35 YEARS.

"But how?" we all cried. "How do you synchronize such an infinity of electrons? We haven't the slightest idea!"

Now at least we knew when he had set off: from 35 years after 1985. From *next year*. We are supposed to know all this by next year! Why has he waited so long to give us the proper clues?

And he is heading for the year 2055. What is there in the year 2055 that matters so much?

(*Sign Nine*) I DO NOT GIVE THIS INFORMATION TO YOU BECAUSE IT WILL LEAD TO YOUR *INVENTING* THE VSTM. THE SITUATION IS QUITE OTHERWISE. TIME IS PROBABILIS-TIC, AS SOME OF YOU MAY SUSPECT. I REALIZE THAT I WILL PROBABLY PERVERT THE COURSE OF HISTORY & SCIENCE BY MY ARRIVAL IN YOUR PAST (MY MOMENT OF DEPARTURE FOR THE FUTURE); IT IS IMPORTANT THAT YOU DO NOT KNOW YOUR PREDICAMENT TOO EARLY, OR YOUR FRANTIC EFFORTS TO AVERT IT WOULD GENERATE A TIME LINE WHICH WOULD UNPREPARE YOU FOR MY SETTING OFF. AND IT IS IMPORTANT THAT IT DOES ENDURE, FOR I AM THE MATRIX OF MAN. I AM THE HUMAN RACE. I AM LEGION. I SHALL CONTAIN MULTITUDES.

MY RETICENCE IS SOLELY TO KEEP THE WORLD ON TOL-ERABLY STABLE TRACKS SO THAT I CAN TRAVEL BACK ALONG THEM. I TELL YOU THIS OUT OF COMPASSION, AND TO PREPARE YOUR MINDS FOR THE ARRIVAL OF GOD ON EARTH.

"He's insane. He's been insane from the start."

"He's been isolated in there for some very good reason. Contagious insanity, yes."

"Suppose that a madman could project his madness—"

"He already has done that, for decades!"

"—no, I mean really project it, into the consciousness of the whole world; a madman with a mind so strong that he acted as a template, yes a matrix for everyone else, and made them all his dummies, his copies; and only a few people stayed immune who could build this VSTM to isolate him—"

"But there isn't time to research it now!"

"What good would it do shucking off the problem for another thirty-five years? He would only reappear—"

"Without his strength. Shorn. Senile. Broken. Starved of his connections with the human race. Dried up. A mental leech. Oh, he tried to conserve his strength. Sitting quietly. Reading, waiting. But he broke! Thank God for that. It was vital to the future that he went insane."

"Ridiculous! To enter the machine next year he must

already be alive! He must already be out there in the world projecting this supposed madness of his. But he isn't. We're all separate sane individuals, all free to think what we want—"

"*Are we?* The whole world has been increasingly obsessed with him these last twenty years. Fashions, religions, lifestyles: the whole world has been skewed by him ever since he was born! He must have been born about twenty years ago. Around 1995. Until then there was a lot of research into him. The tachyon hunt. All that. But he only began to *obsess* the world as a spiritual figure after that. From around 1995 or 6. When he was born as a baby. Only, we didn't focus our minds on his own infantile urges—because we had him here as an adult to obsess ourselves with—"

"Why should he have been born with infantile urges? If he's so unusual, why shouldn't he have been born already leeching on the world's mind; already knowing, already experiencing everything around him?"

"Yes, but the real charisma started then! All the emotional intoxication with him!"

"All the mothering. All the fear and adoration of his infancy. All the Bethlehem hysteria. Picking up as he grew and gained projective strength. We've been just as obsessed with Bethlehem as with Nazareth, haven't we? The two have gone hand in hand."

(*Sign Ten*) I AM GOD. AND I MUST SET YOU FREE. I MUST CUT MYSELF OFF FROM MY PEOPLE; CAST MYSELF INTO THIS HELL OF ISOLATION.

I CAME TOO SOON; YOU WERE NOT READY FOR ME.

We begin to feel very cold; yet we cannot feel cold. Something prevents us—a kind of malign contagious tranquillity.

It is all so *right*. It slots into our heads so exactly, like the missing jigsaw piece for which the hole lies cut and waiting, that we know what he said is true; that he is growing up out there i n our obsessed, blessèd world, only waiting to come to us.

(*Sign Eleven*) (Even though the order of the signs was time-reversed from his point of view, there was the sense of a real dialogue now between him and us, as though we were both synchronized. Yet this wasn't because the past was inflexible, and he was simply acting out a role he knew "from history". He was really as distant from us as ever. It was the looming presence of *himself* in the real world which cast its shadow on us, moulded our thoughts and fitted our questions to his responses; and we all realized this now, as though scales fell from our eyes. We weren't guessing or fishing in the dark any longer; we were being dictated to by an overwhelming presence of which we were all conscious—and which wasn't locked up in the VSTM. The VSTM was Nazareth, the setting-off point; yet the whole world was also Bethlehem, womb of the embryonic God, his babyhood, childhood and youth combined into one synchronous sequence by his all-knowing-ness, with the accent on his wonderful birth that filtered through into human consciousness ever more saturatingly.)

MY OTHER SELF HAS ACCESS TO ALL THE SCIENTIFIC SPECULATIONS WHICH I HAVE GENERATED; AND ALREADY I HAVE THE SOLUTION OF THE TIME EQUATIONS. I SHALL ARRIVE SOON & YOU SHALL BUILD MY VSTM & I SHALL ENTER IT; YOU SHALL BUILD IT INSIDE AN EXACT REPLICA OF THIS LABORATORY, ADJACENT TO THIS LABORATORY, SOUTHWEST SIDE. THERE IS SPACE THERE. (Indeed it had been planned to extend the National Physical Laboratory that way, but the plans had never been taken up, because of the skewing of all our research which the VSTM had brought about.) WHEN I REACH MY TIME OF SETTING OUT, WHEN TIME REVERSES, THE PROBABILITY OF THIS LABORATORY WILL VANISH, & THE OTHER WILL ALWAYS HAVE BEEN THE TRUE LABORATORY THAT I AM IN, INSIDE THIS VSTM. THE WASTE LAND WHERE YOU BUILD, WILL NOW BE HERE. YOU CAN WITNESS THE INVERSION; IT WILL BE MY FIRST PROBABILISTIC MIRACLE. THERE ARE HYPERDIMENSIONAL REASONS FOR THE PROB-ABILISTIC INVERSION, AT THE INSTANT OF TIME REVERSAL. BE WARNED NOT TO BE INSIDE *THIS* LABORATORY WHEN I SET OUT, WHEN I CHANGE TRACKS, FOR THIS SEGMENT OF REALITY HERE WILL ALSO CHANGE TRACKS, BECOMING IMPROBABLE, SQUEEZED OUT.

(*Sign Twelve*) I WAS BORN TO INCORPORATE YOU IN MY BOSOM; TO UNITE YOU IN A WORLD MIND, IN THE PHASE

SPACE OF GOD. THOUGH YOUR INDIVIDUAL SOULS PERSIST, WITHIN THE FUSION. BUT YOU ARE NOT READY. YOU MUST BECOME READY IN 35 YEARS' TIME BY FOLLOWING THE MENTAL EXERCISES WHICH I SHALL DELIVER TO YOU, MY MEDITATIONS. IF I REMAINED WITH YOU NOW, AS I GAIN STRENGTH, YOU WOULD LOSE YOUR SOULS. THEY WOULD BE SUCKED INTO ME, INCOHERENTLY. BUT IF *YOU* GAIN STRENGTH, I CAN INCORPORATE YOU COHERENTLY WITHOUT LOSING YOU. I LOVE YOU ALL, YOU ARE PRECIOUS TO ME, SO I EXILE MYSELF.

THEN I WILL COME AGAIN IN 2055. I SHALL RISE FROM TIME, FROM THE USELESS HARROWING OF A LIMBO WHICH HOLDS NO SOULS PRISONER, FOR YOU ARE ALL HERE, ON EARTH.

That was the last sign. He sits reading again and listening to taped music. He is radiant; glorious. We yearn to fall upon him and be within him.

We hate and fear him too; but the Love washes over the Hate, losing it a mile deep.

He is gathering strength outside somewhere: in Wichita or Washington or Woodstock. He will come in a few weeks to reveal himself to us. We all know it now.

And then? Could we kill him? Our minds would halt our hands. As it is, we know that the sense of loss, the sheer bereavement of his departure hindwards into time will all but tear our souls apart.

And yet . . . I WILL COME AGAIN IN 2055, he has promised. And incorporate us, unite us, as separate thinking souls—if we follow all his meditations; or else he will suck us into him as dummies, as robots if we do not prepare ourselves. What then, when God rises from the grave of time, *insane*?

Surely he knows that he will end his journey in madness! That he will incorporate us all, as conscious living beings, into the matrix of his own insanity?

It is a fact of history that he arrived in 1985 ragged, jibbering and lunatic—tortured beyond endurance by being deprived of us.

Yet he demanded, jubilantly, in 1997, confirmation of his

A—B

safe arrival; jubilantly, and we lied to him and said YES!
YES! And he must have believed us. (Was he already going
mad from deprivation?)

If a laboratory building can rotate into the probability of
that same building adjacent to itself: if time is probabilistic
(which we can never prove or disprove concretely with any
measuring rod, for we can never see *what has not been*, all
the alternative possibilities, though they might have been) we
have to wish what we know to be the truth, not to have been
the truth. We can only have faith that there will be another
probabilistic miracle, beyond the promised inversion of
laboratories that he speaks of, and that he will indeed arrive
back in 1985 calm, well-kept, radiantly sane, his mind com-
posed. And what is this but an entrée into madness for rational
beings such as us? We must perpetrate an act of madness; we
must believe the world to be other than what it was—so that
we can receive among us a Sane, Blessèd, Loving God in
2055. A fine preparation for the coming of a mad God! For if
we drive ourselves mad, believing passionately what was not
true, will we not infect him with our madness, so that he is/has
to be/will be/and always was mad too?

Credo quia impossible; we have to believe because it is
impossible. The alternative is hideous.

Soon He will be coming. Soon. A few days, a few dozen
hours. We all feel it. We are overwhelmed with bliss.

Then we must put Him in a chamber, and lose Him, and
drive Him mad with loss, in the sure and certain hope of a
sane and loving resurrection thirty years hence—so that He
does not harrow Hell, and carry it back to Earth with Him.

ROBERT SHECKLEY

ooooooooooooooooooooooooooooooooooooooooo

Is *That* What People Do?

Eddie Quintero had bought the binoculars at Hammerman's Army & Navy Surplus of All Nations Warehouse Outlet ("Highest Quality Goods, Cash Only, All Sales Final"). He had long wanted to own a pair of really fine binoculars, because with them he hoped to see some things that he otherwise would never see. Specifically, he hoped to see girls undressing at the Chauvin Arms across the street from his furnished room.

But there was also another reason. Without really acknowledging it to himself, Quintero was looking for that moment of vision, of total attention, that comes when a bit of the world is suddenly framed and illuminated, permitting the magnified and extended eye to find novelty and drama in what had been the dull everyday world.

The moment of insight never lasts long. Soon you're caught up again in your habitual outlook. But the hope remains that something—a gadget, a book, a person—will change your life finally and definitively, lift you out of the unspeakable silent sadness of yourself, and permit you at last to behold the wonders which you always knew were there, just beyond your vision.

The binoculars were packed in a sturdy wooden box stencilled, "Section XXII, Marine Corps, Quantico, Virginia". Beneath that it read, "Restricted Issue". Just to be able to open a box like that was worth the $15.99 that Quintero had paid.

Inside the box were slabs of styrofoam and bags of silica, and then, at last, the binoculars themselves. They were like nothing Quintero had ever seen before. The tubes were square rather than round, and there were various incomprehensible scales engraved on them. There was a tag which read, "Experimental —Not to be Removed from the Testing Room".

Quintero hefted them. The binoculars were heavy, and he

could hear something rattle inside. He removed the plastic protective cups and pointed the binoculars out of the window.

He saw nothing. He shook the binoculars and heard the rattle again. But then the prism or mirror or whatever was loose must have fallen back into place, because suddenly he could see.

He was looking across the street at the mammoth of the Chauvin Arms. The view was exceptionally sharp and clear: he felt he was standing about ten feet away from the exterior of the building. He scanned the nearest apartment windows quickly, but nothing was going on. It was a hot Saturday afternoon in July, and Quintero supposed that all the girls had gone to the beach.

He turned the focus knob, and he had the sensation that he was moving, a disembodied eye riding the front of a zoom lens, closer to the apartment wall, five feet away, then one foot away and he could see little flaws in the white concrete front and pit-marks on the anodized aluminium window frames. He paused to admire this unusual view, and then turned the knob again very gently. The wall loomed huge in front of him, and then suddenly he had gone completely through it and was standing inside an apartment.

He was so startled that he put down the binoculars for a moment to orient himself.

When he looked through the glasses again, it was just as before: he seemed to be inside an apartment. He caught a glimpse of movement to one side, tried to locate it, and then the part rattled and the binoculars went dark.

He turned and twisted the binoculars, and the part rattled up and down, but he could see nothing. He put the binoculars on his dinette table, heard a soft clunking sound, and bent down to look again. Evidently the mirror or prism had again fallen back into place, for he could see.

He decided to take no chances of jarring the part again. He left the glasses on the table, knelt down behind them and looked through the eyepieces.

He was looking into a dimly lighted apartment, curtains drawn and the lights on. There was an Indian sitting on the floor, or, more likely, a man dressed as an Indian. He was a skinny blond man with a feathered headband, beaded moccasins, fringed buckskin pants, leather shirt, and a rifle He was holding the rifle in firing position, aiming at something in a corner of the room.

Near the Indian was a fat woman in a pink slip. She was sitting in an armchair and talking with great animation into a telephone.

Quintero could see that the Indian's rifle was a toy, about half the length of a real rifle.

The Indian continued to fire into the corner of the room, and the woman kept on talking into the telephone and laughing.

After a few moments the Indian stopped firing, turned to the woman and handed her his rifle. The woman put down the telephone, found another toy rifle propped against her chair and handed it to the Indian. Then she picked up his gun and began to reload it, one imaginary cartridge at a time.

The Indian continued firing with great speed and urgency. His face was tight and drawn, the face of a man who is single-handedly protecting his tribe's retreat into Canada.

Suddenly the Indian seemed to hear something. He looked over his shoulder. His face registered panic. He twisted around suddenly, swinging his rifle into position. The woman also looked, and her mouth opened wide in astonishment. Quintero tried to pick up what they were looking at, but the dinette table wobbled and the binoculars clicked and went blank.

Quintero stood up and paced up and down his room. He had had a glimpse of what people do when they're alone and unobserved. It was exciting, but confusing because he didn't know what it meant. Had the Indian been a lunatic, and the woman his keeper? Or were they more or less ordinary people playing some sort of harmless game? Or had he been watching a pathological killer in training; a sniper who, in a week or a month or a year would buy a real rifle and shoot down real people until he himself was killed? And what happened there at the end? Had that been part of the charade, or had something else occurred, something incalculable?

There was no answer to these questions. All he could do was see what else the binoculars would show him.

He planned his next move with greater care. It was crucial that the binoculars be held steady. The dinette table was too wobbly to risk putting the binoculars there again. He decided to use the low coffee-table instead.

The binoculars weren't working, however. He jiggled them around, and he could hear the loose part rattle. It was like one of those puzzles where you must put a little steel ball into a certain hole. But this time he had to work without seeing either the ball or the hole.

Half an hour later he had had no success, and he put the glasses down. He smoked a cigarette, drank a beer, then jiggled them again. He heard the part fall solidly into place, and he lowered the glasses gently on to a chair.

He was sweaty from the exertion and so he stripped to the waist, then bent down and peered into the eyepieces. He adjusted the focus knob with utmost gentleness, and his vision zoomed across the street and through the outer wall of the Chauvin Arms.

He was looking into a large formal sitting-room decorated in white, blue and gold. Two attractive young people were seated on a spindly couch, a man and a woman. Both were dressed in period costumes. The woman wore a billowing gown cut low over her small round breasts. Her hair was done up in a mass of ringlets. The man wore a long black coat, fawn-grey knee-pants, and sheer white stockings. His white shirt was embroidered with lace, and his hair was powdered.

The girl was laughing at something he had said. The man bent closer to her, then kissed her. She stiffened for a moment, then put her arms around his neck.

They broke their embrace abruptly, for three men had just entered the room. They were dressed entirely in black, wore black stocking-masks over their heads, and carried swords. There was a fourth man behind them, but Quintero couldn't make him out.

The young man sprang to his feet and took a sword from the wall. He engaged the three men, circling around the couch while the girl sat in frozen terror.

The fourth man stepped into the circle of vision. He was tall and gaudily dressed. Jewelled rings flashed on his fingers, and a diamond pendant hung from his neck. He wore a white wig. The girl gasped when she saw him.

The young man put one of his opponents out of action with a sword-thrust to the shoulder, then leaped lightly over the couch to prevent another man from getting behind him. He held his two opponents at bay with apparent ease. The fourth man watched for a moment, then took a dagger from beneath his waistcoat and threw it. It hit the young man butt-first on the forehead.

He staggered back and one of the masked men lunged. His blade caught the young man in the chest, bent, then straightened as it slid in between the ribs. The young man looked at it for a moment, then fell, blood welling over his white shirt.

The girl fainted. The fourth man said something, and one of the masked men lifted the girl, while the other helped his wounded companion. They all exited, leaving the young man sprawled bleeding on the polished parquet floor.

Quintero turned the glasses to see if he could follow the others. The loose part clattered and the glasses went dark.

Quintero heated up a can of soup and stared at it thoughtfully, thinking about what he had seen. It must have been a rehearsal for a scene in a play. . . . But the sword-thrust had looked real, and the young man on the floor had looked badly hurt, perhaps dead.

Whatever it had been, he had been privileged to watch a private moment in the strangeness of people's lives. He had seen another of the unfathomable things that people do.

It gave him a giddy, godlike feeling, this knowledge that he could see things that no one else could see.

The only thing that sobered him was the extreme uncertainty of the future of his visions. The binoculars were broken, a vital part was loose, and all the marvels might stop for good at any moment.

He considered taking the glasses somewhere to get them fixed. But he knew that he would probably succeed only in getting back a pair of ordinary binoculars, which would show him ordinary things very well, but he could not be expected to see through solid walls into strange and concealed matters.

He looked through the glasses again, saw nothing, and began to shake and manipulate them. He could hear the loose part rolling and tumbling around, but the lenses remained dark. He kept on manipulating them, eager to see the next wonder.

The part suddenly fell into place. Taking no chances this time, Quintero put the glasses on his carpeted floor. He lay down beside them, put his head to one side and tried to look through one eyepiece. But the angle was wrong, and he could see nothing.

He started to lift the glasses gently, but the part moved a little and he put them down again. Light was still shining through the lenses, but no matter how he turned and twisted his head he could not get lined up with the eyepiece.

He thought about it for a moment, and saw only one way out of his difficulty. He stood up, straddled the glasses, and bent down with his head upside down. Now he could see through the eyepieces, but he couldn't maintain the posture. He straightened up and did some more thinking.

He saw what he had to do. He took off his shoes, straddled the binoculars again, and performed a headstand. He had to do this several times before his head was positioned correctly in front of the eyepieces. He propped his feet against the wall and managed to get into a stable position.

He was looking into a large office somewhere in the interior of the Chauvin Arms. It was a modern, expensively furnished room, windowless, indirectly lighted.

There was only one man in the room: a large, well-dressed man in his fifties, seated behind a blonde-wood desk. He sat quite still, evidently lost in thought.

Quintero could make out every detail of the office, even the little mahogany plaque on the desk that read: "Office of the Director. The Buck Stops Here".

The Director got up and walked to a wall-safe concealed behind a painting. He unlocked it, reached in and took out a metal container somewhat larger than a shoebox. He carried this to his desk, took a key out of his pocket and unlocked it.

He opened the box and removed an object wrapped in a silky red cloth. He removed the cloth and set the object on his desk. Quintero saw that it was a statue of a monkey, carved in what looked like dark volcanic rock.

It was a strange-looking monkey, however, because it had four arms and six legs.

Then the Director unlocked a drawer in his desk, took out a long stick, placed it in the monkey's lap, and lit it with a cigarette lighter.

Oily black coils of smoke arose, and the Director began to dance around the monkey. His mouth was moving, and Quintero guessed that he was singing or chanting. He kept this up for about five minutes, and then the smoke began to coalesce and take form. Soon it had shaped itself into a replica of the monkey, but magnified to the size of a man, an evil-looking thing made of smoke and enchantment.

The smoke-demon (as Quintero named it) held a package in one of his four hands. He handed this to the Director, who took it, bowed deeply, and hurried over to his desk. He ripped open the package and a pile of papers spilled over his desk. Quintero could see bundles of currency, and piles of engraved papers that looked like stock certificates.

The director tore himself away from the papers, bowed low once again to the smoke-demon, and spoke to it. The mouth of the smoky figure moved, and the Director answered him. They seemed to be having an argument.

Then the Director shrugged, bowed again, went to his intercom and pressed a button.

An attractive young woman came into the room with a steno pad and pencil. She saw the smoke-demon and her mouth widened into a scream. She ran to the door but was unable to open it.

She turned and saw the smoke-demon flowing towards her, engulfing her.

During all this the Director was counting his piles of currency, oblivious of what was going on. But he had to look up when a brilliant light poured from the head of the smoke-demon, and the four hairy arms pulled the feebly struggling woman close to his body. . . .

At that moment Quintero's neck-muscles could support him no longer. He fell, and jostled the binoculars as he came down.

He could hear the loose part rattle around; and then it gave a hard click, as though it had settled into its final position.

Quintero picked himself up and massaged his neck with both hands. Had he been subject to an hallucination? Or had he seen something secret and magical that perhaps a few people knew about and used to maintain their financial positions—one more of the concealed and incredible things that people do?

He didn't know the answer, but he knew that he had to witness at least one more of these visions. He stood on his head again and looked through the binoculars.

Yes, he could see! He was looking into a dreary, furnished room. Within that room he saw a thin, pot-bellied man in his thirties, stripped to the waist, standing on his head with his stockinged feet pressed against the wall, looking upside-down into a pair of binoculars that lay on the floor and were aimed at the wall.

It took him a moment to realize that the binoculars were showing him himself.

He sat down on the floor, suddenly frightened. For he realized that he was only another performer in humanity's great circus, and he had just done one of his acts, just like the others. But who was watching? Who was the real observer?

He turned the binoculars around, and looked through the object-lenses. He saw a pair of eyes, and he thought they were his own—until one of them slowly winked at him.

Amphitheatre

The retro-thrusters were unpleasantly fierce in operation, setting up vibrations which Bernard Harben could feel in his chest cavity.

He had little knowledge of engineering, but he could sense the stress patterns racing through the structure of the shuttle craft, deflecting components and taking them close to their design limits. In his experience, all machines—especially his cameras—gave of their best when treated with the utmost gentleness, and he wondered briefly how the shuttle pilot could bear to subject his craft to such punishment. *Every man to his trade*, he thought, for the moment incapable of originality, and as if to reward him for his faith the precisely timed burst of power came to an abrupt end. The shuttle was falling freely, in sweet silence.

Harben looked upwards through the crystal canopy and saw the triple cylinder of the mother ship, the *Somerset*, dwindling to a bright speck as it slid ahead on its own orbit. The shuttle was brilliantly illuminated from above by the sun, and from below by the endless pearl-white expanses of the alien planet, which meant that every detail of it stood out with a kind of phosphorescent clarity against the background of space. Up at the front end the pilot was almost hidden by the massive back of his G-seat. He sat without moving, yet controlling their flight. Harben felt an ungrudging admiration for his skill, and for the audacity which enabled him to drive a splinter of metal and plastics down through the all-enveloping cloud layers to a predestined point on an unknown world.

At that moment Harben felt a rare pride in his humanity. He turned to Sandy Kiro, who was in the seat next to him, and placed his hand over hers. She continued to stare straight ahead, but the fullness of her lips altered a little and he knew she shared his mood.

"Let's claim this planet tonight," he said, referring to a secret game in which love-making established their title to any place in which it occurred.

Her pale lips parted slightly, giving him the answer he wanted, and he relaxed back into his own seat. In a few minutes the silence of their descent was replaced by a thin, insistent whistle as they penetrated the uppermost layers of the stratosphere, and the ship began to stir in response. Presently its movements became more assertive, more violent, and when he looked up front Harben saw the pilot had abandoned his God-like immobility and was toiling like any other mortal. Quite abruptly, they were surrounded by greyness and the space shuttle had become an aircraft contending with wind, cloud and ice. Their pilot, his stature reduced in proportion, might have been a twentieth-century aviator trying for a touchdown in an unpredicted storm.

Sandy, unaccustomed to blind planetfalls, turned anxiously to Harben.

He smiled and pointed at his chronometer. "It's almost time for lunch. We'll eat as soon as we set up camp."

His apparent preoccupation with domestic routine seemed to reassure her, and she settled back with a tentative preening of her shoulders. Again his trust in the pilot was justified. The ship broke through the cloud cover and steadied in its course as a grey-green landscape materialized below—ranges of hills, terraces and ramparts formed by broken strata, dark vegetation, and a pewter filigree of small rivers. Harben assessed the view with professional speed, took a panoramic camera from his breast pocket and recorded the rest of their descent. In a surprisingly short time the pilot had grounded the shuttle amid a turmoil of vertical jets, and the three of them were outside and testing their Northampton-made boots against wafers of alien shale.

"That's the Bureau's radio beacon," the pilot said, pointing at a squat, yellow pyramid which clung like a limpet to the rocky surface a hundred metres away. He was a competent-looking boy with fine gold hair and a bored manner which, in view of his extreme youth, Harben thought to have been culti-vated.

"You dropped square on to it, didn't you?" Harben said, testing his theory. "Nice flying."

The pilot looked gratified for an instant, then got back into his vocational stride. "It's ten minutes off local noon. The shuttle will be back here at noon six days from now—that's giving you ten minutes more than the charter called for."

"Generous."

"We're like that, Mr Harben." The boy went on to explain the cost penalties involved if they failed to rendezvous promptly, and to check that their chronometers were properly set to cope with Hassan IV's day of almost thirty hours.

"The shuttle will be here on time," he concluded. "You can be assured of that—though I don't know if I'll be the pilot."

"Oh, I hope it is you," Sandy said, joining in Harben's game. "I was really impressed. David, isn't it?"

"That's right." The pilot was unable to hold back a wide smile. "I have to go now. Good hunting!"

"Thank you, David." They picked up their field packs, retired to a safe distance and watched the shuttle rise vertically for a few metres before vectoring its thrust and swooping upwards into the clouds. It was lost to view long before the irregular, surging echoes from its jets had subsided, but it was not until the final whisper had faded—dissolving their perceptual link with the rest of mankind—that Harben became fully aware of the planet on which he was standing.

Visibility was surprisingly good, considering the amount of moisture in the air, and he could see complex perspectives of grey hills, inter-locking wedges of vegetation, and bodies of water which were leaden, black or soft-glowing silver de-pending on the direction of the light. The temperature was in the region of ten degrees and a breeze was blowing steadily from the east, laden with ozone and the smell of mosses and wet rock. There were no birds, nor any immediately visible signs of animal life—though Harben knew the area was the haunt of one very special creature, the one whose killing technique he had been commissioned to film.

"What a nice boy," Sandy said lightly.

"He's gone," Harben reminded her, gently making the point that it would be best to put the ways of Earth behind them and concentrate on successfully interacting with the new environment. Their marriage covenant had only two months to run and, although he had repeatedly sworn to her that he intended to renew, he suspected she did not fully believe him and had come along on the current expedition with some idea of cementing a bond. He would have been pleased had it not been for the fact that a previous team had disappeared without a trace while filming *E.T. Cephalopodus subterr. petraform.* His attempts to pursuade her not to come had been resisted on grounds he believed were emotional rather than logical, and in the end he had assented on condition that she bore a full working load, both mental and physical.

"Let's go," Harben said. "With any luck we'll find a good site in less than an hour, then we can eat."

Sandy shouldered her pack willingly and they set off in a direction which was virtually due north by their compasses. Harben could actually see the point he was aiming for—a notch in an east-west rampart about eight kilometres away—but he made a careful note of the bearing so that they could return in the foggy conditions which were common throughout the region. In keeping with the agreement that Sandy was not to be sheltered in any way, he insisted that they carry their energy guns at the ready—hers set for a slightly divergent beam which would compensate for any lack of expertise, his own adjusted for maximum convergence at five hundred metres. There was no evidence to suggest that the Visex team of two years earlier had encountered a fate more sinister than, say, falling into one of the numerous underground rivers, but Harben had agreed with his employers that they should take as few chances as possible.

Sandy and he continued north, zigzagging on tilted platforms of sedimentary rock, and gradually reached a softer terrain where the tricky shale gave way to a blackish sand in which thrived shrubs and ground-hugging creepers. In some places the surface was infested with saltatorial insects which leaped from underfoot with audible pops, causing Sandy to flinch away from them. Harben assured her their metallized field suits were proof against much larger creatures, and after a short time she began to take his word for it. She was a travel journalist whose previous experience had been on resort worlds, and he was relieved to see how quickly she adapted to Hassan IV.

Presently they drew near the natural gateway to the north and, as he had hoped, Harben found signs of *E.T. Alcelaphini*, the gnu-like animals which were the principal prey of *petraform*. The tracks fanned outwards from the notch in the encircling cliffs and dispersed into the rocky table-land from which Harben and Sandy had just emerged.

"This is good," Harben said. "I think we're on a main migration route to the south."

Sandy glanced around her. "Shouldn't we have seen some of them?"

"No—that's the whole point. The females slow down a lot when they're getting ready to drop their young, and they and their mates become super-cautious. That could be why our friend *petraform* evolved the way he did."

An expression of distaste appeared briefly on Sandy's classically feminine features. "Don't refer to those things as our friends, please."

"But they're going to bring us a lot of money," Harben protested, smiling. "And that's the second friendliest thing anybody can do for you."

"They're horrible."

"Nothing in nature is horrible." Harben raised his compact binoculars and felt a pang of excitement as he scanned the flat ground immediately south of the pass. The angles were too acute for good observation, and his view was obstructed by boulders and vegetation, but he thought he could see no less than three horseshoe formations of grey rocks. They were like miniature and incomplete versions of terrestrial Druid circles, each about five metres in diameter. Harben's pleasure mounted as he counted the stones and confirmed that there were seven in each circle. Most significant of all was the fact that in each case the gap, where the eighth stone should have been, faced due north—in the direction from which the quasi-gnu came every spring in search of the lush pastures needed by their young.

"In fact, everything in God's garden is lovely," Harben said.

"What do you mean?"

"I think we've hit the jackpot first time. Let's go—I'm hungry."

As they approached the circles Harben discovered that the site was even better for his purpose than he had at first supposed. He had four automatic cameras in his pack and right away could see vantage points in the shape of trees and boulders where they could all be hidden and serviced. There was even a small, wind-hewn monolith just to the north of the group of circles which would enable him to get high-angle shots to improve the visual texture of the completed film. He became so absorbed in plotting camera locations that his attention wandered from Sandy and it was only when he noticed she was unconcernedly walking straight ahead that he became alive to the danger.

"Sandy!" He touched her arm. "Where do you think you're going?"

She froze, sensing the warning in his voice. "What's wrong?"

"Nothing—but stay here with me." He waited until she had positioned herself slightly behind him, then pointed out the three circles. "Those are what we've come to film."

She stared at the flat ground, uncomprehending, for almost a minute before—guided by his gyrating index finger—she picked out the loose patterns among the natural scatter of rocks. Her pallor grew more pronounced, but he was glad to see that she held her ground without flinching.

"I thought they'd look more like spiders," she said. "Or octopuses."

He shook his head. "If they looked like anything but ordinary rock formations they'd starve to death. Their whole survival plan depends on suitable prey walking straight into their arms."

"Then . . . those rocks aren't real."

"No. They're arms in which most of the power of movement has been traded off against the ability to stimulate stone. I suspect you could even tap them with a hammer and not know any difference—as long as you were standing outside the circle."

"What would happen if you were inside it?"

"The eighth arm would probably get you." Harben continued the impromptu lesson in extra-terrestrial zoology by pointing out the shallow depression at the "entrance" to each circle. It was there, under a camouflage of pebbles and grass, that the whip-like eighth arm was coiled in readiness to snap itself around any creature unwary enough to enter the circle.

Sandy was quiet for a moment. "What happens then?"

"That's what we're here to check out and put on film," Harben said. "*Petraform* seems to have the same body plan as an ordinary cephalopod, which means the mouth is in the centre of the circle, but we don't know how long the processes of killing and ingestion actually take. For all we know, when it gets hold of an animal it simply waits until the beast has died of fright or starvation, and then absorbs it." Harben paused for breath, his eyes still assessing the photographic potentialities and limitations of the scene.

"You know, Sandy, this is the big one I've been looking for —the one that'll set me up for life. I can see it going out on every TV network there is."

"I'd like a hot drink now," Sandy said. "Can we put up the shelter?"

"Sure." Harben led the way to a suitable spot, spread out the shelter's base sheet and triggered a built-in gas cartridge to erect the pliant hemispherical roof. He was an exceptionally tall man, with a long back and slightly stiff limbs which did not readily fold into cramped spaces, but he was undisturbed by the prospect of six nights in the tiny inflatable. The rewards promised to be so great that his next field trip, assuming he chose to go out again, would be made in ostentatious luxury. He took twelve flat autotherm trays—guarantee of two hot meals a day—and handed them to Sandy, who stacked them in the shelter with her own supplies. While she was heating cans of coffee he moved off to an appropriate distance and manually dug a latrine, an ancient procedure still in favour because of its superb cost-effectiveness.

He was folding up the lightweight spade when a wisp of sound reached him. With a tingling sense of shock he realized that Sandy, who was a good fifty metres away from him, was speaking to someone in normal conversational tones. Harben ran a short way towards her, then stopped as he saw that—as had to be the case—she was completely alone. She was kneeling with her back to him, apparently opening the coffee cans.

"Sandy," he shouted, not sure of why he was alarmed, "are you all right?"

She turned and he saw the look of surprise on her face. "Bernard? What are you doing over there? I thought you were . . ." Sandy stood up, looked all round her and began to laugh.

He crossed the intervening space and accepted a coffee. "Most people take years of this sort of life before they go crazy."

"I thought you were right behind me." She sipped her drink, somehow managing to look feminine, even fashionable, in the silver-grey quilting of a field suit, and her eyes steadied on the flat space dominated by the stone circles. "Bernard, why are there no animal bones over there?"

"They get eaten. If they were left sitting about they might scare off other prey, but it's most likely that they get absorbed for the mineral content. Hassan IV has some funny gaps in its geochemistry, especially where metals are concerned."

"What a place!"

"All part of nature's rich tapestry, lover." Harben finished his coffee, appreciating its warmth, and put the can down. "I'm going to set up the auto-cameras in case there's some action soon."

"I'll stay here and put some notes together for an article." Sandy gave him a wry smile. "I might as well make some money too.'

Harben nodded. "I'd want you to stay here anyway. It's best to leave as little spoor and scent as possible around the place."

He took the four automatic cameras from his pack, slung the rifle on to his shoulder and walked towards the circles. The cloud ceiling had come down low enough to hide the tops of the tallest trees, but close to the ground the air had the clarity of glass. He kept his gaze fixed on the innocuous-looking rock formations, wondering if the bizarre creatures waiting below ground could feel the vibrations of his footsteps and were preparing themselves in anticipation of his walking into a trap. *Tough luck, rocktopus*, he thought. *I'm not going to feed you—you're going to feed me.*

There were two trees conveniently positioned on each side of the subject area, and he clamped cameras to their trunks, checking the coverage they provided as he did so. The small monolith to the north was easy to climb by the outer face and he installed a third camera on top of it. Two largish boulders were available on the south side as camera mounts. He chose one which was beside a deep-looking pool, hoping that some of the quasi-gnu would be attracted towards the water, thus providing extra film sequences he could use. An advantage of the holofilm system he employed was that it had unlimited depth of focus and a very wide recording angle, which meant that long shots, close-ups, panoramas and framed sequences could be prepared afterwards, at will, through selective processing of one roll of film. Harben was leaning on the boulder and smoothing out the plastic dough of a mounting pad when he became aware of Sandy standing behind him.

"What do you want, Sandy?" he said, not hiding his annoyance. There was no reply. He turned to remind her that she should have kept away from the area, but there was nobody near him. A sudden heightening of his senses made the moisture-laden breeze cooler and the murmur of streams louder. He allowed the strap of his rifle to slip from his shoulder, transferring the weight of the weapon to his hand, and at the same time he scanned the vicinity, satisfying himself there were no places of concealment. A full minute dragged by while he held the defensive pose, but there was no movement except for the slow drift of downward-reaching fingers of mist.

Finally, with the clamour in his nerves gradually abating, he turned back to the camera and completed the task of setting it up. When he had finished he checked the operation of the hand-held remote controller and walked thoughtfully back to the shelter. One explanation for what had happened was that Sandy and he were more jumpy than they realized—walking the face of an alien world was a supremely unnatural experience; another was the possible presence of hallucinogens in the atmosphere. Official survey samplings had indicated a standard mixture of gases, but that did not exclude local or temporary variations. He decided to monitor the performance of his own sensory apparatus for a few hours before saying anything to Sandy.

As soon as he had rejoined her she triggered one of the auto-therm trays and they ate their first meal on Hassan IV. Harben periodically checked the approach from the north with his binoculars, and between times tried to decide if he was per-ceiving his surroundings in a completely normal manner. There was no repetition of the delusion, but as he moved around the camp there were moments, always as he was relaxing his vigilance, when he got an unaccountable feeling he was in a party of three. The impressions were so vague and fleeting that they could have been a consequence of his edginess, and he learned to dismiss them. Sandy, dictating notes into a recorder, appeared to be untroubled.

Late in the afternoon Harben detected a movement in the folds of grey rock to the north, and he made ready with his main camera, snorting with excitement as he checked its settings. A few minutes later two animals which bore a superficial resemblance to antelope came through the pass, delicately picking their way over the broken ground. One was a doe, and even at a distance it was obvious she was soon to give birth.

Being careful to remain in cover, Harben filmed their progress. As the animals began to draw level with him he saw that what he had taken to be the doe's tail was actually two spindly legs of her nascent fawn projecting from the vagina. His heart began a steady pounding as the animals reached the flat area where the *petraforms* lay in waiting. He pressed a button on his remote controller, setting the four automatic cameras in operation, and watched through his viewfinder as the quasi-gnu reached the deadly circles.

As though guided by a powerful instinct, they threaded a path through the danger zone—passing within a metre or so of the ill-defined perimeters—and continued southwards into the safety of the higher ground. Harben shut down his cameras, wondering if the disappointment he felt was being shared by the three immobile predators lurking below the surface. He turned to Sandy, who had been watching the animals through her own binoculars.

"Too bad," he said. "Still, we couldn't really expect to connect first time."

She looked at him with sombre eyes. "Bernard, was the female giving birth?"

"She wasn't far off it."

"But that's awful! Why don't they stop and rest?"

Harben smiled at her concern, suddenly reminded of how little she knew about wildlife. "Animals like that, which stay alive through being able to run fast, usually keep on the move. Especially if they feel threatened. When she drops the fawn it'll have maybe five minutes to learn to walk—then they'll be on their way again."

Sandy glanced about her and shivered. "I don't like this place."

"It's the same on any Earth-type planet," he told her. "You can see the same sort of thing back in Africa."

"Well, I'm glad that one got away. It would have been too horrible if those monsters had caught the mother."

It was not a good time for an argument, but Harben decided he should straighten out Sandy's thinking before she actually witnessed a kill. "In nature there aren't any monsters," he said. "There aren't any good guys or bad guys. Every creature is entitled to take its food, and it doesn't matter whether that creature is a robin or a rocktopus."

Sandy shook her head, lips compressed. "There's no comparison between a robin and one of those . . . things."

"They both have to eat."

"But a robin is only a . . ."

"Not from a worm's point of view."

"I'm cold," Sandy said, looking away from. him All at once she seemed absurdly small and defenceless, and he felt a pang of remorse over having allowed her to accompany him to a world which was so foreign in every way to her own milieu.

There were no more sightings that day, and as soon as it began to get dark Harben laid out the alarm cord in a large circle around the shelter. Sandy crawled into their artificial cave almost immediately, but Harben sat on the ground outside it for another hour, staring into the total blackness and listening to the complex, conflicting whispers of nearby streams. Once he developed a conviction that he was being watched, but none of the green-glowing needles on the alarm panel even trembled, and he concluded there was still some tension lingering in his nervous system.

When he moved in beside Sandy she moulded her body into his so that they fitted together as neatly as two spoons. The love-making they had planned earlier in the day would have relaxed Harben and made it easier for him to sleep, but—sensitive to her mood—he made no advances. He lay awake for a long time, enduring the stretched-out hours and waiting impatiently for the morning.

The return of daylight, the aromas of hot food and coffee, the purposeful domesticity of the morning chores—all combined to elevate Sandy's spirits, and Harben felt a corresponding lift within himself. He moved around a lot, driving the stiffness from his limbs, and talked rather more than was necessary about their plans for the next few years. Sandy may have realized he was scheming to influence her attitude towards his work as a whole, and to the Hassan IV expedition, but there was no adverse reaction on her part. She even started a running joke based on the notion of treating the planet as a luxury resort in an article for a travel magazine.

Harben's principal concern while this was going on was that during the night the cloud ceiling had descended almost to ground level. He kept a watchful eye on it as he ate and was relieved to find that the sandwich of clear air was—in response to the action of the invisible sun—gradually growing wider, revealing more and more of the high branches of trees. It gave him the sense of being at the bottom of a glass of aerated water which was steadily clarifying from the base upwards. As soon as the northern hill slopes beyond the pass had come into view he raised his binoculars and at once saw a small herd of quasi-gnu patiently filtering down through rocky obstacles.

"I think we're in business," he said, sliding his hand

through the wrist-strap of his main camera. "Perhaps you should stay here."

He doubled over and ran to a hummock from the lee of which he had a good view of the flat area and the sentient circles. A glance at the remote controller told him the automatic cameras on their vantage points were ready to function and, as a precaution against being forgetful in the forthcoming excitement, he switched them on early. He sensed Sandy taking up a position close behind him, but was too busy getting long shots of the approaching herd to speak to her. The quasi-gnu were emerging from the pass and their leaders were heading straight for the waiting circles.

Harben watched the entire scene in enlargement through his viewfinder as the herd of about twenty came level with him and began crossing what, for them, was the danger zone. Again, as though protected by an extra sense, the animals threaded tangential courses between circles. He was beginning to think none of them would make the fatal mistake when a large buck, which was being followed by a pregnant female, walked into the nearest circle. Harben's mouth went dry as the creature, unaware of its peril, stepped over the depression marking the *petraform*'s eighth arm. It crossed the ring of stones which were not stones and, moving with a stately nonchalance, passed safely out the other side.

Harben's disappointment was as sharp as a blow. *Could the petraform be dead? Would he have to look for another site?*

He tensed again as the doe followed her mate's footsteps into the circle. There was an explosive flurry of movement in the entrance depression. A slim black tongue snapped upwards and, with an easily audible whipcrack, coiled around the legs of the partially-born fawn which protruded from the doe's haunches. The doe screamed in terror and immediately came to a standstill.

I'm going to be rich, Harben exulted, as he jumped to his feet to improve his camera angle.

At the doe's cry of pain and fear the rest of the herd, with the exception of her mate, bolted off to the south. Their hooves drummed briefly, then there was silence broken only by the plaintive bleating and snuffling of the captured animal.

The buck watched her, helplessly, from a safe distance as she shifted her feet, inching backwards as the leathery black arm of the *petraform* increased its tension, threatening to drag the fawn from her womb. Harben guessed she could have ejected it easily and made her escape, but that the maternal instinct in the species was too strong to permit the sacrifice of her young. And as he watched, keeping his camera trained on the struggle, the doe's dilemma became more urgent—the *petraform*'s other seven legs had begun to stir like giant snails. The living stones churned the wet soil as they closed in on the trapped animal.

"Bernard!" Sandy's voice came from some distance behind Harben, and was followed by the sound of her footsteps as she ran towards him. On one level of his consciousness he was slightly surprised—he had been certain Sandy was close by him—but his attention was concentrated on the natural drama being enacted before him.

"Bernard!" Sandy arrived at his side, breathing heavily. "You've got to *do* something!"

"I'm doing it," he said. "I'm not missing a thing."

As the doe became aware of the arms closing in on her, elongating as they came, she gave a convulsive movement and the full length of her fawn's forelegs came into view, followed by its head. Sandy gave a low sob and stepped past him, and from the corner of his eye he saw the metallic lustre of the rifle in her hands. He risked looking away from the viewfinder long enough to grasp the weapon, and used his superior strength to twist it out of her grasp.

"You've got to help her, Bernard." Sandy beat ineffectually on his shoulder with her fists. "I'll never forgive you if you don't help her."

"There's no point." He fended Sandy off, knowing that subsequent processing would eliminate the effects of camera movement. "This is the way nature intended the rocktopus to provide for itself. What you're seeing now has happened billions of times before we got here, and it'll happen billions of times after we've gone."

"I don't care," Sandy pleaded. "Just this once . . ."

"Look at that, for God's sake!" Harben shouted.

Through the viewfinder he saw the ground suddenly begin to open beneath the doe's feet. The rocktopus was ready to feed. As the surface supporting her began to shift and dissolve, the doe's courage failed her and she lurched towards safety. The fawn fell behind her and, on the instant of being born, disappeared into the waiting mouth. Freed of her constraint, the doe leaped effortlessly over the advancing arms of the *petraform* and galloped to the waiting buck. Both animals fled into the surrounding greyness and were lost to sight.

"I've got to have this." Harben was only dimly aware of Sandy's whimpering as he ran forward, past a tree, into the flat area to get a downward view into the predator's maw. She kept beside him, pulling desperately at the rifle in his left hand.

He pushed her away, intending to continue running to the centre of the flat area, but his wrist was gripped with a force which brought him to a standstill with an arm-wrenching jolt. Sandy screamed his name with a new urgency. Harben swung round angrily and found he had been snared, anchored to the ground, by a thin black cord. He tugged at it disbelievingly and an identical cord sprang from another point and encircled his ankles. Within a second a dozen others, pulsing with eager life, had coiled themselves around his limbs, rendering him helpless. He looked about him in desperation and saw that Sandy was going to her knees amid a similar web of tendrils.

"*The gun!*" Her voice shrilled into the topmost registers. "Burn them off!"

As though her words had been understood by a mind other than his own, new cords wrenched the rifle out of his grip. Harben was barely aware of this—because all of the flat space surrounding the three stone circles had begun to writhe with black feelers which waved in the air like wind-blown grass. And then, as the ultimate horror, the trees and boulders forming the outer circle began to change shape, to move inwards. Even the surface of the dark pool humped upwards into a pseudopod of black jelly.

The shifting and loosening of the ground beneath his feet brought a total, though belated, understanding to Harben—

the entire area was part of one huge, complex and hungry beast of prey.

He fell to his knees as the glistening cords increased their multiple tensions, and he felt the surface gently parting to receive him, yearning, beginning to exert suction. Sandy was almost hidden from view by skeins of black threads. A strange, sad humming filled the air.

Harben raised his gaze skywards as he gave vent to one last bellow of fear and despair, but the protest died in his throat as he saw something—something incredible—moving in the cloud ceiling above him.

There was a humanoid figure, unnaturally tall, difficult to focus on because it slanted in and out of visibility in a way which had nothing to do with obscuration by mist. It was sheathed in prismatic colours and carried glimmering artifacts. A tongue of blue-white incandescence stabbed downwards from it, a scream which Harben felt rather than heard vibrated through the vastness of the plasm beneath him, and suddenly he was free to move. The thickets of black tendrils had vanished into hidden pores.

He staggered to his feet, caught Sandy's hand, and they half-ran, half-waded towards the safety of the firm ground beyond the circle of boulders and trees. As they passed a weirdly misshapen, but now immobile, tree Harben glanced back and glimpsed the rippling, polychromatic figure suspended among a swirl of vapours. He could not distinguish the eyes, but he knew the being was looking directly at him, into him, through him.

Know that you were wrong, my friend. The door to an intellectual furnace was opening, and its fire washed through Harben's mind. *I, too, am a recorder, but my experience far surpasses yours. Entropy demands that all living things shall die— but Life is counter-entropic, and that must apply in particular as well as in general. If you surrender the ability to sympathize with the individual, you will become isolated from Life itself. . . .*

There was a shifting of super-geometries, and the figure vanished.

By the time Harben had broken camp the arena in which they had almost died looked exactly as it had done before. The trees

looked like ordinary trees, the boulders and pool were indistin-
guishable from natural features of the landscape, and in the
centre the three stone circles were quiescent. A thin, steady
drizzle was gradually erasing all signs of disturbance from the
surface layer of soil.

The sedatives she had taken had quelled the trembling of
Sandy's limbs, but her face was pale and distracted as she
looked at the deceptively peaceful scene. "Do you think," she
said, "that it's all part of the same organism?"

"I doubt it," Harben replied as he opened a valve to deflate
the shelter. "I'd say the three in the middle have some kind of
symbiotic relationship with the big brute."

"I don't see why it let the herd pass on through, then went
for us."

"Neither do I—yet. It might be because it's mineral-hungry
and we carry so much metal. Look at the way the material of
our suits perished in a matter of seconds." Harben got to his
feet as the shelter subsided. "Can you roll this up?"

Sandy nodded, and her troubled gaze steadied on his face.
"Where are you going?"

"To pick up the automatic cameras."

"But . . ."

"It's all right, Sandy. I'll be safe as long as I stay outside the
circle."

She approached him and took his hand in hers. "Are you
going to take the film back with you?"

"You're still in shock, little girl." Harben laughed incredu-
lously, withdrawing his hand. "That stuff is worth a fortune,
especially if our visitor registered on it. Of course I'm taking
it back."

"But. . . don't you remember what he said?"

"I'm not sure that he said anything, and what there was of
it didn't make too much sense to me."

"He said we all have to die—but not for the benefit of an
audience."

"I told you it didn't make sense."

"It's very simple, Bernard." Sandy's eyes were dulled with
drugs, and yet were oddly intent. "When you point your camera
at any creature you make it special. You enlist the sympathy

of millions of viewers, and if our sympathy isn't worth anything
. . . what are we worth?"

"I've never had myself valued."

"He was filming us, but he didn't let us die."

"Sandy, this is just . . ." Harben began to walk away, then
he saw that she was crying. "Listen to me," he said. "The fawn
is dead and gone, and there's nothing anybody can do about it.
And you'll notice that *he* didn't kill that brute off. It's all right
again, and it's going to go on feeding itself in the only way it
knows how. For all we know, that's what happened to the Visex
team a couple of years ago."

"It's a pity you weren't here to film that."

"You'll feel better when I get you away from here," Harben
said curtly. He turned from her and collected his cameras at
the points where they had fallen, being careful not to set foot
within the circle of menace. Sandy's last remark had stung him,
but his thoughts were becoming preoccupied with new plans
for the future. Quite apart from having yielded the fleeting but
newsworthy contact with the super-naturalist, Hassan IV was
an even richer treasure house than he had dreamed, one which
could only be exploited through years of dedicated work.
Already it was obvious that Sandy would not want anything to
do with it, and that fact posed serious problems with regard to
their marriage covenant.

Later, as they were crossing the uplands on the approach to
the radio beacon, he realized he had come to a decision. He felt
unexpectedly guilty at the prospect of broaching the subject
while she was still so badly shaken, but he was entering a
vital phase of his career and would have to learn to move
quickly in everything he did.

"Sandy," he said quietly, taking her elbow, "I've been thinking things over, and. . ."

She pulled her arm away from him without turning her head.
"It's all right, Bernard—I don't want to stay married to you,
either."

Harben stood still for a moment, staring at her retreating back,
experiencing an emotion compounded of puzzlement and relief;
then he adjusted his camera pack to a more comfortable position
and continued picking his way across the wet, grey shale.

The Negation

Dik would listen for the train every evening he was not on patrol. Sometimes, when the mountain winds had temporarily stilled, he could hear the rhythmic drumming of the wheels while the train was many miles from the depot, but he always heard the blast of steam as it arrived, and the shriek of its whistle when it left. To Dik it was a melancholy reminder of home, because roads were few in the mountains and he knew he would leave the frontier as he had arrived, on one of those nightly trains.

He had once written a few lines of verse about the train, trying to maintain a lifeline to his identity that had existed before conscription, but he had destroyed them soon afterwards. They were the only writing he had done while serving in the Border Police, and he felt it was unlikely he would try any more.

For the last two weeks he had been listening for the train with extra interest, because he knew that Moylita Kaine, the novelist, should be arriving soon. He hardly expected that the sounds of the train would be any different for her being on it, but it seemed appropriate that he should be waiting for her. As events turned out, though, her arrival in the village was signalled by something else. He was leaving the canteen one evening, half an hour before the train was due, and he noticed that several of the burghers' limousines were parked in the centre of the village. They were lined up outside the civic hall, their engines running and the hired drivers sitting in readiness. Dik walked by on the other side of the street, smelling the gasoline fumes and hearing the soft puttering of the muffled exhausts: both unusual phenomena in the isolated village.

The large double doors of the civic hall opened, and a beam

of orange light from within fell across the polished cars and the trodden snow. Dik hunched his shoulders, and walked on towards the constabulary hostel. He heard the burghers leaving the hall, the car-doors slamming, and in a moment a slow convoy of vehicles passed him, turning from the village street on to the narrow, unmade track that led towards the station further down the steep valley. It was only then that Dik guessed at the possible meaning of the burghers' excursion, and when he reached the entrance to the hostel he paused to listen for the train. It was still too early, and with the wind it would be impossible to hear the wheels in the distance.

He changed quickly out of his uniform, then went alone to the outside balcony on the first floor. No fresh snow had fallen that day, and his frozen footprints from the night before led to the corner of the balcony and lost themselves in a confusion of stamping and shuffling. He followed them and stood in the corner, thrusting his hands into the pockets of his greatcoat.

From this position he could see up the narrow street that led to the centre of the village, but most of the buildings were dark and seemed uninhabited; from somewhere came the sound of an accordion band, and men were laughing drunkenly. In the other direction, looking across the sharply angled roofs of the houses on the edge of the village, was a panorama, breath-taking by day, down the wintry valley. The night was dark, and Dik could only just make out the pine-forest clinging to the frozen scarps that rose on either side. On the northern ridge, three thousand feet above the village, the frontier wall overlooked the valley, but Dik knew without looking that no trace of it could be seen from here.

He waited, stamping his feet and shivering, until at last he heard a jetting of steam, echoing up through the chill, blustery air of the valley, and he felt again the familiar pang of homesickness.

Dik went inside at once and joined his friends in the hostel common-room. The talk was boisterous and rowdy: the last few days at the frontier had been eventful, and there was much suppressed tension to release. Dik was soon shouting and laughing with the rest. A few minutes later one of the lads by the window let out a shrill whistle, and the others ran to cluster around him. Peering with them through the film of condensation into the street outside, Dik saw the convoy of burghers' cars returning from the depot, the engines purring, the wheels crunching softly across the compacted snow.

Dik had been about to enter college when he was conscripted. He could imagine no one less suitable for any kind of military service than himself, and had taken all the usual steps to try for deferment. It was unlucky for him that his draft-papers arrived more or less coincidentally with the first of the enemy's air-raids on Jethra, and when, a few weeks later, there was an unsuccessful invasion in the south, the pressures of conscience grew and he signed on with as much goodwill as he could muster.

His intention had been to read Modern Literature at Jethra University, and it had been the writing of Moylita Kaine that had prompted the decision. Although he had been reading fiction and poetry for as long as he could remember, and had written many poems of his own, one book—a novel entitled *The Affirmation*—had so impressed him that he counted the reading of it as the single most important experience of his life. In many ways a deep and difficult work, the book was little known or discussed. For Dik, the book's apparent obscurities were among its greatest joys; the novel spoke to him in an intensely clear, wise and passionate voice, its story an elemental conflict between deceit and romantic truth, its resolution profoundly emotional, and its understanding of human nature so perceptive and candid that he could still recall, three years later, the shock of discovery. He had read and re-read the book more times than he could count, he had urged it on his few close friends (though never once allowing his precious copy out of his possession), and tried, as far as was humanly possible, to live his own life within the philosophy of Orfé, the chief protagonist.

He had, of course, looked for other books by the same author, but had found nothing. He had instinctively assumed the author dead—because of the common assumption that books found in secondhand shops are always by dead authors—but a letter to the publisher had elicited the enthralling information that not only was Moylita Kaine still very much alive, but she (Dik had assumed the author was male!) was presently working on a second novel.

All this was before the political dispute with the neighbouring countries, and before the fighting broke out along one of the frontiers. As a growing boy, bookish and isolated, Dik had been vaguely aware of the impending war, but his conscription had placed him, literally, in the front line. Since joining the Border Police all his hopes and plans had had to be suspended, but he had kept his much-used copy of *The Affirmation* with him wherever he went. It was now, like the nightly arrival of the train, a link with his old life and his past, and in another sense a link with his future.

The fact that a government-sponsored writer had arrived in the village was posted on the notice-board in the common-room, and Dik applied at once for a pass to see her. Much to his surprise, it was granted with only the slightest hesitation.

"What do you want it for?" the platoon serjeant said.

"To improve my mind, sir."

"No relief from duties, understand."

"In my own time, sir."

That night Dik slipped the piece of paper into the pages of the novel, choosing as its place the passage describing the momentous first meeting between Orfé and Hilde, the captivating wife of his rival Coschtie. It was one of his favourite scenes in the long book.

Before he could use the pass, Dik was sent on patrol again. There was an exchange of mortar-fire and grenades—six constables from another platoon were killed, and several more were injured—but then the weather closed in and Dik was sent back to the village.

The streets were blocked by drifting snow, and the blizzard continued for another two days. Dik stayed inside the hostel with the others, watching the grey-black sky and the driven snow. He had grown used to the variable weather in the mountains and no longer saw it as an expression of his own moods. Grey days did not dispirit him, clear days did not cheer him;

rather to the contrary, indeed, for he had sufficient experience of the patrols to know that enemy attacks were fewer when the sky was heavy, that days that began bright with winter sun often finished bright with spilled blood. It was curiously exciting to know that Moylita Kaine was somewhere in the village, but also depressing that he could not use his pass to visit her.

The next day was clearer and by noon the snow had stopped. Dik was detailed to a shovelling team, and worked alongside the tractors to clear the streets once more. Digging with the others, his arms and back straining with the heavy work, Dik spent most of the time obsessively wondering why the burghers did not lay electric warmways through the village, as they had done along the approaches to the frontier, and on the wall itself. But beneath the snow were the ancient cobbles of the village streets, grating against the metal edge of the spade as Dik laboured on at the futile task.

Repetitive work induced repetitive thoughts, but it relieved him of some of his bottled-up resentment against the burghers. He knew little of what life must have been like in this village before the frontier was closed, but he detested what he knew of it now. The only civilians were the burghers and their servants, the only distractions those provided by grace of the Police authorities.

He slept deeply that night, and in the morning, as he set off up the steep warmway to resume patrol-duties, Dik felt the agony of his over-used muscles. The pack on his back, and his rifle and grenade-thrower, and his snow-shoes and ropes, felt as if they had the entire weight of the snow he had shifted.

The chance to see Moylita Kaine had come and passed, and now it would have to wait until his next spell of leave. Dik was resigned to this with the weary stoicism of the part of him that had become a soldier. He accepted that by the time he came down again from the frontier wall, if he wasn't killed or injured or had been captured, she might have finished her work in the village and left on the train.

The wall was quiet, and a few days later Dik returned unharmed to the village. He had two days to himself, and the

A—C

time which normally would be spent in lassitude or tomfoolery in the hostel suddenly had a meaning and purpose.

The pass the serjeant had given him allowed him access, during daylight hours, to the old saw-mill on the edge of the village; this was presumably where Moylita Kaine was working or living. Dik knew the saw-mill, and during the long hours of patrol he had rehearsed the walk to it in his mind perhaps a score of times. This aside, he didn't know what to expect, either of himself or of the writer. He had nothing that he had prepared to say; it would be enough to meet her.

As he left the hostel, Dik made sure his copy of *The Affirmation* was in his greatcoat pocket. An autograph was the only definite thing he wanted from her.

At the edge of the village, where the street became a path, Dik was surprised to discover that a warmway had been laid on the ground, cutting a winding black swathe up through the stiff pine-trees towards the mill. White vapour rose from it in the frosty air. He stepped on to it, his feet slipping slightly as the snow and ice he had picked up on his boots melted beneath him.

As he approached the old mill he saw someone standing by a window high up in the front wall. It was a woman, and when she saw him climbing the warmway she opened the window and leaned out. She was wearing a huge fur hat, with flaps that fell over her ears.

"What do you want?" she called, looking down at him.

"I've come to see Moylita Kaine. Is she here?"

"Yes. What do you want her for?"

"I've got a pass," he said.

"There's a door . . . round there." The woman withdrew her head, and closed the window firmly.

Dik walked obediently towards the corner she had indicated, leaving the warmway and stepping along a narrow path where the snow had been trodden. It was only as he rounded the corner, and saw a door set into the side of the building, that he realized he had just spoken to Miss Kaine herself!

It was quite a surprise. While he had never built up a mental picture of the author, and had envisaged her neither young nor old, he suddenly knew that he had not imagined her looking quite like that. The glimpse of her had been of a woman in her early middle age, rather plump and fierce-looking, quite unwriterlike.

The author of *The Affirmation* had been, in Dik's mind, more ethereal, more a romantic notion than an actual person.

He opened the door and walked into the saw-mill. The old building was unlit and cold, but he could see the angular shapes of the benches and saws, the storage racks and conveyor-belts. The smell of pinewood and sawdust was in the air: dry and distant, sweet and stale.

He heard the hollow clumping of feet, and the woman appeared at the top of a flight of wooden stairs that were built against the wall.

"Are you Miss Kaine?" Dik said, still hardly believing that it could be her.

"I left a message at the civic hall," she said, coming down towards him. "I don't want to be disturbed today."

"Message . . .? I'm sorry. I'll come again later." Dik backed away, reaching behind him for the door-handle.

"And tell Clerk Tradayn that I shall be engaged tonight as well."

She had reached the fourth step from the bottom, and halted, waiting as Dik fumbled for the handle. It seemed to have stuck . . . so he took his other hand from his pocket to get a better grip. As he did so, his copy of *The Affirmation* fell to the ground. The pass, still wedged between Orfé and Hilde, slipped from the pages and fluttered away. Dik stooped to pick them up.

"I'm sorry," he said again. "I didn't know—"

As he stood up, Moylita Kaine came quickly to his side and took the book from his hand.

"You've got a copy of my novel," she said. "Why?"

"Because . . . I was hoping I might talk to you about it."

Holding the book, looking at him thoughtfully, she said: "Have you read this?"

"Of course I have. It's—"

"But the burghers sent you?"

"No . . . I came because, well, I thought anyone could see you."

"So they tell me," she said. "I suppose we should go up-stairs and talk."

"But you aren't to be disturbed."

"I thought you were from the burghers. Come up to where I'm working. I'll sign this copy for you."

She turned and went up the stairs. After a moment, with his eyes fixed disbelievingly on the back of her trousered legs, Dik followed.

The room had once been an office in the saw-mill, and the window looked down the valley and across to the distant snow-caps beyond. It was a bare, grubby room, furnished with a desk and a chair, and a tiny one-bar electric radiant heater. It was not much warmer here than it had been downstairs, and Dik understood why Miss Kaine wore her furs as she worked. She went to the desk, moved some papers aside and found a black fountain-pen. As she opened his copy of the book to the title-page, Dik saw that her hands were clad in gloves, with the woollen fingers cut away.

"Would you like me to dedicate it?"

"Yes, please," Dik said. "Whatever you think is best."

In spite of the moment, Dik's attention was not wholly on the signing of his book, because as she spoke he had noticed that in the centre of the desk was a large, old-fashioned type-writer, with a curl of white paper coming out of the roller. He had found her actually writing something!

"Then what shall I say?" Moylita Kaine said.

"Just sign it," Dik said abstractedly.

"You wanted me to dedicate it . . . what's your name?"

"Oh . . . Dik."

"With a 'c'?"

"No, the usual way."

She wrote quickly, then passed the book back to him. The ink was still wet. Her handwriting was very loose and wild, and it looked as if she had written: 'To Duk . . . will evey beet wisl, Moylilo Kine'. He stared at it in joyous incomprehension.

"Thank you," he said. "I mean . . . er, thank you."

She went behind the desk and sat down, stretching out her hands towards the fire.

Dik looked at the paper in the typewriter. "Excuse me . . . is that a new novel you're working on?"

"A novel? I should think not! Not at the moment."

"But your publishers said you were writing one."

"My publishers told you that? What—?"

"I wrote to them," Dik said. "I thought *The Affirmation* was the best novel I had ever read, and I wanted to find out what else you had written."

She was looking at him closely, and Dik felt himself beginning to redden. "You really have read the book, haven't you?"

"Yes, I told you."

"Did you read it all the way through?"

"I've read it several times. It's the most important book in the world."

Smiling, but not patronizingly, she said: "How old are you, Dik?"

"Eighteen."

"And how old were you when you read the book?"

"Fifteen, I think."

"Did you find some of it rather, well, bizarre?"

"The love scenes?" Dik said. "I found them exciting."

"I didn't mean those, but . . . good. Some of the reviewers—"

"I looked up the reviews. They were stupid."

"I wish there were more readers like you."

"I wish there were more *books* like yours!" Dik said, then instantly regretted it. He had vowed to himself that he would be dignified and polite. Miss Kaine was smiling at him again, and this time Dik felt that his enthusiasm had made him deserve it.

"If that isn't a novel," he said, pointing at the page in the typewriter, "do you mind telling me what it is?"

"What I'm being paid to write while I'm here. A play about the village. But I thought everyone knew what I was doing here."

"Yes," Dik said, trying not to reveal the disappointment he felt. He had seen the leaflet setting out the writer-sponsorship scheme, and knew that visiting writers were commissioned to write drama for the communities they visited, but he had retained an irrational hope that Moylita Kaine would be somehow above that sort of thing. A play written about the village

didn't have quite the same appeal as a novel like *The Affirmation.*
"Are you writing another novel, though?"

"I started one. I could finish it, but it wouldn't be published . . . not until the war is over. There's no paper available.
A lot of saw-mills have been closed."

He was staring at her, unable to look away. It was almost
impossible to believe that this was Moylita Kaine, someone
who had been on or at the back of his mind for three years. Of
course she didn't *look* like Moylita Kaine, but she didn't even
talk like her either. He remembered the long philosophical
dialogues in the novel, the subtleties of debate and persuasion,
the wit and the compassion. The woman who was here was
speaking openly but ordinarily, she was friendly but somehow
reserved.

His first impression of her appearance had been hasty, and
partly the product of circumstances. It was her bulky clothes
that made her seem plump, because her hands and face were
slender and delicate. She was no longer a girl, but neither was
she matronly; Dik tried to guess her age, and thought she was
probably older than thirty but younger than forty. It was difficult to tell, and he wished she would take off her fur cap so he
could see her face properly. A wisp of dark-brown hair fell
across her forehead.

"Is the play what you want to write?" he said, still staring
fixedly at her.

"No . . . but it's a way of making a living."

"You're paid well I hope!" And again he flinched inside
from his own forthrightness.

"Not as well as your burghers are being paid for having me
here. But . . . I didn't want to give up writing altogether." She
had turned away from him, pretending to hold her hands nearer
the fire. "I have to wait for the war. A fallow period will be
good for me in the end."

"Do you think the war will be over soon?"

"I'd make it end tomorrow, if thinking it would do it. But
you should know better than me. You're a soldier, aren't you?"

"A policeman. It's the same thing, I suppose."

"I suppose so too. Look, why don't you come and stand
here? You'll be warmer."

"I think I should be returning to the hostel. You must be busy."

"No, I'd like you to stay. I want to talk to you."

She turned the electric fire slightly, indicating that he should go nearer, so he went to her side of the desk and sat awkwardly on the corner, letting the heat play on his legs. From this position he could see some of the words she had been typing on the paper, and he looked curiously at them.

As soon as she noticed this, Moylita Kaine pulled the page from the machine. She laid it face down on the desk.

Taking it as a rebuke, Dik said: "I didn't mean to pry."

"It isn't finished yet, Dik."

"It'll be marvellous," he said, sincerely.

"Maybe it will be, and maybe it won't. But I don't want anyone to read it yet. Do you understand?"

"Of course."

"But you might be able to help me," she said. "Would you?"

Dik felt an urge to laugh, so ridiculous and thrilling was the notion that he could offer her anything.

"I don't know," he managed to say. "What do you want?"

"Tell me about the village. The burghers aren't interested in me, except for the prestige and money they get because I'm here, and I haven't been allowed to see anybody else. I have to write a play . . . but all I can write about is what I see." She gestured towards the window, with its view of the frozen valley. "There aren't many dramatic possibilities in trees and mountains."

"Couldn't you make something up?" Dik said.

"You sound like Clerk Tradayn!" When she saw his expression she added quickly: "I want to write about things as they really are, Dik. Who lives in the village, for instance? Is there anyone here who isn't a soldier?"

Dik thought. "There are the burghers' wives," he said. "But they live outside the village. We never see them."

"Anyone else?"

"There are still a few farmers in the valley, I believe. And the men at the railway-depot."

"So it is just soldiers and burghers. I might as well write about trees and mountains!"

"But I thought you had already started," Dik said, glancing at the pile of pages beside the typewriter.

"It's proceeding," Moylita Kaine said, explaining nothing. "What about the frontier wall? Do you ever go up there?"

"On patrol. That's what we're here for."

"Will you describe it to me?"

"Why?" Dik said.

"Because I haven't seen it. The burghers won't let me go up there."

"You couldn't put it in your play."

"Why not? Surely it's at the heart of this community."

"Oh no," Dik said, very seriously. "It's along the top of the mountains." As Moylita Kaine laughed he squirmed with embarrassment, then laughed too. "I see what you mean."

"The wall goes right round our country, Dik. We're imprisoned by it, but how many ordinary people have ever seen it? It's what the war is about, and so for anyone writing today it's a very important symbol. And it's the same here. To understand this community, I have to know about the wall."

"It's just a wall. It's made of . . . concrete, I think. It's high, about twice the height of a man. There's barbed wire along parts of it, and machine-gun posts and towers. The enemy have put up floodlights on the other side."

"And it runs along the old frontier?"

"Exactly," Dik said. "Right over the peaks of the mountains. It's very . . . symbolic," he added, using her word.

"Walls always are. What do you do up there?"

"We make sure nobody tries to get across. Nothing much happens for most of the time. We've got warmways laid in the snow, to stop the ground freezing. In theory we can turn them off quickly in case the enemy tries to invade, but I don't think that's ever been done. Every now and then someone on the other side throws grenades at us, and if they do we throw some back. Sometimes it doesn't lead to anything, sometimes the fighting goes on for days."

"Is it frightening?"

"Sometimes. It can be very boring."

As he talked she was looking at him sympathetically, her

hands resting lightly on the desk and idly fingering her type-script. "Do you know who built the wall, Dik?"

"They did."

"Do you know that that's what they say?" she said. "That we put up the wall?"

"That's ridiculous. Why should we do that?"

"It's what they say." Dik was going to ask how she knew, but she went on: "I've read their literature. Some of it has been smuggled in. They believe we put up the wall to prevent people from fleeing the country. They say we are living under a dictatorship, and that our freedoms are restricted by the tithe-laws."

"Then why are they trying to invade? Why do they bomb our cities?"

"But Dik, *they* say they are defending themselves, because we, our government, are trying to impose our system on them!"

"Then why accuse us of building the wall?"

"It doesn't matter who built the wall . . . don't you see it shouldn't be there at all! It's a symbol, as we agree, but a symbol of stupidity."

"Are you on their side?" Dik said, coldly.

"Of course not. I'm on no one's side . . . I just want the killing to end. Didn't you find this in *The Affirmation*?"

Her unexpected mention of the novel took Dik aback; while she was talking about the war she was venturing into his territory, was on a subject about which he knew rather too much. But suddenly to relate the book to it . . .

He said: "I don't remember."

"I thought I made myself clear. The duplicity of Hilde, and her lies. When Orfé—"

"I know!" Dik said, seeing at once. "The first time he makes love to her . . . they are talking. Hilde wants him to be treacherous, to excite her, and Orfé claims she will be the first to betray them."

He would have gone on, letting his detailed memory of the book's plot carry him forward, but Moylita Kaine said: "You really did read it closely. You see what I mean then?"

"About the wall?"

"Yes."

He shook his head. "I know what happens in the book . . . but it was written before the war started!"

"There have always been walls, Dik!"

Then she began to talk about the novel, leaning slightly to one side as she did so, dangling her fingers before the fire to warm them. She was guarded at first, watching Dik's response to her words, but as she saw his eager interest, as he revealed that his reading of the novel had been close and intelligent, she talked more freely. She spoke quickly, she made deprecating jokes about herself and her story, her eyes sparkled in the snowy light from the window. Dik was more excited than he could remember: it was like reading the book for the first time again.

She said that there was a wall in the novel, a figurative barrier that lay between Orfé and Hilde. It was the dominant image in the book, if never directly described. It was there from the outset, because of her marriage, but after Coschtie's death it continued because of the betrayals. As first Orfé and then Hilde tried to draw the other closer, because each found infidelity sexually stimulating, the wall became higher and more impregnable. The labyrinthine involvements of the lesser characters—fulfilling Coschtie's demands on them in his lifetime, revenging themselves on his memory when he was dead —formed a pattern of moral attitudes. Their influence was divided: some controlled Orfé, some Hilde. Every conspiratorial action further fortified the wall between the two lovers, and made more inevitable the final tragedy. Yet the book was still the affirmation of the title: Moylita Kaine said she intended the novel to make a positive statement about the human condition. Orfé's final decision was a declaration of freedom; the wall fell as the book ended. It was too late for Orfé and Hilde . . . but the wall had nevertheless fallen.

"Do you see what I was trying to do?" she said.

Dik shook his head vaguely, still lost in this new insight into the book, but when he realized what he was doing he nodded emphatically.

She regarded him kindly, and sat back in her chair. "I'm sorry, Dik. You shouldn't have allowed me to talk so much. I get carried away when I talk about my writing."

"Please . . . tell me more!"

"I thought I'd said it all!" she said, laughing.

It was Dik's opportunity to ask the questions he had been storing up since his first reading of the book. How she had had the original idea, whether any of the characters were based on real people, whether she had ever visited the Dream Archipelago where the story was set, how long the book had taken to write. . . .

Moylita Kaine, obviously flattered by his interest, gave replies to them all . . . but Dik was unable to judge how literally she was answering. She made more jokes, and sometimes was deliberately vague, raising more questions than he could ever ask.

It was after one such self-effacing joke that Dik suddenly took stock of himself, and realized that his barrage of questions was sounding like an interrogation. He lapsed into awkward silence, staring down at the battered old typewriter she had been using.

"Am I talking too much?" she said, to his surprise.

"No! I'm asking too many questions."

"Then let me ask some of you."

Dik had little enthusiasm for himself, and answered in an uninterested voice. He told her about the degree-course he had been offered, but he was uncertain of what might have followed that. He nurtured secret ambitions to write—and probably to write a book like *The Affirmation*—but he would never reveal that to Moylita Kaine.

There was only one thing he had left to say to her, and that was something else he would never volunteer to her, even though he hugged its secret to himself like a beloved animal. The question that would have let him tell her did not seem to be forthcoming, so Dik moved away from the desk-top and stood up.

"Can I come and see you again tomorrow?" he said.

"If you are able to."

"I have another day's leave. If you're not too busy—"

"Dik, the government intends these residences to allow people like you to meet writers. Yes, please come again tomorrow . . . and bring some of your friends."

"No . . ." Dik said. "Not unless they ask."

"Won't you tell them?"

"If you'd like me to."

"They have been told I'm here, haven't they?"

Dik remembered the announcement on the notice-board. "I think so."

"You seem to have found out without any difficulty." She looked suddenly at his copy of *The Affirmation*, which he had put under his arm again. "As a matter of interest, how *did* you know I was coming to the village?"

And just as he thought his secret would stay intact, she had come to it.

"I saw the scheme announced in the Police magazine," he said. "Your name was there . . . and I wanted to meet you."

He confessed all. The scheme was intended to encourage the arts during the emergency, and in theory was open to any community on or near the front line. Dik, lowliest constable— or so he imagined himself—in one of the lowliest platoons in the Border Police, felt that any request he made would be refused automatically, but seeing Miss Kaine's name listed as a participant had encouraged him at least to try. His request to the platoon-serjeant must have reached the burghers, because a few weeks later a notice had appeared in the common-room, describing the scheme and asking for nominations. Dik, who sometimes felt he was the only constable who ever looked at the notice-board, had written Moylita Kaine's name on the form, and, for good measure, had written it in three more times in different hands.

He hadn't known it at the time, but an additional grant was paid to the administrators of the communities—in this case, the Council of Burghers—and this unexpected way of receiving money and prestige was probably what had decided the burghers. Moylita Kaine as writer would be of no interest to them; any writer or artist would have been sufficient.

She listened to his account—half-proud, half-shy—smiling faintly.

"So it's you I have to thank?" she said.

"I'm sure I had very little to do with it," Dik lied, his face burning again.

"Good," Moylita Kaine said. "I wouldn't like to think that you were responsible for giving me this."

She waved her gloved hand to take in the grimy room, the one-bar heater, the frosty view.

"Are you sorry you came to the village?" Dik said.

"I was until today. I'm glad we've met. You will come tomorrow?"

"Yes, Miss Kaine."

"It's . . . Mrs Kaine," she said.

"Oh. I'm sorry. I didn't know—"

"You had no reason to know. It doesn't matter."

But it did, unexpectedly, to Dik. That night he could hardly sleep for thinking about her, and loving her with a passion that astonished him.

A time for reflection, unwelcomely. Dik's intention had been to return to the saw-mill straight after breakfast, but he was "volunteered" for cookhouse duties by a sharp-featured caporal who waylaid him outside the canteen. Given a morning of tedious chores, Dik retreated into his usual state of inner contemplation, and in the clattering, steamy cookhouse he saw the conversation of the previous day in a new light. Far from the heady euphoria of his night's dreams, Dik thought more analytically about what Moylita Kaine had said.

While he was preparing himself for college, Dik had taken to reading literary criticism in the hope of gaining new insights into the literature he read. One book had made a particular impression on him. In it, the author made out the case that the act of reading a book was just as creative an act as writing one. In some respects, the reader's reaction was the only reliable measure of the book. Whatever the reader decided became the definitive assessment of the book, *whatever* the intentions of the author.

To Dik, who was largely untutored in literature, this approach to reading struck him as being of great value. In the case of *The Affirmation*—a novel not mentioned once in any of the criticism he read—it gave further weight to his belief that it was a truly great novel; by this critical method, whatever objective values might be placed against the book by other people, it would remain a great novel because *he* interpreted it as such.

Putting his conversation with Moylita Kaine into this light, not only were her intentions irrelevant to his enjoyment, but it was arrogant of her to impose them on him by explaining.

The instant Dik thought this he regretted it, because he knew her motives had been kindly. Even to think it was to place himself as her equal, when it was abundantly clear that she was superior to him in every way. Chastened by his own arrogance, Dik resolved to make amends in some way, without revealing why.

But as he worked on in the kitchens, waiting for his duties to finish with the serving of the midday meal, the thought would not go away. In explaining her novel to him, had Moylita Kaine been trying to tell him something?

Walking up the warmway to the saw-mill, Dik passed one of the burghers. Automatically, he stepped into the snow at the side and stood with eyes humbly lowered as the man swept past.

Then: "Where are you going, boy?"

"To see the writer, sir."

"By whose authority?"

"I have a pass, sir." He fumbled in his pocket, thanking the stars that he had remembered to take it with him. The burgher examined it closely, as if trying to find the least irregularity. Then he passed it back.

"You know who I am, Constable?"

"Yes, sir."

"Why did you not salute?"

"I . . . didn't see you approaching, sir. I was watching where I placed my feet."

There was a long silence, while Dik continued to stare at the ground. The burgher was breathing stiffly, as if seeking some excuse to bar him from the mill. Then at last, without a word, he walked on down towards the village.

After what to Dik seemed a respectful few seconds, he regained the warmway and hurried up to the saw-mill. He let himself in and went up the stairs. Moylita Kaine was standing by the window, and as he opened the door she turned towards him with an expression of such anger that he almost fled.

But she said at once: "Oh, it's you. Come in, close the door." She turned back to the window, and Dik saw her hand was clenched tightly, the knuckles white. He assumed that her anger was directed at him—had she somehow sensed his uncharitable thought?—but after a moment she looked back at him. "Don't take any notice, Dik. I've just had a visit from one of your burghers."

"Is there something wrong?"

"No . . . not at all." She went to her desk and sat down, but almost at once she stood up again and paced about the room. At last she went back to the desk.

"Was he ordering you about?" Dik said, with a feeling of kinship.

"No, not that sort of thing." She sat forward. "Yesterday, you said the burghers were married. All of them?"

"I . . . think so. When my troop arrived there was a function at the civic hall for the officers. I saw a lot of women then."

"Clerk Tradayn . . . is he married?"

"I don't know." Suddenly suspecting what might have happened, for it had been Tradayn Dik had met on the warmway, he wanted to hear no more about it. He reached under his weatherproof cape, and brought out the object he had been carrying.

"Moylita," he said with some hesitation, for it was the first time he had used her first name, "I've brought you a present."

She looked up, then took it from him. "Dik, it's beautiful! Did you carve it?"

"Yes." As she turned it in her hand, he went and sat on the edge of the desk, as he had done before. "It's a special wood. I found it in the forest. It's easy to carve."

"A hand holding a pen," she said. "How did you know . . .?"

"It was the way the wood had grown. It looked a bit like that before I started. I'm sorry it's crude. All I've done is smooth it down."

"But it's exactly right! May I really keep it?" When he nodded she stood up, and, leaning across the desk, kissed him on the cheek. "Dik, thank you!"

He started to mumble about the inadequacy of the gift, thinking of his repentant motives, but Moylita moved some of her papers aside and set the wood-carving firmly on the desk in front of her.

"I asked how you knew," she said, "because it's a coincidence. You see, I have a present for you too."

"For me?" Dik said, stupidly.

"I wrote something for you last night. Just for you."

"What is it?" Dik said, but at the same moment Moylita produced a few sheets of white paper, clipped together in one corner.

"It's a story . . . I wrote it for you after you left yesterday. I don't think it's very good, because I wrote it so quickly, but it happened because of what we talked about."

"May I see?"

She shook her head. "Not yet. I want you to promise me something first: that you won't read it until I've left here."

"Why not?" Dik said, then added with a flash of insight: "Is it about me?"

"Well, there's someone in it who's a bit like you . . . you might recognize one or two things he says."

"I don't mind that!" Dik said eagerly. "I'll read it now."

He held out his hand.

"No. I want to tell you about it first. I don't want you to think I'm trying to impress you . . . it really isn't a good story. It's not very original, and I think the writing isn't polished enough. I did it quickly."

"That's how I made my carving."

"Maybe . . . but there's something else. If anyone found this, you could get into trouble. You see, the character in the story is someone who's on the other side . . . beyond the wall. If the burghers found this, they would wonder what you were doing with it, and where you got it from. Do you still want it?"

"Of course. I can hide it . . . our kit is never searched."

"All right, then. But another thing. The story isn't set here, in the mountains. I've set it in the south. Do you know where I mean?"

"Jethra," Dik said.

"No . . . not even in the south of the country. The southern continent, on the other side of the Midway Sea."

"Near the Dream Archipelago!" Dik said, thinking of the novel.

"That sort of area. I've got to warn you, because although it probably sounds innocuous to you, and even rather unlikely, if the burghers saw this they would assume you were a spy."

Dik said, not understanding: "Moylita, how can—?"

"Listen, Dik. Just before I came to the village, there were a lot of rumours in Jethra about the progress of the war. Some of my friends suspect there have been secret negotiations with the enemy, because the air-raids have been doing a lot of damage. It's been said that the theatre of war will be moved to the south, to fight it out where there are no cities." Dik opened his mouth, but Moylita went on: "I know it sounds nonsensical; it does to me too. Why they can't just declare a ceasefire, I don't know. But the war is getting worse, not better, and to save our precious way of life they're going to make war elsewhere. For the story, I've assumed this will happen, and in the very near future . . . so the story takes place on the southern continent."

"A lot of books have been set there," Dik said.

"Yes, but not books dealing with the war, with *this* war."

Moylita fell silent, and seemed to be studying Dik's face, trying to divine his reaction.

"Do you still want to have the story?" she said.

"Oh yes," he said at once, because his reaction was one of even greater interest in seeing it.

"Very well, then. Look after it, and don't read it now. Do you promise?"

He nodded emphatically, so Moylita Kaine pressed the thin typescript out across the desk and scrawled her signature on the top sheet. Then she folded it in two, and passed it over. Dik took it, and as if the paper were the skin of a living animal it seemed that every fibre was alive and throbbing with organic electricity. He could feel the typewritten words indented in the paper, and he ran his fingers along the reverse side, like a blind man feeling for meaning.

"You interrupted the play to write this," he said.

She looked at him with unconcealed surprise. "It doesn't matter."

"But surely that's more important?"

"I'm writing the play because I'm paid to, Dik, and I'm writing it for the burghers. They'll get their play, but I don't feel I'm really writing it. I'm following a formula I worked out years ago. I just change names and places . . . it's easy. I thought you'd realized that."

"I suppose I had guessed," Dik said, nevertheless a little disappointed. Holding the new typescript, feeling the pressure of its words against his hand, and all the mystery and promise they held, he remembered his thoughts of the morning. Yesterday, Moylita had disappointed him about the play, and soon afterwards had told him about her ideas about *The Affirmation*. He didn't want her to do that to this story.

Even so, a great curiosity was growing in him; he so wanted to understand it properly.

"Moylita, is this story . . . symbolic?"

She didn't answer straight away, but looked at him with a strange and shrewd expression. Then: "Why do you ask?"

"Because . . . please don't tell me what it means!" It stumbled out, not at all what he had meant to say. He wanted her to tell him about it; he might never see her again. She had made him understand the novel, when before he had only loved it.

But she was smiling, and said: "Don't worry, Dik. It's very simple. It's about a soldier who reads a book, and later he becomes a poet. Nothing symbolic at all."

"What I meant—"

"I know . . . because yesterday I was carried away by my own brilliance, and talked about the walls? There's only one wall in this, and it's built of bricks and it's just a wall."

"And this soldier, this . . . poet, he climbs it?"

"Dik, I think you should wait until you've read the story. I don't want you to give it meanings it hasn't got."

"But he does climb the wall, doesn't he?"

"How did you know?"

"Because—"

Then the door opened without warning, and the burgher

Dik had seen earlier came quickly into the room. He slammed the door behind him.

Because of what you said; Dik's intuition, tailing away.

The burgher said: "Mrs Kaine, would you—?" He saw Dik, who had moved back against the wall, and turned at once towards him. "What are you doing here, Constable?"

"I told you, sir . . . I have a pass." He reached into his pocket, groping for it.

"I've seen the pass. What are you doing here, in this room?"

Moylita said: "He has every right to be here, Tradayn. While I'm writing, the troops—"

"The Border Police are under the orders of the Council, Mrs Kaine. Passes issued by non-commissioned officers have to be approved by me."

"Then you can approve it now. Have you got it there, Dik?"

While they spoke, Dik had found the slip of paper and held it out towards the burgher. He had never heard anyone ever speak back to a burgher, and it was awe-inspiring to see the confidence with which Moylita did it.

Clerk Tradayn took no notice of him or his pass, but went to the desk and leaned across it, resting his broad, plump hands on the edge.

"I want to see what you've been writing," he said. "All of it."

"You've seen the play . . . I haven't done any more since yesterday."

"You were using the typewriter late into the night."

"Have you been spying on me, Tradayn?"

"Mrs Kaine, while at the frontier you're under military law. Let me see what you've been writing."

She scooped up the sheaf of papers from the desk and thrust them at him. Meanwhile, Dik, still standing with his back against the wooden wall, could feel her secret typescript hanging conspicuously in his hand. He wished he could slip it under his cape, but any movement would draw the burgher's attention.

"Not this, Mrs Kaine . . . the rest of it. What are you holding, Constable?"

"Just the pass, sir,"

"Give it to me."

Dik glanced helplessly at Moylita, but she was staring at the burgher with frank hostility. Reluctantly, Dik held out the pass, but Clerk Tradayn reached behind him and snatched the typescript from his other hand. He moved to the window, and unfolded it in the light.

" 'The Negation'," he said. "Is that your title, Mrs Kaine?" Moylita's steady gaze did not flicker, and the burgher read on, adopting a scornful, mocking voice: " 'It no longer mattered which side had first breached the pact that prohibited the use of sense-gases. They had been in illegal use for so long that they were no longer questioned. What the ordinary soldier perceived as real could not be trusted, because his sense of vision, touch and sound had been . . .' " The burgher stopped reading aloud, looked sharply at Moylita, then turned back to the typescript. He read quickly down the first page, silently mouthing the words, then flicked it over and read the second. "Have you been reading this, Constable?"

"No, sir—"

"The boy has no knowledge of it. I've lent it to him . . . it's something I wrote several years ago."

"Or several hours ago." Tradayn squinted again at the first page, his small, deep-set eyes moving quickly across the lines. He held out the typescript for Moylita to see. "Is this your signature?"

"Yes."

"Good." He stuffed the typescript into an inner pocket. "Constable, return to your quarters at once."

"Sir, I—"

"Quarters, Constable!"

"Yes, sir." Dik shuffled hesitantly towards the door, looking back at Moylita. She was watching him now, her eyes steady and calm. He wondered if she was trying to signal some message to him, but if she was it was something so subtle it was lost on him. When he reached the frosty air outside he started to walk down the warmway, but halted after a short distance. He listened, but he could hear nothing. He hesitated a few seconds longer, then left the warmway and ran across the snowfield towards the nearest trees. Here the snow had drifted deeply, and he jumped down and hid behind the trunk of a broad fir.

He had only a few minutes to wait. Moylita and the burgher soon appeared, walking down the warmway towards the village. Moylita went first, walking with her head bowed, but she was carrying under her arm the carving Dik had given her.

Dik hid in his hostel room for the rest of the day, waiting for the inevitable summons to Clerk Tradayn's office in the civic hall, but it seemed nothing in life was inevitable, for the summons never arrived. By nightfall, Dik was more in terror of the uncertainty than he would have been of punishment.

The story he had never read seemed, for reasons he did not fully understand, as potentially explosive as one of the enemy's flatcake mines. She had said it herself, and the burgher's reading of it had confirmed it. She would be charged with spying and treachery, and she would be imprisoned or exiled or shot.

The fact that this sort of retribution might also be taken on him was of less importance.

The constant nagging fears and worries sent him into the streets of the village as soon as the evening meal was done with. He had eaten virtually nothing, sitting in silence as the other lads shouted and laughed.

The night was clear, but a strong wind was up, lifting the powdery snow from the roofs and sills and sending it stingingly into his face. Dik walked the length of the main street, hoping for a sight of Moylita or some clue as to where she might be, but the street was empty and dark and the only light showing was from windows high under the gables. He returned slowly, halting when he came to the civic hall. Here the tall windows showed light, gleaming in horizontal slits through the wooden shutters.

Hardly thinking what the consequences might be, Dik went to the main doors and walked inside. There was a narrow hallway, cold and brightly lit, and opposite him were two more doors, made of wood and heavy glass, ground-cut with ornate curlicues. A caporal was standing before them.

"What's your business, Constable?"

"I'm looking for Moylita Kaine, sir," Dik said, with simple truth.

"There's no one here. Just the burghers."

"Then I'll see them, sir. Clerk Tradayn summoned me."

"The burghers are in session. They summoned no one. What's your name and number, Constable?"

Dik stared back silently, fearing the caporal's authority but still compelled by his anxiety about Moylita, and he backed away. He returned to the street, closing his ears and mind to the caporal's voice, shouting behind him. Dik expected to be followed, but once he had let the main doors swing closed behind him the shouts ceased. Dik ran away, sliding on the icy ground as he reached the corner of the building. He came into the tiny square which lay beyond. This was where local farmers could petition the burghers during the day-time, and where, before the war, there had been weekly markets. The square was divided up into a number of pens where the tithe-livestock would be kept while the petitions were heard. Dik vaulted over two of these pens, then paused to listen. There was no sound of pursuit.

He looked up at the shuttered windows of the civic hall, behind which was the Council Chamber. Dik climbed on to one of the pens, and shuffled forward until his hands were resting on the cold brick of the building. He raised himself as high as he could go, and tried to peer through the shutters into the Chamber. The shutters behind the glass were slatted, and all he could see was the ceiling, richly ornamented in plaster mouldings and delicate, pastel-coloured renderings of religious tableaux.

Dik could hear the indistinct sound of voices from within, and after several unsuccessful attempts to see he pressed his ear against the glass. At once, he heard the sound of Moylita's voice, high-pitched and angry. A man said something Dik couldn't hear, then Moylita shouted: "You know the sense-gases are being used. Why won't you admit it?" Several voices were raised against her, and she was shouting. Dik heard: ". . . they have a right to know!" And: ". . . drive them mad, it's illegal!" The Chamber was in uproar, and Dik heard a series of loud thuds and the sound of wood falling hollowly against wood. Moylita started to scream.

Then Dik was found by the caporal. He was dragged down from his precarious place by the window and fell kicking and struggling into the snow. The caporal cuffed him painfully until he stopped, then hauled him away. He was taken to a guardroom by the entrance to the hall, where he was given another beating and two platoon-serjeants were summoned.

The sky had clouded over and the wind had risen, and by the time Dik had been dragged through the streets to the hostel, the gale was bearing thick, suffocating snowflakes, piling them up against the walls and posts.

Bruised and dispirited, Dik was locked in his room for the rest of the night, and for all the day following. He had much on which to ponder, and nearly all of it was concerned with Moylita and the possible fates that he imagined could be delivered to her; they were all awful, and he could barely countenance them. For the rest, he wondered about the little story he had held, unread, for those few moments. All Moylita had told him directly was that it concerned a soldier who became a poet; what he had later learned about it implied that its content was much more intricate. The few short sentences the burgher had read aloud: sense-gases, distortion of perception. Later, what he had overheard from the Chamber: the right to be told, the illegality, the madness.

But Moylita had written it exclusively for him. She had not talked about the background, she had told him only about the poet. This was, for her, the true statement of the story, and so it should be for him.

He had never told her of his own literary aspirations, of the bundles of unpublished verse that lay in a cupboard somewhere at home. Had she somehow guessed? In the same way that she had interpreted her novel for him, was she trying, with the story, to tell him to reinterpret his own life?

Dik didn't know. Whatever part of him had once been a poet had been beaten out of him by the military; he could not forget the failure of the verse he had tried when he arrived in the village. The studious boy who had never had many friends was a long way behind him now, beyond the wall of conscription.

His precious copy of *The Affirmation* was safe in his room, and in the late afternoon he had worked enough of the resentments and angers out of his system to feel calm, and he lay on his bed and read a part of it. He selected the passage he always found the most intriguing: the last five chapters. This was the part of the story where Orfé had escaped from the conspiratorial machinations of Emerden and the other minor characters, and was free to go in search of Hilde. Orfé's quest through the exotic landscape of the Dream Archipelago quickly became a journey into self-exploration, and Hilde became ever more remote.

Reading the book again for the first time since Moylita had talked about it, Dik was suddenly aware of the wall-symbolism, and he cursed his lack of perceptiveness in not seeing it for himself. As Orfé sailed from one island to the next he encountered one barrier after another; the author's images, her dialogues, her choice of words, reflected the fact that Hilde had retreated behind the wall of Orfé's own making. Even Moylita Kaine's choice of locale for the end of the quest—the island of Prachous, which in Archipelagan argot meant "the fenced island"—was appropriate.

He finished the book with a sense of satisfaction, but his thoughts returned at once to the short story. Moylita had been trying to tell him something with it; did he know enough about it to try to imagine what that could be?

Affirmation/negation: opposites. Orfé had failed to climb his wall when he had had the chance, and thereafter it was too late. In the story, the soldier climbed a wall and became a poet, so the chance was there. In the novel, Orfé started as a romantic idler, a dilettante and a sybarite; because of his failures and involvements he became a haunted ascetic, obsessed with purpose and guided by moral principle. In the story . . . what?

Dik, drawing on his own inner strengths of rational contemplation, began to understand what Moylita Kaine wanted of him.

On the mountain frontier there was no greater punishment than wall-patrol, and so Dik was unsurprised when he was restored to normal duties. By mid-afternoon of the next day he was pacing an allotted sector of the wall, high and remote and lost in cloud. It was bitterly cold: every minute or two Dik had to chip away the encrusting ice from his goggles, and work the breech-mechanism of his rifle to prevent it from jamming.

While climbing up to the frontier in the morning, Dik had been able to see the saw-mill from the slopes above the village. There had been no lights on that he could see, and the unbroken snowfield beneath it was proof that the warmway that once led to it had been taken up.

During his leave certain changes had been made to the defences along the wall. The beginnings of a floodlight system were evident near some of the guardposts, and several immense drums of electric cable had been dumped on the slopes. In addition, there had appeared several bulbous metal shapes, half-buried in the snow beside the warmway. Complicated arrangements of pipes and nozzles led from these across the warmway and up to the parapet of the wall; Dik tripped over the pipes several times in the murky light, until he learnt to watch out for them.

He was allowed a short break at dusk, when he drank a ferociously hot soup in one of the guardposts, but after nightfall he was back in his sector, pacing to and fro in numb misery, trying to count the minutes that remained until relief.

Night-patrols were especially nerve-racking, for he was alone in the hostile alliance of dark and cold and unexplained noises. On this night the enemy had not turned on their floodlights, so he could hardly even see the bulk of the wall looming beside him. All that was clear was the dark strip of the warmway against the white snow, and the sinister, half-buried cisterns.

He wondered, as he always wondered, where the enemy were and what they were doing or planning on the other side. Was there someone like himself, a few feet away on the other side, stamping to and fro, hoping only to survive the cold night long enough for patrol to end?

Here, at the place where the two countries met, where two political ideologies clashed, he was physically closer to the enemy than anyone other than the rest of the patrolling constables. And yet the frontier united him with the enemy; the men on the other side obeyed the same sort of orders, suffered the same fears, endured the same hardships, and they, presumably, were defending their country to support a system that was as remote from them as the burghers were remote from Dik.

He worked the breech-mechanism to free it. There was a pause in the whining of the wind, and in the brief silence Dik heard, from the far side of the wall, someone working a breech-mechanism. It was something often heard at the wall: at once alarming and comforting.

Dik could feel the weight of Moylita Kaine's novel in his pocket. He had brought it with him, in defiance of standing orders. After the events of the last two days he felt that even temporary separation from it would be a breach of the responsibility he owed her. He had no idea of what had happened to her, and knew only that her life would have been changed drastically. Carrying her book was the only way he knew of accepting her ideas. She talked in symbols, and Dik was prepared to act in symbols. He could not act in reality, because he knew at last what she had been telling him.

Climb the wall, Dik.

He glanced up at the bleak, unsymbolic wall beside him. It was known to be booby-trapped. Flatcake mines had been laid by both sides. The trip-wires and scramble-fence were touch-triggered and electrified. A man had only to show his hand above the top of the wall and a fusillade of shots would come from the other side. In the short time the war had been in progress, there were already scores of stories about grenade-attacks brought on by nothing more than the sound of sliding snow.

He walked on, remembering the momentary resentment he had felt about the way Moylita had interpreted her novel for him. This was the same. In her negation of ideals, a man could climb the wall and write verse about it afterwards; Dik was making his own negation.

Then he remembered the sound of her voice coming from the Council Chamber. She had taken a risk in writing the story; punishment had been meted out to her. Conscience and the sense of responsibility returned, and Dik thought again about climbing the wall. He glanced up at the dark bulk beside him. It was high here, but there were firing-platforms further along, where one could climb if necessary.

He was abruptly aware that somewhere around him was a hissing noise, and he halted at once. He crouched down, holding his rifle ready, and looking about him in the gloom. Then, from a long way away, from the depths of the valley, a shrill, thin sound reached him, distorted by the wind and the distance: the train was in the depot, letting its whistle be heard. Dik stood up again, relieved by the familiarity of the sound.

He walked on rattling the bolt of his rifle. On the other side of the wall, someone else did the same.

And the hissing continued.

Another hour passed, and the time for the relief-sentry to come had almost arrived, when he saw the figure of one of the constables walking along the warmway towards him. Dik was frozen through, and he stood and waited gratefully for the other to reach him. But as the figure came nearer, Dik saw that he was raising his arms and holding his rifle above his head.

He halted a short distance from Dik, and said, in a foreign accent: "Please not shoot. I wish surrender."

It was a young man of about his own age, the sleeves and legs of his protective clothing ripped and torn by the barbed wire. Dik stared at him in astonishment. They were near one of the cisterns, and the hissing of gas was loud above the wind.

Dik himself could feel the bite of the freezing wind through the gashes in his jacket and trousers, and as a floodlight switched on he saw a smear of blood below his knee. He looked at the young soldier standing amazed before him, and said again, much louder: "Please don't shoot. I'm surrendering."

They were near one of the cisterns, and the hissing of gas was loud above the wind.

The enemy soldier said: "Here . . . my gun."

Dik said: "Take my rifle."

As Dik passed him his, the young man handed his own over and raised his hands again.

"Cold," said the enemy soldier. His goggles had iced over, and Dik could not see his face. "That way," said Dik, pointing towards the distant guardpost and waving the muzzle of the captured rifle. "This way," said the young soldier, pointing to the guardpost.

They walked on slowly in the wind and snow, Dik staring at the back of his enemy's caped head in admiration and envy.

▼▼▼▼▼▼▼▼▼▼▼▼▼▼▼▼▼▼▼▼▼▼▼▼▼▼▼▼▼▼▼▼

The Greening of the Green

"Be careful with that dinghy, you idiots," the admiral bellowed in a whisper. "It's the last one we have."

He looked on anxiously while the sweating sailors lowered the dinghy from the deck of the submarine into the water. There was no moon, but the crowded stars in the clear Mediterranean sky glowed like tiny light bulbs.

"Is that the shore, Admiral?" the passenger asked. His teeth chattered as he spoke, probably from fear since the night was warm.

"Captain," the admiral said. "I'm captain of this sub so you call me captain. And, no, that is a fog bank. The shore is over there. Are you ready?"

Giulio started to speak, then, sensing the trembling of his jaw, nodded instead. He felt as scruffy as he looked with his ancient beret, decaying corduroy trousers and decayed jacket. Felt even scruffier next to the crisply uniformed figure of the admiral: in the dark the patches and darns of his uniform did not show. Giulio nodded again when he realized the admiral had not seen his nod the first time.

"Good. Then you know your instructions?"

"Of course I don't know my instructions," Giulio said with petulant irritation, trying not to stammer the words. "I only know that there is a piece of paper in my pocket with a word on it and I'm to read that word then eat the paper. At dawn."

"Those are the instructions I'm talking about, you idiot." The admiral grumbled like a volcano, his authority insulted.

"You can't talk to me like that," Giulio squeaked, realized he squeaked and lowered his voice. "Do you know who I am. . . ?"

He choked himself into silence. No, the admiral did not know who he was, and if he told him then the C.I.A. would kill them both; they had promised him that. No one was to know.

"I know you are a goddamned passenger and a goddamned nuisance and the sooner you are off this vessel the better. I have far more important things to do."

"What?" Giulio tried and succeeded in getting a sneer into his voice. "Sail a desk? What's an admiral doing in charge of a crummy sub? Too many brass hats, that's what!"

"No, not enough ships. This is the last pig boat." A little tear of self-pity formed in the admiral's eye, for he had been hitting the vodka bottle hard. "My last command. After this the beach. I should consider myself lucky even for this. . . ." He swallowed and gulped and shuddered away from this topic, which obsessed him night and day. "Here is your bag. I wish you good luck on your mission, whatever it is. Here is a receipt form—sign here."

Giulio scratched his name as well as he could in the darkness, clutched the battered but exceedingly large and heavy suitcase to him, then was half-carried into the bobbing dinghy. As soon as he was aboard the line was cast off and the four sailors began rowing furiously. An officer crouched in the bow with a compass and muttered instructions in arcane nautical terms. The beans and salt fish that Giulio had wolfed so hungrily an hour earlier now fought each other for a return journey up his throat. The dinghy bobbed and splashed through the waves, Giulio groaned aloud, then almost fell overboard as they grated to a stop. Horny hands seized him in silence, slid him over the side into a foot of cold water, then grabbed up paddles again and pulled hastily away.

"Good luck, buddy," the officer whispered as he vanished back into the darkness. A wave slapped cold water over Giulio's crotch. He gasped and turned and staggered up on to a sandy beach, holding the massive suitcase to him like an old friend. Once above the water he dropped the bag and sat upon it and tried not to groan aloud. He had never felt as alone and helpless before. He didn't even know where he was. Well that could be changed quickly enough. Dragging the suitcase after him he stumbled through the sand towards a looming dark structure.

There was no sound, other than the susurration of the waves on the shore behind him. The dark structure proved to be a row of bathing shacks, unlocked as he discovered when he rattled the door of the nearest one. Perfect for his purposes. He dropped the bag inside and pulled the door shut behind him, grinning wickedly into the darkness. Screw the instructions. Right now was when he wanted to know where he was and what happened next. A feeble flap towards personal freedom. This was why he had stolen the book of matches in defiance of all instructions and logic. He dug them out now, and the piece of paper, and fumbled to strike one in the darkness. It flared up suddenly, he squinted at the paper, at the word. It was upside down. He turned it over and read *shamrock*—then jerked his hand, burning his fingers, as memory rushed in. The match went out, he sucked his hand and almost spoke aloud the words that were dredged from his memory, hidden there by hypnotic suggestion until he read the word that had triggered their release.

YOU ARE ON THE BEACH OF MARINA PICCOLA ON THE ISLAND OF CAPRI. IT IS NOW LIGHT AND YOU WILL WALK UP THE ROAD TO THE TOWN OF CAPRI. IN THE PIAZZETTA YOU WILL GO TO THE PHARMACY ON THE RIGHT. A MAN WITH A GREY BEARD THERE WILL ANSWER *BUCCA* WHEN YOU GIVE THE PASSWORD *STUZZICADENTI*. EAT THIS PAPER.

He ruminated on the paper and the words. Capri, isle of joy in the Bay of Naples, or that is what they said. He had never seen it before, or Italy itself for that matter. Land of his fathers. He wondered what it was like and, for the first time, forgot to be afraid. He would find out soon enough. And the message was wrong about it being light; he felt a small triumph over this. A tiny blow struck against the system. Nor was he going to wait here until dawn. The further inland he was before he was seen, the less chance of his being suspected of landing on the beach. The logic of this was suspect but he still felt that way and he was going.

After a good deal of stumbling against invisible objects, he found stone steps that led up through a wall. The road was on the other side, with houses flanking it. All the windows were tightly shuttered against the poisonous dangers of the balmy night air and he tiptoed past them silently. The suitcase was heavy as lead and he had to keep changing hands. Only when he was around the second bend of the steep road, with no houses in sight, did he drop the thing and sit on it. He was panting and dripping with sweat and wondered how far away the town was.

Guilio was still struggling up the road when it began to get light in the east. The sky burned red as fire behind the mountains across the bay, and it was suddenly dawn. He felt vulnerable under the open sky and he hurried on. But it was a brief spurt and he had to stop, panting, and set the bag down again. Just as he did so a man came around a bend in the road carrying a great bundle of grass on his head. He looked up at Giulio with a very suspicious eye, made even more suspicious by the fact he was cross-eyed, as he passed.

"*Buon giorno*," Giulio said, forcing a smile.

The man grunted, a deep porcine sound, and Giulio's stomach churned. Was he really in Italy, on Capri? Then, when he was well past, the man released a reluctant, "*Buon gio'*."

The first encounter was the worst. A few other peasants passed, some in silence, others with a good morning, and he began to feel a certain security. He himself looked like a peasant, Christ, his parents had been peasants, and he could talk Italian. This thing might work yet.

Staggering with fatigue he made the last climb up the narrow road to the opening of the piazzetta. Early as it was most of the shops were open. On the far side was a bold sign over a shopfront that read *Farmacia*. Below the sign were only heavy steel shutters. The pharmacy was closed.

A cold chill swept through Giulio as he realized, a little too late, why he should have waited until dawn to read the note. He was too early and, he felt, obvious and suspicious. Wasn't that policeman looking at him, chewing the toothpick and wondering who he was? Fear rattled the teeth in his head and sent him stumbling into the mouth of the nearest street. It was narrow and dark and there were steps down which he half fell. Around the first corner and into a narrower alleyway. Were there footsteps behind him? A dark storefront opened before him and he stumbled through it, blinking in the darkness.

"*Sì?*" a voice rumbled, almost in his ear. A dark man with a two-day growth of beard stood there looking at him quizzically.

"Aspirin," Giulio said. "I need some aspirin."

"*Pazzo,*" the man growled, the sour odour of rough wine washing out on his breath. "Get out of here."

Giulio peered into the cavernous gloom and saw the box with a few old potatoes, the crate of tomatoes next to it. "I thought this was the pharmacy," he said. So unconvincingly that he didn't even fool himself. "What time does the pharmacy open?"

"Out!" the proprietor said loudly, and made a dismissing and insulting gesture with the fingers of his right hand. Giulio went out and retraced his steps towards the piazzetta. There was no sign of the policeman; that did not lessen his fear.

When he came back into the sunlight he saw a man with a long pole rolling up the steel shutter of the pharmacy. Giulio's heart beat rapidly as he dragged the heavy bag with him across the cobbles and towards the safety of the entrance. "*Stuzzicadenti,*" he said as the man turned towards him.

He was young and clean-shaven and had the same suspicious eye as the greengrocer. An answer was beneath him and he just jerked his thumb towards the grocery store behind him.

"Aspirin?" Giulio asked hopefully, trying to smile and not succeeding. The young man looked him up and down slowly in economic appraisal. Apparently Giulio looked as though he could at least afford an asprin or two. The young man shouldered the pole and silently led the way into the shop.

A fat man with a grey beard was behind the marble counter opening a package. He glanced up when Giulio entered, then turned his attention back to untangling the thick string. Fear was replaced by joy in Giulio's heart. He hurried to the man, leaned close, and whipered *stuzzicadenti* in his ear.

"Marco, did anyone see him come in?" the man asked, talking over the top of Giulio's head.

A D

"Only half the town," the young man answered.

"*Stuzzicadenti?*" Giulio asked, hopefully.

"It's always that way, they send people who know nothing."

"*Stuzzicadenti* . . . ", in an unhappy moan.

"Toothpicks?" grey beard asked, looking at Giulio for the first time. "Oh, yes, the stupid password thing. Wood? Nose? Tooth? No. Yes! Mouth. *Bucca!*"

"You took your time about it," Giulio muttered, put out by the reception.

"Shut up and follow me. Stay well back and look as though you are *not* following me. When they come looking for you I want everyone to know you left my shop."

He pulled on a natty pinstripe jacket, seized up a Malacca cane from the corner, then strode out of the door and across the piazzetta. Giulio started to follow and was restrained by the strong arm of the youth. "Not so close. Watch where he goes."

Only after grey beard had disappeared in a narrow alley did he release Giulio who hurried after. Rushing while trying not to rush, panting with the weight of the suitcase. He followed at a distance and, after a number of turns, was rewarded with the sight of his quarry entering a building. He strolled slower now, stopped and looked back. No one in sight. He pushed into a dark hallway and heard the door thud shut behind him. Another door opened and he followed the man into a cheerful room where wide-open double windows displayed a breath-taking view of the Bay of Naples. Grey beard waved him to a chair near the window, flashed a sudden gold-filled smile through the jungle of his beard, then seized up a bottle of wine from the sideboard.

"Welcome to Italy, Giulio. You may call me Pepino. How was the trip? You will have some of this wine, the native wine of this island, you will love it."

"How did you know my name?"

The smile vanished for a second, then aurously reappeared. "Please. I arranged all of this. I have your passport and papers here, with your picture on them. Tickets as well. I did all this and I tell you, it was not cheap." He glanced at the suitcase and his smile broadened. "So I am happy to see that you brought payment. May I have the case?"

Giulio held it tighter to him. "I was told to hand it over only when told a certain word."

"Your C.I.A. has seen too many old spy films! Who else but me . . . " With mercurial ease Pepino's temper changed and he was smiling again. "But of course—that's not your fault. The word is . . . *merda* . . . there are so many of the stupid words to remember. This one is . . . *shamarocka*! There, got it right the first time."

With no more ceremony he pulled the suitcase to him, dropped it flat on the floor and flipped the catches. It was locked. He muttered something nasty under his breath and produced, rather quickly Giulio thought for such a fat man, a large black knife that flicked open with a very nasty sound. A few twists with this and the locks flew open, the knife vanishing as quickly as it had appeared. He threw the lid open and Giulio leaned forward to look, for he had no idea what he had been burdened with.

The suitcase was tightly packed with bundles of pantyhose. Chuckling with pleasure, Pepino broke a bundle open and waved the diaphanous limbs in the air. "I'm rich, I'm rich," he whispered to himself. "More precious than gold."

Giulio nodded an amen to that. There was a fortune in the suitcase. Years earlier when petroleum had started to run out it had not only spelled the death of the auto and allied industries, but put paid to the petrochemical factories as well. What little supplies remained were reserved for essential pharmaceutical and industrial chemicals, and little or none for the manufacture of plastics. From being the most common material plastic had become the rarest, and non-industrial nylon the rarest of all. Of course a blackmarket did exist, which only helped push up the price of such non-essentials as pantyhose.

"This is for you," Pepino said, passing over a battered wallet that had been tucked between the bundles. Giulio opened it and looked at the tightly wadded banknotes. He took one out and stared at it. A squat man, robed to the ears, stared back. The printing was in a strange language, and alphabet, and read something like *NOTA AUTHAIRGTHE AUIG PHUNT*.

"Put them away," Pepino ordered. "For expenses and bribes when you get there." He dumped the contents of the suitcase into a high wardrobe, then locked it. From a drawer, at the bottom of the same wardrobe, he took underclothes, socks, shirts, all of them ancient, faded and patched, and stowed them in the suitcase. In place of the broken clasps he sealed it with a length of rope tied round, then handed it over to Giulio.

"Time to go," he announced. "On the north side of the piazzetta are steps leading down to Marina Grande. Descend, neither too slowly nor too quickly, and in the harbour there you will find the ferry to Naples waiting. Here is a ticket, put it in an outside pocket if you please. This envelope contains your passport and all the other papers you will need. The ship will be easy enough to find. You may board any time today and I suggest you proceed there as soon as you land. You will only get in trouble if you stay in the city. Good luck, that's it, finish your wine, and good luck with your mission whatever it is. If you get back alive tell your C.I.A. what a fine job I have done. They are one of my best customers."

Moved on by these encouraging words, and a firm hand in the small of his back, Giulio carried the now lightened suitcase down the seemingly endless steps to the harbour. He had a clear view of the ferry tied up at the mole and saw that they were shaking out the sails. He could not miss it! Hurrying, as fast as he could, he reached the harbour in a rush, then staggered to a walk, streaming with sweat, when he saw that people were still boarding. But he was none too early, for soon after he had dropped wearily to the deck they cast off the lines, with a good deal of shouting, and the ferry moved out into the bay. There was a brisk following wind, thankfully since his stomach did not enjoy the voyage at all, and they were soon gliding by the docks of Naples.

Empty of course, except for some fishing boats and coastal traders. The world could not convert quickly from power to sail. The ferry moved past the rusting hulk of *Ark Royal*, flight deck canted at a sharp angle where she sat on the bottom. Sunk by sabotage the rumour had it, though holed through by rust was probably more likely. In the midst of these tiny sailboats and rusting despair, the great green bulk of the *St. Columba* loomed large and impressive.

She stretched on and on, sleek metal and smooth paint, like something out of a history book. At her stern flapped an orange, white and green flag, while from her funnel trickled a thin streamer of pungent brown smoke. In a crumbling world she was a monument to the might of man and, suddenly, Giulio felt very happy. He was going to board her, travel on her, see this powerful machine in action. Since he was a child of the world's declining years he had known only grounded planes, skeletal cars, silent machines. Despite the danger of his mission he could not help but look forward with anticipation.

It was all he had ever dreamed of—and more. The only formality was the actual boarding of the vessel. Sharp-eyed soldiers, weapons ready, guarded the dock against unwelcome visitors, and a uniformed officer examined his papers, stamped them, removed some, and waved him on. A cursory glance through his suitcase followed, then he was aboard. It was like entering the gates of paradise.

A ruddy, smiling purser checked his name on a list and assigned him to a bunk. The man had a few words of basic Italian and a large vocabulary of gestures. Giulio made an effort not to understand the English.

"There you are, my lad, cabin number 144. *Uno, quatro, quatro*, do you have that? *No kabeesh*, ey. Sleep my old son, kip, *dormir* there down below, bloody *sotto*, you know. Catch on? That's grand. Nod away, that's it, cools the brain. And here's a few quid against your month's wages. *Soldi*, got that? Can't have a man going thirsty. Fine now, move off, bugger *avante*. Just follow the sounds of revelment and you can have a few jars with your mates to celebrate your voyage to the chosen land. Next."

The roar of masculine voices and laughter grew louder and louder as Giulio progressed down the corridor, until he pushed open the swinging doors of the saloon where the noise burst over him in a cloud of tobacco smoke and shouted Italian. Red-faced men, in shirts and neckties, were serving up great tankards of some dark, foaming beverage to dark-skinned, black-haired men who drank it at a ferocious rate. There were also smaller glasses of an amber fluid that was mixed with water from a jug. As Giulio pushed through to the bar he heard appreciative comments that, while it was not good wine and heady grappa, it certainly was worth drinking in its own right. Roll on the ship. Giulio passed over one of the bank notes he had been given, the same, though of a smaller denomination, as those packed into his inner pocket. The Italians were right, the drinks were different but very palatable.

So were the meals. He went through the first one in a bit of a haze, but had joyous memories of a piece of meat big enough to feed a family of ten back home in Hoboken, floury potatoes, golden plates of butter, dark bread. All a dream—that was not a dream. But all too quickly the journey passed. He gained a few pounds on the voyage, enjoyed some massive hangovers and undoubtedly did immense damage to his liver.

The Italian passengers had very little contact with the crew of the ship. This did not appear to be a matter of policy, just that this was a working ship, a freighter for the most part, and the sailors were quite busy. This and the linguistic barrier kept them apart. Though Giulio did volunteer for a working party when one was requested; who knew what technical secrets lay in the bowels of the ship! He discovered little other than that the *St. Columba* was steam-powered, peat-fired, and built in Cork. All of which he was sure the C.I.A. already knew. In exchange for this fragment of information he spent an exhausting afternoon shovelling peat past a broken conveyor belt from the bin. It was little solace that all of the others suffered as well, and returned to their quarters complaining bitterly and comparing the blisters on their hands.

Then the voyage was over. Gentle hills and an undulating coastline appeared ahead. The *St. Columba* moved slowly between the outstretched granite arms of the two great breakwaters and into the harbour. *Dun Laoghaire* a large sign said on the dock-side building, but there was no clue as to how it was pronounced. With little ceremony the men, carrying their few belongings, were moved off the ship and boarded the waiting double-decker buses. *An Lar* read the destination on the display boards, and all of the men chattered excitedly at the thrill of riding in a power-operated vehicle. The buses were silent too, obviously electrically powered, and moved out in a lumbering convoy for a short ride through narrow streets. There were green trees and small houses, gardens with flowers and parks with smooth, rich grass. The journey ended before a high wall and a tall, impressive-looking gate that opened to admit the fleet. The men unloaded in a large court-yard surrounded by interesting-looking buildings, and Giulio tried to remember all of the details as he had been trained to do. As soon as the buses had left, with a cheery wave from the last driver, the gates swung shut again and a man mounted a plat-form and blew into the microphone there. His magnified breath echoed like a wind from the walls and the Italians grew silent and turned to look at him. He wore a dark suit with matching waistcoat, a gold chain draped across the full front of this, and smoked a large-bowled pipe which he pointed at them to emphasize a point. It was pointing now.

"My name is Mr O'Leary," he said, "and I am in charge of this establishment. Some of you may speak English now and all of you will learn it if you intend to stay here. Gino here is the translator and he is going to translate now. But there are English classes every evening and you will be expected to attend. Tell them that, Gino."

O'Leary produced a lighter and proceeded to fire up his pipe while the translation was in progress. Then he nodded, whether at the translation or the tobacco was not made clear, and went on.

"You gentlemen are guest workers of Ireland. There are valuable jobs to be done here and I know you will enjoy doing them. The work is not hard, you will be fed well, will have a good deal of leisure time, will be permitted to send your salary home if you wish, will go to the church of your choice which of course will be the Roman Catholic Church. As we discover your qualifications and abilities you will find the best work suited to you. Some will become street sweepers, for we pride ourselves on the cleanliness of our cities, and others will have the pleasure of being dustmen and riding the great and power-ful vehicles that perform this vital function of the community. There are opportunities galore for you." He tamped down the smouldering tobacco with his thumb and appeared not to hear the mutter that muttered across his audience.

"Yes, I know that you applied for skilled jobs, masons and carpenters and the like, but if my experience of past drafts is correct there isn't an honest working man here." There was steel in his voice now and a new hardness in his eyes. "Nor a single callous on the soft hands of the lot of you. But that's all right. We know that you all are rich or know someone rich enough to enable you to afford the bribes and forgeries of papers that got you here. It'll not be held against you. You will be expected to work hard and measure up. And if you do not you will be shipped home forthwith. But live up to the terms of your contract and we will live up to ours. You will enjoy your stay on our shores. Remember, you will be permitted to send food parcels and manufactured articles to your families at home. You will prosper on the healthy diet of the land. You will drink Guinness and grow strong. You will assemble here at half-seven tomorrow morning to begin carrying bricks for the construction of the new powerplant."

At this O'Leary turned away—was there a twinkle in his eye?—and left before the translation was finished so that the groan that greeted his final words exited him through a small door. His audience went, somewhat crestfallen, to their quarters.

But not Giulio. Depressed? Never! Powerplant! This was the best luck ever.

It was drizzling next morning and in groups of ten, damp and cold, they stood in the courtyard. Each group next to a large pile of singularly massive-looking bricks. A squat and solid man with large red hands talked to Giulio and his companions and held out an object towards them. It had a long wooden handle that supported two boards, set edge to edge to make a V.

"This," he said, "this, my good lads, is a hod. Got that? Hod, hod. Let me hear you say it. Hod?"

"Hod," one man said, then others, "hod, hod."

"Very good. You're a bright lot and you'll learn fast. Now this is a wee bit of a hod as anyone who knows about such things will tell you, but that is because the bricks are not the normal, weak, crumbling things that you are used to in your foreign lands."

The men listened, puzzled, and Giulio tried to appear as unknowing as the others. The mere fact that no one understood their instructor did not seem to bother him nor halt the flow of his words.

"Time was when you had to carry a great hod just heaped with bricks, but now there are but three in a load. Why, you might ask, only three? Well I'll be happy to tell you. There are but three because they're bloody heavy, that's why, seeing as how they are now the Irish Standard Brick and made of solid granite and good for the centuries. Just pick one up—if you can that is, you there, Tony my lad, smile away, but this is no bag of pasta, that's it. Touch of the old hernia there if you don't learn to lift better. . . ."

"Paddy," a voice called out. "I need a pair of brawny lads to unload a lorry. Got any to spare?"

"They're a puny lot and you can have them all. Take what you will for I despair of ever making good union hod carriers out of any of them."

The newcomer stood behind them and pointed to the nearest man. "You then, Tony, come-o with me-o. Got that. And you too, Tony." He jabbed a finger at Giulio and waved him over. Giulio went through a pantomime with him, of pointing to his chest and nodding and so forth, then followed meekly. Excited.

Through a small gate and then another. Towards a great, windowless building that dominated all the others around it. From high on the wall, standing forth on hulking, white insulators, great electric cables reached out to a tall pylon and beyond. This was it!

"Grand sight, isn't it, Tony? Nothing like that back in the land of pasta, is there? But work first then. Boxes off lorry-o, on to handcart. And bloody smart if you don't mind. Like this. Got it?"

It did not take long and the lorry pulled away and two men pushed off the handcart. "More lorry, got that?" Their guide shouted, waving and pointing at the ground at the same time. "Take a kip and we'll be back."

The drizzle had stopped and the sun was out. Giulio's companion curled against the wall and was instantly asleep. Giulio pulled a blade of grass that was growing from a crack in the paving, chewed on it, and looked around. No one in sight, very lax, but the Irish were always this way. Their weakness, and he had been instructed how to take advantage of it. Look around. He strolled towards the high wall near by and to the small door bearing the legend, KEEP OUT—POWER-PLANT PERSONNEL ONLY.

Did he dare? Why not, that was what he was here for, sooner or later he would have to make the attempt. The door was locked but he recognized the brand of lock; he had been well instructed on it. The lockpick was concealed behind his belt buckle and dropped into his fingers at a touch. Still no one in sight. Insert, lift, press . . . turn.

The door swung open. He was through in a second and it closed behind. A brightly-lit passage stretched away before him; his heart beat like a hammer in his chest. Carry on, he could do nothing else. Down the corridor. Doors. All closed. Numbered. They could be anything. Then, another one. He stopped, still, quavering at the sign on it.

TECHNICAL MANUALS STORE.

He had done it! The same kind of lock, twist and open, darkness beyond, a glimpse of shelves before he closed the door behind him. Grope for a light switch, there, flick it on . . .

"Do come in, Giulio," the man said. "Sit down, here across the desk from me. Cigarette? No, I forgot, you don't smoke, do you."

Numb, unbelieving, Giulio slid into the chair and tried not to gape at the smiling man on the other side of the desk. He wore a uniform of some kind, three pips on his shoulder straps, and nodded in a most friendly manner across his tented fingers. "There, that's better," he said. "I suppose you're C.I.A., but not career I hope. Could I have your correct name?"

Giulio finally found his voice. "*Scusi, signore, no cap . . .*"

"Please, Giulio, don't waste our time. You see we found this in your pocket. We do make searches, you know." He held up a blue matchbook with white lettering that read *United States Navy*.

Giulio gasped and his spine softened and he slumped even more.

"No co-operation? Oh dear, oh dear, but you are being difficult. My name is Power, Captain Power. And yours? Oh well, if I must."

The Captain came around the desk and in a sudden lightning motion secured Giulio in an unbreakable grip. He even managed to have a hand free with which he pressed Giulio's fingers on to a white card on the desk; fingerprints appeared on it an instant later. Power released Giulio, took the card by the edge and looked at the prints critically, nodded, then dropped it through a slot in the desk's top.

"That should do. While we're waiting for results we'll go look at the powerplant. Well don't gape like that—that's why you're here, isn't it? Ireland's pride and joy, and the envy of the world at large." He opened the door for Giulio and showed him out, and continued to talk as they strolled down the corridor. "In a world of declining resources and failed power supplies we here find ourselves quite happy on this fruitful island of ours. The crops and the herds are the best, sure we've always grown more than eno ugh for our own needs, and a bit over. And peat, all we could ever need, we've been generating electricity with it for years, now we use it in our ships. But power, that's our secret, isn't it? The reason why you're here. And steel too, for we've enough of that. We prosper in an unhappy world and help others where we can, but we are a small nation after all. In here if you please." He eased open a massive door. "Now, I ask you—isn't that a glorious sight?"

It was indeed something. They stood on a balcony high up on the wall of an immense chamber. The sound and heat and motion at first made it hard to understand what was happening. Steam hissed and curled up from the floor where great turbines spun. A conveyer belt carried an endless stream of stone bricks from an opening in one wall, to vanish through an opening in the other. Giulio blinked, trying to make sense of it all. Captain Power explained.

"When the granite bricks drop into the steam chamber they are practically still molten, temperature in the thousands of degrees I understand. We had lots of trouble in the beginning with them fracturing, blowing up like bombs and that sort of thing. All licked now of course. After they leave the steam, and are a bit cooler, they fall into the water and generate more steam and on and on. And the steam drives the generators and that's really about all there is to it."

"But . . . no, that cannot be." Giulio was stammering, confused. "Where do the bricks come from?"

"I thought you would never ask. If you will walk this way you will meet one of the men responsible."

The walk was shorter, and the room they entered larger than the first, and filled with odd equipment. A tall man with a shining bald head, fringed with remnants of red hair, sat on a couch reading a computer print-out.

"Giulio," Power said. "I want you to meet Sean Raftery."

"A pleasure," Sean said, standing and taking Giulio's hand and giving it a hearty shake. "You're a brave man to come this far, and with a good education too, as I have been reading. Giulio," he glanced at the print-out, "Giulio Balietti. Born in Hoboken, New Jersey—what an unusual name for a city—college . . . university . . . ahh, a doctorate in physics, atomic physics. And quite young too."

"Atomics," Captain Power said. "They're still looking in that direction. Well, more strength to them."

"Then . . . you know . . ." Giulio said.

"Of course. We pride ourselves on our records. You're not the first, you know. We used to try to keep them out, then we discovered it was much easier to let them in and take care of them then."

"You're going to kill me!"

"Nonsense—we're not the C.I.A. after all. This is a civilized country. We are going to show you Ireland's great secret, then remove—with no pain—your memory of today. You have worked so hard to get this far we thought it only fair to let you find what you are seeking after. Also, we have discovered that after the memory removal process the agent is much more relaxed having once actually *known* what he wanted to know. Somewhere in the subconscious there is a feeling of success and this is most important. Sean, if you please."

"Of course. Our secret, Giulio, is the tapping of an immense strength in the Irish personality and character that has always existed, has always been seen, but never channelled in the right direction. The poets and the authors have taken from this mighty stream and profited thereby. Someone once said about an Irish author, with cruel intent but nevertheless it holds a germ of truth, that anyone could write that way if they abandoned their mind to it. Perhaps. But only the Irish can do it without scarcely trying."

Giulio watched, eyes widening, as Captain Power wheeled a black suit, like a parody of a medieval suit of armour, before Sean Raftery. It was ugly as an Iron Maiden but seemed to raise no fears in Sean who voluntarily pushed his arms into the extensions of the thing. He even smiled as it was locked around his body.

"The flow of wit and Irish humour is famous, our actors known worldwide, their abilities to express themselves famous." But his powers of expression seemed to be lagging. He stumbled over words and began to repeat himself. "Please excuse . . . excuse if you will. You see this is sensory deprivation suit. I cannot feel anything with my body or hands, I cannot use them . . . But, praise be to God, I can still talk . . ."

Sean's eyes widened and his words were muffled into silence as Captain Power slipped a soft but strong gag over his mouth. The captain continued.

"And there you have it. Complete sensory deprivation so the subject cannot gesticulate or point his fingers or walk about. Communication is damaged by that. Communication and the flow of language dammed up completely by the gag. So what do we have, you ask? We have, I answer, a mighty torrent of expression seeking a way out. We have a genius for communication without an outlet. But—wait, an outlet is still left. The brain! With no other way of expressing the pressure of thoughts churning in the mighty Irish brain, the mighty Irish brain expresses itself by direct contact with the outside world. That glass on the table—would you please, Sean?"

The glass lifted suddenly into the air, swooped about like a bird and landed again on the table with ease.

"Direct manipulation of matter by the mind. But much graver than conjurer's tricks like this one. Sean, and the others on his team, reach deep into the molten heart of the earth with their minds, miles deep, and open a hole to the surface. The magma, liquid rock, is forced through this hole, a solid rod of lava being ejected into the tank out there. Or rather it would be a solid rod if the opening was not opened and closed regularly to cut the rod into the bricks you have already seen. At other times, delving deeper, they tap the molten iron core of our planet and bring the purest iron into our rolling mills. It is a wonder indeed."

He smiled at Giulio and signalled to Sean. "Now, lightly, touch his memories and excise this day."

Giulio jumped to his feet, tried to run, to flee, but blackness fell.

"*Chi è lei?*" Giulio said to the officer behind the desk, who was industriously studying a computer print-out.

"No games, please, this is a busy office," Captain Power told him. "We have your complete record here. You are Dr. Giulio Balietti, an atomic physicist. You were sent here by the C.I.A. to unearth our technical secrets. This is espionage and you could be shot for it . . . Here sit down, you're so pale. A glass of water? No? That's better. But we are a kindly people and we are giving you a choice. You may return home now and tell the C.I.A. to leave us alone. Or you may remain here as long as you refrain from further espionage. There is an opening for a lecturer in atomic physics at Trinity College. Just part-time I'm afraid, a few hours a week. Until there is a better position you will have to do other work as well. We have found that academics enjoy peat-cutting. Healthy, out-door occupation, very relaxing when you are used to it. A lot of our older people like to have peat fires of handcut turf and it is not too much of an effort to indulge them. So what do you say?"

What did he say? A memory of Hoboken, the endless grey poverty, the plankton and soy food, the drab existence. Stay, why not, he wasn't being asked to give his word. He could still keep his eyes open, look for the Irish secret, bring it back to the U.S. if he could. His duty was to stay.

"Trinity and the peat bog," he said, firmly.

"Good man. Here, this way, I want you to meet Herr Professor Doktor Schmidt. A physicist also . . ."

"Nein, you forget, my captain. It is Ivan who is the physiker. I am simple chemist. Come—Giulio is your name?—we have a good chat and I show you how to use the peat shovel. A most satisfactory tool."

They left, arm in arm, out into the falling rain.

THOMAS M. DISCH

□□

Mutability

["Mutability," which is excerpted from a novel-in-progress, is set in the year 2097. The human race has become immortal as a result of genetic alterations caused by a plague that swept the world late in the twentieth century. However, a small but genetically dominant minority of mortals has survived and perpetuates itself in this world. Most of the mortals live apart in island enclaves, but a few, such as the protagonist of this story, lead a makeshift existence on the fringes of the larger immortal society.

Other excerpts from the novel have appeared in the *ORBIT* series ("The Pressure of Time"), *AGAIN, DANGEROUS VISIONS* ("Things Lost") and *IMMORTAL* ("Chanson Perpétuelle").]

Tübingen, 2 July 2097.

The free university city of Tübingen (*alt. 315m; population
2090: 140,400) is situated on the banks of the Neckar thirty-five
kilometres south of Stuttgart. It is chiefly renowned in modern
times for its university, founded in 1477 by Count Eberhard im
Bart of Wurtemberg. Melancthon lectured at the Bursa from
1514 to 1518. In 1536 Duke Ulrich founded the Protestant
seminary, where Kepler later studied under the astronomer
Mästlin. Kepler's first work, the* Mysterium cosmographicum,
*was published in Tübingen by the Gruppenbach Press. During the
19th Century the university regained the high reputation it had
lost during the devastations of the Thirty Years War. Hegel,
Schelling, Hölderlin, Uhland, and Mörike (all identified with the
Swabian 'renaissance') studied and taught at the seminary, which
was also, a few decades later, the centre of the critical movement
in Protestant theology, exemplified by Baur and Strauss.
Inevitably the long decline of Protestantism during the unification
and expansion of the German Reich under Bismarck and Hitler
affected the stature of the university, but it once again came into
prominence in the first decades of this century when its faculty
and students spearheaded the Pan-Germanic Anarchist movement. In 2024 it became the capital of the independent state of
Baden-Schwaben, and in 2039 the United Nations granted its
petition for free-city status. In 2096 the university enrolled
21,300 students in its graduate faculties (approximately half of
this number receiving stipends) and 243 undergraduates. In
recent years the faculty of history (enrolling more than 8,000
students) has won world-wide recognition for its achievements,
and the "bifurcating bibliographies" of the Tübingen school have*

revolutionized modern historical methodology. This faculty was the first at the university to abolish voluntarily, in 2019, the increasingly meaningless distinction between the teaching staff and the body of graduate students. Despite the controversy that still attaches to its uniquely democratic government, Tübingen attracts eminent scholars from all fields and from all countries. No university in Europe and only California in America can boast an alumni of equal distinction.

from Baedecker's The German States,
2097 edition

1 p.m.

Antennae adither, the ant seeks its fellows on the hinderside of her hand. She turns her hand palm up. With angst the ant considers the index fingers, then veers off along the lifeline. The middle finger, gilded with nicotine, bends forward and crushes the ant, or pismire (from the Danish *myre*, though long, long before the Danes there had been Myrmidons, and before Myrmidons a plague.):

HCOOH.

Meanwhile they poured up out of the floorboards in their multitudes. Avoiding the suitcases, the column followed the crack to the west wall, ascending the wall as far as to the wainscoting that concealed the power cable, and followed this traverse northwards and then, at the corner, to the east. Where a doorway interrupted the wainscoting the ants once again ascended. Against the age-dark wood of the beam they became invisible. Reaching the south wall they descended, slanting left, to the counter where that morning Veronica had left the unwashed spoon, their fleece of Golden Syrup.

A journey, she estimated, of fifty feet: an ideal itinerary would not have exceeded seven. It was allegorical.

"Fools," Veronica said, not without affection.

Michael Divine, who'd lost interest in the ants half an hour ago, seemed uncertain how to interpret this remark. He smiled faintly, faint wrinkles forming about his eyes and mouth.

Aligning himself (she thought) *on the side of wisdom.*

She rubbed the smear of formic acid off on her tee-shirt and returned to her worktable, where a random compost of notes and artifacts, quanta of history, confronted her: Doctor Emeritus Veronica Quin.

She inserted the tape of *12 August 1998, 7.30 p.m. E.S.T., N.B.C., "Beware, Babylon!"* and speeded through the first minutes, making a monkey gibber of the opening hymn. She slowed at the first close-up of the blurred ghostly chiliast, who crackled portents of the Days to Come. His Leonardesque finger pointed to the handwriting on the wall. The audience was made to consider whether they were sheep or goats, grain or chaff. Then came the show-stopper, as he clawed away the numeral days from a giant calendar.

The estimates for that first show had been twenty-two million, and the ratings increased steadily until February of 2000, a month after the terminal date of the universe. In the interim months Reverend Delmont had been elected Governor of the state of Nevada (where the Elect had been asked to assemble) and Mayor of Los Angeles, (where they'd been assembling already for eighty years). "Beware, Babylon!" was an essential datum in any consideration of millennialism.

She observed:

1) The *frisson* of the Apocalypse; hell's sex-appeal.
2) The seduction of numerology. We are all Pythagoreans.
3) The secret suicidal wish (Freud, the Cold War, *et al.*).

Beyond these partial causes there had been the memory of the Plague, of decimations, of landscapes more vivid than Bosch, providing both a portent and a model of the universal wrack. How much more satisfying to the moral sense than the nescient speculations of Ph.D.s if this should be the *meaning* of the Plague—that all those million deaths had been accomplished as a word to the wise.

"Who is he?" Michael Divine asked.

She had forgotten, so seldom did she have visitors in the day, to localize the sound.

"Baptist Delmont, who promised us that time would stop. To his chagrin, it wouldn't. Inertia, I guess."

"Never heard of him. Was he important?"

So the lad would chatter. Then to oblige Joseph she would for a while chatter too. She touched a finger to HOLD, stopping time within the microcosm of the viewer. A plosive froze on Baptist Delmont's lips.

"He was representative. For my purposes that's better than being important. There were hundreds of Baptists in those days, big and little, and tens of millions of believers. Workers stopped working, the crime rate rose, and the market dropped."

"Oh. Is that what you had in mind when you said 'Fools'?" He caught exactly the tone she'd used.

"Can anything so big really be foolish?" (Though it *might* have been at the back of her mind. What was society, after all, but one vast formicary? Black ants waging war on red ants. Milking aphids. Building tunnels.) "You see, it wasn't just the zealots who felt the end was coming," she added. "The *fin de siècle* had begun a century before. Some of the best minds of the time were convinced the end was at hand. If not of the world, then of history, of the West, of us."

She touched, illustratively, the cast-bronze first edition of *Der Untergang des Abendlands* that weighted down a sedimentary heap of her primary sources. From such muck as this, compacted for years by the pressure of thought, the rocks of history are made.

Michael came up to the table and lifted the metal book in one hand. His movements were quick and crisp, but seen this close his flesh betrayed the cells' inexorable attrition. Small fulciform pouches had begun to form beneath his eyes. Eyes of hazel, that shifted into an improbable red when the sunlight caught them at an oblique angle.

"Well, in a way, wasn't he right?" Michael said. "A lot of that did come to an end."

"Every age, however, feels that it's a culmination, the tonic chord that resolves the imperfect progressions of the past." *I am doing this* (she thought) *for Joseph's sake. Only for him.*

"I don't feel that way. But maybe that's because I'm a fossil."

For the first time since Joseph had brought him round that morning Veronica regarded Michael Divine with some interest. His remark indicated a degree of intelligence, a quickness, that she never took for granted in a mortal. Or, for that matter, in any of Joseph's featherweight *liebhabers*.

"A fossil? In the Toynbeean sense, perhaps. On the other hand, most immortals feel much the same. The past has lost its hold on all of us. It may be from a sense that the larger historical process has stopped. The red armies and the black armies have declared a truce. There's no turnover in the personnel department. Kings don't die. Did you know that Charles IV is still alive? He works at an undersea development station off the Japanese coast. Once a year he comes back to Hampton Court and entertains. So much for History with a capital H."

"Well, it hasn't lost its hold on you, anyhow. Or on Joseph. He's obsessed with the past."

"That's because we both represent a kind of intermediate species. We were already adults before we began to suspect we were immortal. For a long time it was only a small doubt. Agerasia was no proof of immortality. In fact, it remains to be proved. But after a century or so, the conviction takes root anyhow. People younger than us grew up with that conviction. For them the present is absolutely discontinuous with the past. Even for Joseph and me the past that interests us has been the past we've lived through ourselves. This man, for instance—I might have seen his debut on N.B.C. If my mother hadn't forbidden it."

"How old were you?"

"Nine."

(Was he tallying it up? $9 + 2 + 97$. Old, old, old.)

"And what is his interest now?" He pointed at the pouting face of Baptist Delmont.

"He's one of my facts. Paul and I are putting together a kind of sequel to *2000+*. About the decline of religion since 1900 till now. When the world refused to end, there was some disillusionment."

"Which you shared?"

"Never completely, or I wouldn't have become an historian. It's a profession that still has more in common with theology than with science. It's so easy to make patterns. I tend to confuse my patterns with the world's facts. In that respect I probably preserve more illusions than you."

Michael blinked. In contrast with other movements of his

face and body, there was a tiredness in this unconscious gesture that pointed to a possible retardation of the neural response. He was probably closer to forty than to thirty, which had been her first guess.

"That would be difficult," he said.

The tonic chord. Neither felt any need to say more. Michael crossed the room to stare at his face in the empty aquarium. Veronica reanimated Baptist Delmont, but first she noted on her shorthand pad the tidy simile of the rocks and the muck.

2 p.m.

Time was tangible in this room not simply in the absolute sense that this was a very old room, but also in the way that whole eras of geology can be encapsulated in a single conglomerate rock. The constituent pebbles (the books, the photographs, the tins of film, the rusted Spandau, shelves and boxes of kitsch and curios) were cemented together by a dross adhesive of the contemporary: empty tetrahedrons of Lowenbrau, vases of dried and moulting blooms, her own filthpackets of wiring, cheeserinds, butts and ashes, Niobe's kitty litter, cast-off clothes, the polychrome debris of her typed and scribbled notes.

The world with metaphors. But dried up. Herself dried up, a sack of dust.

A memory: cleaning out the East 11th Street apartment, the half-empty box of Kotex in the cabinet underneath the sink in which the mice had made their comfy nest. She ought to have preserved that for her stock of souvenirs. It seemed unlikely that Oliver, to whom she'd mailed it in the same spirit she'd sent him cartoons clipped from magazines, would have saved it. (And if he had, how many light-years away would it be now?)

If Michael Divine *were* forty, he would still be too young, by twenty years, to have been the son she'd never had.

He was, distinctly, a handsome boy. A pleasure to look at. She looked at the small motions of enforced idleness, the restless flicker of his gaze, the quick snap of his wrist that made the face of his silver bracelet lie flat against the back of his hand.

She bent down to take his hand in hers. "What does it say?"

So wary of her he was: the young Adonis.

"Your bracelet," she explained. He let her lift his forearm to read the inscription. She laughed. She released him, and he leaned back in the chair, safe.

"Beer? Coffee? Tea?"

"No, thank you."

"You'll excuse me if I make some for myself." She went into the utility room, drew water from the tap, and lighted the Volkswagen. "A marvellously inconvenient place, this," she commented from the doorway. "No room. Draughty in winter. And Paul knocks himself silly at least once a week on the rafters. How tall are you, Michael?"

"Five foot eight."

"Then you're safe."

Let him think so anyway.

She held up two cups. "You're sure?"

"Well, if it's already made. . . ."

"Draughty and—" Turning back to the console. "Oh, a dreadful nuisance, but it is stone-old. That's its charm for a historian. The Gruppenbach Press used to be down on the ground floor, and the building goes back before even that."

She poured out the potion, gave him his cup.

"Really?" he said, without interest.

He took a sip, saw the stains all round the inside edge of the cup, grimaced. Veronica didn't take much trouble with the decorative side of cleanliness.

"Is it that bad?" she asked.

"Bad? No, it's delicious."

She laughed. "Not the coffee, Michael. Your life."

"Oh, that."

"Are you furious with Joseph?"

"I've no cause to be angry with him. Only grateful. He must have told you how we met."

"No." (Or if he had, she'd forgotten.)

"Good. I won't either. It was nasty and a bit ridiculous, but the upshot of it was that Joseph pretty much saved my life. I was going under and he put me on my feet. I am on my feet, still. For that I'm grateful, still."

"And do you love him, still?"

"Do you?"

Unfair.

She shrugged off the question as though it were some bulky, unseasonable cardigan and sprawled on a pile of pillows on the floor. She could lose twenty pounds of her slipshod flesh in a month, if she made the effort. How long had it been since she was wholeheartedly physical?

"Do you?" he insisted.

"I was thinking. It's a difficult question. I guess I'd have to say no. We've had our moments, of course. Most of them a long time ago. Nearly a century's gone by since we met. I was his secretary at Freedom Mutual. He used to work in insurance then, you know, on the investment end."

"I know."

"I was twenty-one. Joseph was forty. He wasn't getting on with his wife. It was exactly the sort of thing one used to see all the time on teevee. Had it been anything else, I wouldn't have been able to follow the script. Life was so much simpler then. But you've probably heard the whole thing from Joseph already."

"Some of it, though never that much about you. About the wife."

"Hope?"

"No, the other one. Emma?"

An ant, or emmet, strayed across the cushion. Had she ever, in fact met Emma? She remembered her eyes, a deep brown, solemn with accusation, but no actual confrontation.

"Emma. It was a tragic case. She killed herself, you know."

"How old was she?"

"Forty. Maybe forty-one."

"Premature," Michael said. "I give myself much longer than that."

"I should hope you do." She squashed the ant, or emmet: HCOOH. "Are you going off with Joseph to London?"

"Is that where he's going? Then I'll go there. At this point, you know, I'm just holding on and hoping. What else did he say?"

"That your father is dying."

"Yes. He's always dying. He's fairly rich. He can afford doctors. He used to be quite rich, twenty years back, but geriatricians are expensive. I fairly hope he does die this time. I'd like there to be a little something left for me."

"How old is he?"

"Eighty-one."

"My mother held out till she was eighty-eight. For the last five, six years she watched teevee from a stuffed recliner. Her mind went, and every time she exhaled a breath she made a sort of whistling sound. Quite unnerving. One summer there was a power failure that lasted twelve hours. We thought she was going to die with the set blank. She got all fussed. But Joseph came up with the most wonderful idea. He took the insides out of the set, and we took turns the rest of the day talking to her from inside. It was enormous fun."

"Did she die?"

"Not then. A week later, during the Senate Committee hearings on contract labour. If you don't want to go off to London right away, you can stay on here for a while. We have room."

"Wouldn't Mr Regnier mind?"

"Paul is very permissive. Besides, we have boxes of things that have to be catalogued, so you could pick up a bit of cash. Assuming you need some. It's interesting work."

"I'll consider it."

"And Joseph would probably be pleased, Not at being rid of you, mind. But to know you were in good hands." She smiled a sly, nose-wrinkling, rabbity smile.

And Michael (in his element again) leaned forward to take the taste of her mouth. She closed her eyes, and the waters of the past rippled over her lax flesh, the ghostly caresses of a hundred vanished lovers, mortal and immortal, men and women.

"In a month or so, I could lose twenty pounds."

"I like you better this way," he said. Then, as a machinist will begin as a matter of course to test the tolerances of a new piece of equipment, he added: "Sluttish."

"Ah!" It wasn't necessary to say what it was she found attractive in him. Even so, she framed an ambiguous compliment: "Have you always been a grasshopper, Michael?"

"How is that?"

"A grasshopper, as opposed to an ant."

"No one *wants* to be an ant."

Once on the wall of one of those characterless European rooms she'd taken after Joseph had left her the second time she'd made a chart or model to represent the structure of her own life. Wishfully, she had gerrymandered the contours until its form had approximated a crystal structure. SiO_2. That mural was now painted over, or the wall demolished, but the map had remained with her, to become encrusted with baroque embellishments or reduced to the cubical simplicity of copper according as her life seemed to her various or plain.

She rose to her feet, walked to the bookshelf, lifted the chunk of what she'd been told was Martian rock. "My valence is rising," she said. But these little mystifications were no longer enough to put Michael off his form.

"Because," he said, pursuing the previous metaphor, "they get squashed."

Observant too. She began to see why Joseph had let it drag on so long.

"Michael, *zeig er mir jetzt die Zunge!*"

Before he could obey, the phone rang. It was Joseph. She localized the sound and hunched in front of the screen to keep him to herself.

"What did he say?" Michael asked.

"He's on his way over."

They regarded each other closely. Already he'd sensed she was lying to him.

3 p.m.

Michael was in the alcove exploring a sonnet of drawers in a massy Teutonic catchall, emptiness rhyming to emptiness. ("You can see," Veronica said, "I have nothing to hide.") But the fifteenth drawer yielded a holly warping from a glorious garland of cloisonné and florentined gold.

"And this?" he asked.

A platoon of office workers in sad long-ago clothes arranged themselves in the (count them) three dimensions of a fluorescent space. This was to holography what tintypes were to photography—and conveyed by its stiffness a similar pathos.

"The nothing in question," she answered, and almost told him to put it back.

"Which is you?"

She pointed to two tiny blue eyes staring eighty-six years straight ahead at these hazel eyes that shifted to red. "I was in love then."

"That very moment? You don't look it." The comment and his inflection were mediate between cruelty and a finicking regard for the instant's inner truth, a tone he must have picked up from Joseph, who was an enthusiast of the abstracter virtues: honesty, clarity, *esprit*, and whatever else might be ranged against Duty.

Without quibbling, she took the holly from him and pressed it flat into its incongruously fine frame. Six of the twenty-six faces showed signs of age. Dorothy Jerrold, who'd been supervisor of the typing pool then, and Larry Noonan, who took over from Dorothy a few years later, and Mr Whewell, who read all the best-sellers, and Yolanda—or was it Eula?— Sloane. The names of the other two black women she'd forgotten. All six of them would be dead by now, and the building itself turned into some kind of dorm, or so she'd heard. The clouds roll by. She put the picture back where it belonged.

Meanwhile he was into another drawer, poking at a pretty jumble of electronic junk resembling a spilled bracelet or the shingle of a beach. "I love other people's souvenirs," he said, "much more than my own. What else is there?"

She told him about the Kotex box and the mice; then (he had discovered the motel ashtray) about her momentous weekend of adultery in the Florida Disneyland.

"He took *me* to Belgium," Michael said, not to be outdone.

"He would. He loves anything *wiederaufgebaut*, not to say fake. He's wild over what they've done to the Colosseum."

"Which is Greek for?"

She thought. "Latin, isn't it? For gigantic."

"No, before that, what he loves—Diderot's cow?" Sounding the *t*.

The latch began to lift and Michael's hand, from gesturing airily, fell into Veronica's lap.

Paul came in, and with him Niobe.

"Paul, this is Michael Divine."

Paul's psyche was borne, smiling, toward the sofa by his dowdy soma, rather as the Baptist's head might have been carried in to Herod by the axeman. Arriving, he bent down, lifted Michael's hand and kissed it. (He was French.) "I've heard so much about you."

"No, Niobe!" Veronica called out to the very enceinte cat, who was furtively making her way underneath the Volkswagen. Then, to Paul: "Michael and I are waiting for Joseph. We thought, as you came in, that *you* might be he."

This was ironic. It was their understanding, Paul's and Veronica's, that he and Joseph were opposites something along the lines of Mind and Matter: Paul having been the Pygmalion to her Galatea, while Joseph was the bull to her Europa. There was a further irony in that they both knew Joseph had already left Tübingen.

Michael's antennae were out, however. He'd understood what had passed between them as clearly as if it had come in on his own police radio. "He's left. Hasn't he?"

"Left?" Paul echoed. He was easily stared down. "Well, yes, he has. He was afraid, you see, that you might—as you'd followed him here—that you might follow him . . . away."

"Away where?"

"He didn't know. To a mountain perhaps. He wanted to unfuzzy his mind."

"He couldn't tell me himself?"

"Hasn't he been trying to?" Veronica asked, taking over for Paul, who had no talent for confrontations.

"So he just up and leaves all that here?"

"All that" was the two polly suitcases with their sunbursts of cheap glitter. It had been their presence in the corner all through the afternoon that had allowed Michael to feel that Joseph was still safely shackled to him. But really! Would anyone who identified with his own suitcases have bought two such sleazy specimens as these?

"Did he want us to *keep* them for him?" she asked Paul. "He knows there isn't room, and the last time we had those awful boxes of his for two years. We never could figure out where that smell was coming from—remember?"

Paul waved the question aside. Michael, standing in the

middle of the littered room, had begun to cry, and Paul studied this process with panicky fascination, as though, visiting a zoo, he'd suddenly encountered a beautiful tiger on the gravelled path. Then, as if the tiger were calmly to walk back into its cage, Michael stopped.

"I think if we were to leave Michael alone for a minute—"

Paul was more than willing to be led away. He collapsed into his bed with his all-purpose curse. "Holy fucking moly!"

"You know what it is?" Veronica said soothingly.

"Glänzende Götterlufte!"

"It's their goddamned vulnerability. *They're* always so wide open, and they make *us* feel the same way."

"Oh, I don't blame him, poor thing. But they do take it out of you somehow. Look at the shape Joseph's in. One minute he's going to do this, the next moment it's something else, going on like a flittermouse. And all for what? For a boy."

"Michael is scarcely a boy."

Paul was too pleased with "flittermouse" to notice what she'd said. "I'll admit he's attractive in a rather *unheimlich* way. But even so, Joseph is old enough to know better."

"By the by, I've told Michael he can stay on here a while, so if he should—"

"It's not as though he even *cared* for boys. He doesn't, as a rule."

"Be *nice* to him."

Michael was standing in the doorway in his underwear. He knocked on the open door. "I feel dirty. Can I take a bath?"

Paul became Arabian in his courtesies. The apartment belonged to Michael. He could stay on a week or a month. He explained, twice, how the console worked, found a fresh bar of soap, and dug into the wardrobe for a fresh towel. As Michael accepted it Paul squinted at the writing on his bracelet, and laughed. "Oh, I like that! Did you see this, Ronny?"

"Yes, I saw it."

"Your name. That's precious."

Michael released the catch, and the bracelet glissaded down the folds of the towel. Paul tried to catch it, missed.

"You like it," Michael said, with a smile of stony insincerity, "it's yours."

"Oh but—"

Michael stepped round him, entered the bathroom, and locked the door.

5 p.m.

Bursting with new kittens and well content, Niobe lay beside Michael on the rumpled bed. From time to time Veronica would reach across his knees to ruffle the fur of her throat and she would purr. People (she thought) should be more like cats.

Sleep had smoothed the grosser signs of age from his face, but gradually in the half-light of the hall she was able to decipher, in the pebbling of the skin, in the pulse of a vein, in a breath, the tragic implications wound into his genes. Was it worth it? worth the pain of reading, always more clearly, the same portents? Of growing every day a little guiltier until her heart was ripe to betray him? And for what? For love? She would not have called it that, but it was there, inside of her, by whatever name, the reason for it.

A hollowness. As though some creature, intelligent yet inarticulate, compounded of volatile gases, were pushing and prodding at her inner organs, writhing in the oily machineries of her imperishable flesh. Not a child. (Of those regrets no particle remained.) An anti-child perhaps, which Michael's sperm, dying within her, might cause to die as well.

He woke at last, all fuzzy and mild from the sedation.

"You're in my bed. You'll be all right."

"Oh." Slowly his mind added it up; he grimaced at the sum. The worst of it seemed to be not that he'd failed but that it would be supposed he'd meant to fail. "Jesus. I'm sorry. I really didn't mean to—"

"You *did* mean to, I think," she reassured him. "You have your own good looks to blame. There's a hole in the wall near the flush mechanism. Paul was watching you every moment. When you blanked out we broke in. Five minutes, he said, would have done the trick. You made it quite deep enough."

He touched the bandage round his left wrist. "Who?"

"Paul. Ages and ages ago, when I was typing in that typing pool, Paul was a chirurgeon in Grenoble."

"I might as well have gone straight to the Emergency Ward to kill myself. Christ."

"Well, you weren't to know."

Niobe, moved either by suspicion or by appetite, was attempting delicately to take the bandage off his right wrist. He swatted her, and winced with pain.

"Niobe, no! *Bad* Niobe. Would you like something to eat? Paul said you should."

"Maybe later."

"What a flutter you put *him* in. Once he'd sewn you up, it was all I could do to get him not to call in the University's health service to cart you off. I said it would be better just to find you a nice pill that will see you through the next week or two. You *won't* try again, will you? You said before that forty-one was premature."

"I promise not to kill myself. Now would you make some soup or something? Or if you've got to stare at me, do it from another peephole. Okay?"

"Okay. But Michael?"

"What?"

"Nothing."

Was it only what he seemed to think—morbid curiosity? Wasn't it at least as much the case that she liked Michael? She balked at the word "love". But Joseph, evidently, had fallen in love with him. Why couldn't she, eventually?

She raised one partition and lowered another, turning the bathroom into the kitchen. As she rolled the Volkswagen to the tap, the bloody water sloshed about inside. She turned the faucet: not a drop. Recycling what was in the sac seemed tantamount to vampirism, but it was Michael's own fault for having taken two days' worth of water for his bath. Before she switched on the purifier she dipped a cup down into the water.

The transparent pink of a red balloon blown up almost to bursting. She could taste soap, but of his blood there was not a glimmer.

7 p.m.
"And where," Paul asked, blundering daintily in, "is our young

Werther?" He put down a beribboned baggy on the Martian rock. Niobe came up to sniff at it.

"Gone. For good, I think."

"Oh damn. And I just made such an ass of myself with Marilyn insisting on *three* of these. Niobe, get off that."

"We can split the third one between us."

"And I meant to thank him for this." Jingling the bracelet. "Well, let's hope he hasn't gone and jumped into the Neckar. I wish, though, he had waited till he'd swallowed something to make him cheerful. Maybe you'd better swallow it."

"Me?"

"Life goes *on*, Ronny. Tomorrow and tomorrow and tomorrow. As you just said yourself, it's for the best. If he'd stayed you'd only have got entangled. You're well out of it. You know you are. Here, look." He snapped the ribbon, spread the yellow paper apart like the crinkly petals of some November flower, to reveal three wedges of sacher torte. "You see. Even in the midst of affliction Earth pours forth her blessings. I don't suppose there are any clean forks?"

"Use your fingers."

He already was.

"Guess what he— Oh, these are delicious."

"Then remember to say so—" he sprayed crumbs across the desk "—to Marilyn."

"Guess what he stole."

"All my notes."

"No, not as bad as that."

"All yours."

"That picture of Joseph—the one I've kept all this time, that his wife painted."

"Oh, the little shit. That enamel frame must be worth a year's rent. I *told* you to hide all those things away. The minute Joseph called to say they were coming, I said put *that* where they won't see it."

"I did. He found it. I'd fixed an old holly of me in the frame, but it had come half-way out. He must have noticed. I just wish I knew if it were the picture or the frame that he wanted. If it was the frame I could feel righteous."

"I'm glad now I *didn't* get to thank him for the bracelet."

"Otherwise it's my just dessert."

"*Our* dessert," he said primly, breaking the third wedge in half. He compared the pieces carefully and took the larger for himself.

"Because *I* stole it when Joseph had just thrown *me* over. With, as I recall, a perfectly clear conscience."

Paul shook his head. "Love."

"Joseph does that to people."

"Apparently. But I don't see how. He's rather thick, he has *no* discernible gifts, and he's that homely he's almost grotesque. An indifferent physique. A complexion like a Matisse."

"A nose like a Brancusi," Veronica added.

"It's all he has. A noble nose. That's it."

"He's irresistible."

"*Ihr Gewaltigen!* Does that mean you let him have it? The whole, overweening amount he asked for?"

"He always pays me back. With interest."

"How much this time, Ronny? How much?"

"Five thousand. He asked for ten."

"I throw up my arms," he said, though this was only a figure of speech, for his arms hung, as ever, lifelessly at his sides, "and ask no more. You are a fool for love."

11 p.m.

As he wound back the tape, Paul's hand brushed the acoustics control, and when the music began again the whole room resounded with the doctor's abrasive triumphings: "*Oh! meine Theorie! Oh mein Ruhm. Ich werde unsterblich! Unsterblich! Unsterblich!*" Immersed and unaware, he didn't notice that *Wozzeck* had spilled over into Veronica's part of the room until, at the start of Act Three, the phone rang. "Oh! Oh, I'm sorry." He pulled back the sound just as Veronica answered. "If that's Joseph," he said warningly.

The screen was blank, allowing her to hope that Paul had guessed right. A long silence and the screen still dead. Could it be Michael?

"Ronny? Hello?"

"Loren? Is that you, Loren?"

"Ronny, your screen is jammed. Can you hear me?"

A—E

"Loren?"

"I can't hear you, and there's no image."

"Loren, I think we have a bad connection. Why don't you"

"I'm going to hang up and"

"hang up dial again?"

"dial again."

She hung up and sat beside the phone waiting for it to ring. It didn't. This is what comes, she thought, of living in a country run by anarchists.

She checked to see if the phone was still tied on a line to the library. No. Then she located the problem: RECORD was on, and the tape had come to an end. As she removed it from the slot, half of the holly she'd put in front of Joseph's picture came out with it. Every face a little dimmer, every edge a little duller, as though Time had just taken a bite of her mind.

In ballpoint on the back of the holly someone—Michael—had written: "This is just to say 'Thanks for a lovely time!' and 'Till we meet again!' The tape is for Joseph. Please see that he gets it. Ever, Michael D."

She put the tape back in the phone (Loren, evidently, had given up), reversed it, and pushed REPLAY.

First the time—5:58—and date—2/7/97—flashed red on black as an operator chirruped: ". . . through your call to New York, sir." The screen was blank while the phone rang: an unlisted number.

Then, a clown's face. A most literal and traditional clown it was—with a bright red bulb of a nose, maniac eyes, a broad, foolish frown, and tonsured crimson hair sprouting vividly from chalk-white flesh. "Blessed be the holy name of Jesus," the clown piped in a piercing falsetto.

"Hi Lulu," Michael said. (His own features unrecorded throughout the call.) "Is Cole there?"

"Michael! Michael Divine?" the clown shrilled. "Where *are* you?"

"Germany. Is *Cole* there?"

"Just a moment, Michael. Oh, Father Severson! Yoo-hoo, Father Severson! Michael, if you would hold the line just one minute I will see if I can find him. I think he may be hearing

confession. Oo La La!" He rolled his eyes and tongue about in
a parody of *voluptas*.

"I'll hold the line."

"I won't say who it is. I'll let you surprise him!" The clown's
face moved out of the camera's eyes, revealing a few square
feet of sandalwood wall and a severe, silver-on-teak crucifix.

Then—another phone, a smoother voice: "Sassahty of
Jesus, Fathuh Severson speakin!" Before black drapes, Cole
Severson, blond and blandly Byronic, regarded the screen of
his own phone with a smile of cautious satisfaction.

"Hi Cole."

"Wail, wail, wail. As ah live an' breathe! If it ain't my old
frayend Michael Dee-vahn! Long tom, no see."

"Yeah."

"What *can* ah do for yahl? In a word."

"I guess you know."

Cole dropped his accent. "And I guess *you* can say."

"What you didn't do the last time."

"Through no fault of my own, dear child. You rather
disappeared."

"I'm willing to come back now. On one condition."

"It isn't for you to be making conditions."

"On one condition."

"And what is that, Michael?"

"That you document the whole thing, as it happens, all the
gory details. And that you send the instalments to someone
who—whose address I'll—I don't have it now but—"

"Oh-ho. It's like that, is it?"

"That's my condition."

"A pleasure to fulfil it, Michael. Tears? Are you crying real
tears? Bless your soul. But you still haven't said, have you,
just what it is you want me—the Society, rather—to do?"

"I want you to kill me."

"Gently, lad, gently. Even on telstar, you know, there are
monitors. We don't live, like you Europeans, in a state of
anarchy. *We* have a government, for which I daily give thanks
to God."

"I want to join the Society of Jesus. Is that better?"

"You'll take the three vows?"

"However many you like."

Cole raised his voice: "Lulu!"

And the falsetto: "Father?"

"You may join us on the other line."

The screen divided: Cole on the right, Lulu on the left. His costume now included a little straw hat with a big floppy fuchsia daisy sticking up from it.

"Lulu, Michael will be coming to live with us at the rectory. He wishes to return to a religious life."

"Oh!" Lulu squealed. "How simply divine!"

"Why don't you sing a song for Michael—to welcome him home."

Lulu bowed his head submissively. Then, looking earnestly into the telephone he broke into a florid, forlorn rendition of Schubert's *Ave Maria*. Tears rolled down from both his eyes, and, triggered by tweaks of his bulbous nose, his little straw hat lifted off his head each time he reached a particularly high note. The daisy wobbled on its wire stem.

Veronica turned it off.

Paul was standing beside her. "God," he said, "don't they break your heart?"

●●

One Afternoon at Utah Beach

"Do you realize that we're looking down at Utah Beach?"

As he took off his boots and weather cape, David Ogden pointed through the window at the sea wall. Fifty yards from the villa the flat sand ran along the Normandy coast like an abandoned highway, its right shoulder washed by the sea. Every half-mile a blockhouse of black concrete presented its shell-pocked profile to the calm Channel.

Small waves flicked at the empty beach, as if waiting for something to happen.

"I walked down to the war memorial," Ogden explained. "There's a Sherman there—an American tank—some field guns and a commemorative plaque. This is where the U.S. First Army came ashore on D-Day. Angela . . .?"

Ogden turned from the window, expecting his wife to comment on his discovery. She and Richard Foster, the pilot who had flown them over to Cherbourg for a week at this rented villa, sat at either end of the velvet settee, watching Ogden with a curious absence of expression. Dressed in their immaculate holiday wear, brandy glasses motionless in their hands as they listened politely, they reminded him of two mannequins in a department store tableau.

"Utah Beach . . ." Angela gazed in a critical way at the deserted sand, as if expecting a military exercise to materialize for her and fill it with landing craft and assault troops. "I'd forgotten about the war. Dick, do you remember D-Day?"

"I was two." Foster stood up and strolled to the window, partly blocking Ogden's view. "My military career began a little later than yours, David." Glancing down at Ogden, who was now staring at a blockhouse six hundred yards away, he said, "Utah Beach—well, you wanted some good shooting.

Are you sure this isn't Omaha, or one of the others—Juno,
Gold, what were they called?"

Without any intended rudeness, Ogden ignored the younger
man. His face was still numb from the sea air, and he was intent on his communion with the empty sand and the blockhouses. Walking along the beach, he had been surprised by
the size of these concrete monsters. He had expected a chain of
subterranean pill-boxes hiding within the sea wall, but many
of them were massive fortresses three storeys high, larger than
the parish churches in the near-by towns. The presence of the
blockhouses, like the shells of the steel pontoons embedded
in the wet sand, had pulled an unsuspected trigger in his
mind. Like all examples of cryptic architecture, in which form
no longer revealed function—Mayan palaces, catacombs, Viet
Cong sanctuaries, the bauxite mines at Les Baux where
Cocteau had filmed *Le Testament d'Orphée*—these World War
II blockhouses seemed to transcend time, complex ciphers
with a powerful latent identity.

"Omaha is further east along the coast," he told Foster
matter-of-factly. "Utah Beach was the closest of the landing
grounds to Sainte-Mère-Église, where the 82nd Airborne
came down. The marshes we shoot across held them up for
a while."

Foster nodded sagely, his eyes running up and down Ogden's
slim but hyperactive figure for what seemed the hundredth
time that day. Throughout their visit Foster appeared to be
sympathetically itemizing a catalogue of his defects, without
in any way being insolent. Staring back at him, Ogden reflected in turn that for all the hours Foster had logged as a
salesman of executive jets his sallow face remained remarkably
pallid, as if he were plagued by some deep *malaise*, some un-
resolvable contradiction. By noon a dark stain seemed to leak
from his mouth on to his heavy chin, a shadow that Foster had
once described to Angela as a blue tan from spending too much
time in bars.

As if separating the two men like a referee, Angela came to
the window. "For someone who's never been in the army or
heard a shot fired in anger, David's remarkably well-informed
about military matters."

"Isn't he—for a non-combatant," Foster agreed. "And I don't mean that in any critical spirit, David. I spent five years in the army and no one ever told me who won the battle of Waterloo."

"Weren't you a helicopter pilot?" Ogden asked. "Actually, I'm not all that interested in military history. . . ."

Strictly speaking, this wasn't true, Ogden admitted to himself during lunch, though in fact he had not thought of the D-Day beaches when Angela first suggested the week in Normandy. Under the pretext of a demonstration flight in the twin Comanche, Foster had offered to fly them gratis, though his real reasons were hard to define. The whole trip was surrounded by ambiguities, motives hidden inside each other like puzzle boxes.

This curious threesome—the aircraft salesman, the provincial film critic in his late forties, and the young wife ten years his junior, a moderately successful painter of miniatures —sat in this well-appointed villa beside a long-forgotten battleground as if unsure what had brought them here. Curious, not because of any confrontation that might occur, any crime of passion, but because three people so ill-assorted had formed such a stable relationship. At no time during the six months since their meeting at the San Sebastian festival had there been the slightest hint of tension, though Ogden was sure everyone took for granted that his wife and Richard Foster were well into an affair. However, for various reasons Ogden doubted this. For her own security Angela needed someone around her who had achieved a modest degree of failure.

His young wife . . . Ogden repeated the phrase to himself, realizing as he watched Angela's sharper chin and more prominent jaw muscles, the angular shoulders inside the chiffon blouse, that she was not all that young any more. Soon she would be older than he had been when they first met.

"I'm taking Angela into Sainte-Mère," Foster told him after lunch. "Do you want to come along, David? We can try the calvados."

As usual, Ogden declined. The walk that morning had exhausted him. He stretched out in an armchair and watched the slack sea shrug itself against the beach. He was aware of the complex time-table of apparently arbitrary journeys that Foster and his wife embarked upon each day, but for the moment his attention was held by the blockhouse six hundred yards away. Despite the continuous sunlight the concrete was drenched in spray, gleaming like wet anthracite as if generating its own weather around itself.

An hour after his wife and Foster had gone, Ogden pulled on his boots. He had recovered from the lunch, and the silent villa with its formal furniture felt like the stage-set of a claustrophobic drama. The strong afternoon light had turned the beach into a brilliant mirror, a flare-path beckoning him to some unseen destination.

As he neared the blockhouse Ogden visualized himself defending this battered redoubt against the invading sea. An immense calm presided over the cool beach, as if nothing had happened in the intervening thirty years. The violence here, the scale of the conflict between the German armies and the allied armada, had pre-empted any further confrontation, assuaging his own unease about Foster and his wife.

Fifty yards from the blockhouse he climbed the scrub-covered dune that rose to its seaward flank. The sand was scattered with worn-out shoes, cycle tyres and fragments of wine bottles and vegetable crates. Generations of tramps had used these old forts as staging-posts on their journeys up and down the coast. The remains of small fires lay on the steps of the concrete staircase at the rear of the blockhouse, and pats of dried excrement covered the floor of the munitions store.

Ogden walked across the central gunnery platform of the blockhouse, a rectilinear vault large enough to house a railway locomotive. From here a heavy-calibre naval gun had lobbed its shells at the invasion fleet. A narrow stairway set into the solid wall climbed to the observation deck, and gave access to the barbette of a small-arms weapons platform below the roof. Ogden climbed the stairway, tripping twice in the darkness. The worn concrete was slick with moisture sweating from its black surface.

As he stood on the roof, lungs pumping in the cold air, the sea already seemed far below, the villa hidden behind its high

privet hedges. Looking around, though, he immediately
noticed the white Pallas parked behind the sea wall two hundred yards along the beach. The car was the same colour as
the Citroën they had hired in Cherbourg, and Ogden took for
granted that it was their own vehicle. A tall man in a hunting
jacket was steering a woman companion along the broken
ground behind the wall. They approached a wooden boathouse
at the end of a slipway above the beach, and Ogden could see
clearly the patterns of the woman's musquash fur and recognize her gesture as she reached a gloved hand to the man's
elbow.

Ogden stepped down into the stairwell. Watching them
calmly, his shoulders hidden by the parapet, he knew that he
had deliberately encouraged Angela and Richard Foster to
come together. His own solitary walks, the private excursions
he had made to the D-Day museum at Arromanches, had been
part of a confused and half-conscious attempt to bring matters
to a head and force a decision on himself.

Yet when he saw them unlocking the door of the boathouse
together, briefly embracing in the sunlight as if openly trying
to provoke him, Ogden felt a profound sense of loss. He knew
too that the months of self-control had been wasted, and that
from the beginning he had deluded himself that all was well.

Without thinking, he turned quickly from the parapet. With
luck he could pack, call a taxi and have caught the ferry from
Cherbourg before they returned to the villa. He started to run
down the concrete steps, lost his footing on the damp diagonal
sills, and fell backwards down the stairway on to the floor of
the barbette ten feet below.

Sitting in the half-light against the wet concrete wall, Ogden
massaged his bruised hands. By luck he had been able to protect his head, but he could feel the raw skin of his arms and
shoulders. Some sort of viscous oil stained his fawn trousers,
and a leather button torn from his jacket lay like a burst chest-
nut at the foot of the stairway. Immediately to his left was the
embrasure of the fire-sill, the quiet beach below. There was
no movement from the boathouse, and the white Pallas was
still parked behind the sea wall.

At this moment Ogden realized that he was not the only person keeping a close watch on the beach. Six feet away from him, almost hidden by his grey uniform in the shadows behind the parapet, a man lay against the concrete wall. He was resting on one elbow, face turned towards the open sea, and at first Ogden assumed that he was dead. His blond hair had been bleached to an almost arctic pallor. He appeared to be no more than nineteen or twenty years old, his pale skin stretched across the bony points of his face like wet parchment around a skull.

His thin legs, encased in a pair of heavy boots and ragged serge trousers, stuck out in front of him like poles strung with rags. Lying diagonally across them, its long barrel supported by a bipod, was a light machine-gun, stock pressed against the young man's right shoulder. Around him, arranged like the décor of a shabby military display, were an empty mess tin, a spent ammunition belt, the half-rotted remains of a field pack and webbing, and a grease-stained ground sheet.

A few feet from Ogden, lying on the fire-sill within his reach, was a spring-action flare-pistol of a type he had seen only the previous afternoon in the D-Day museum at Arromanches. He recognized it immediately, like the uniform and equipment of this young Wehrmacht soldier whose corpse he had stumbled upon, in some way preserved by the freezing air, or perhaps by the lime leaking from the hastily mixed concrete. Curiously, the machine-gun still appeared to be in working order, a spiked bayonet fitted under the barrel, the butt-stock and receiver greased and polished.

Confused by this macabre discovery, Ogden had already forgotten his wife's infidelity. He was about to pick up the flare-pistol and fire it over the parapet in the direction of the boathouse. But as his bruised hand touched the frozen butt Ogden became aware that the young soldier's eyes were watching him. Of a blanched blue from which almost all pigment had been washed away, they had turned from the beach and were examining Ogden with a tired but steady gaze. Although the soldier's white hands still lay passively at his sides, his right shoulder had moved against the wall, swinging the machine-gun fractionally towards Ogden.

Too frightened to speak, Ogden sat back, taking in every detail of the German's equipment, every ammunition round and piece of webbing, every pore in the cold skin of this young soldier still defending his blockhouse on Utah Beach as he had done in 1944.

After a moment, to Ogden's relief, the machine-gun barrel turned towards the sea. The German had shifted his position slightly, and was once again scanning the beach. His left hand moved to his face, as if he were hoping to transfer a morsel of food to his mouth, and then fell to the floor. A ragged bandage circled his chest, covering a blackened wound partly hidden by his tunic. He took no notice of Ogden as the latter climbed to his feet, both hands pressed to the wall as if frightened that it might collapse on him at any time.

But as Ogden stepped over the machine-gun a white claw moved across the floor, about to seize his ankle.

"*Hören Sie. . . .*" The voice was flat, as if coming off an almost erased recording tape. "*Wieviel Uhr ist es?*" He looked up with a kind of exhausted impatience. "*Verstehen Sie? Quelle heure . . .? Aujourd'hui? Hier?*" Dismissing Ogden with a wave, he murmered, "*Zu viel Larm . . . zu viel Larm. . . .*"

Pulling the stock of the machine-gun into his shoulder, he stared along its barrel at the beach below.

Ogden was about to leave, when a movement on the beach caught his eye. The boathouse door had opened. Richard Foster stepped into the sunlight, and swung his arms lazily in the cool air as he waited until Angela appeared thirty seconds later. Together they walked across the dunes to the parked Pallas, climbed into the car and drove off.

Ogden paused by the staircase, watching the young soldier with the machine-gun. He realized that the German had seen neither Foster nor his wife. The boathouse and sea wall were hidden from him by the parapet of the barbette. But if he recovered from his wounds, and moved forward to the edge of the fire-sill. . . .

By the time he reached the villa ten minutes later Ogden had already decided on both the tactics and strategy of what he knew would be the last military action of World War II.

❋   ❋   ❋

"Have you seen the blankets from the children's room?" Angela flicked through the inventory, her sharp eyes watching her husband as he played chess with himself by the sitting-room window. "I didn't bother to check them when we arrived, but Mme Saunier insists they're missing."

Ogden looked up from the chessboard. As he shook his head he glanced at the blockhouse. For the three days since his discovery the suspense had become exhausting—at any moment he expected a wounded Wehrmacht soldier to appear on the roof among the wheeling gulls, a pink blanket around his shoulders. At lunch he had changed his place, sitting by himself further down one side of the table so that he could keep the blockhouse under observation.

"Perhaps they were never there," he said. "We can replace them."

"They were here all right. Mme Saunier is scrupulous about this sort of thing. She also said something about one of the decanters. David, are you in a trance?"

Irritably, Angela pushed her blonde hair from her forehead, then gave up and picked up her coat. Richard Foster was waiting by the car in the drive, one of the two shot-guns they had hired cradled under his arm. Ogden noticed that he had taken to carrying the weapon everywhere with him, almost as if he detected a change of atmosphere in the villa. In fact, Ogden had gone to strenuous lengths to maintain the good humour of the first days of their holiday.

He waited patiently for them to leave. Half an hour later Mme Saunier set off in her Simca. When the sounds of the car had faded Ogden stood up and moved swiftly across the villa to the conservatory at the rear of the dining-room. He removed the pots of bright winter plants standing on the wooden dais, eased back the platform from the wall and pulled out the cheap suitcase he had bought in Sainte-Mère that morning while Angela and Foster were lounging over the breakfast table. Taking the blankets from the empty bedroom had been a mistake, but at the time he had been concerned only to keep the young soldier alive.

Inside the suitcase were adhesive tape, sterile lint and antiseptic cream, one bottle of Vichy water and a second of schnapps, a primus stove, six cans of assorted soup, and a pull-through he had purchased from the town's gunsmith. However carefully the German had oiled the machine-gun, its barrel would need a thorough reaming-out.

After checking the contents, Ogden replaced the dais and let himself through the conservatory doors. Protected by the high privets, the garden was warm, and the air coming off the beach had an almost carnival sparkle. As usual, though, by the time he reached the blockhouse the temperature had dropped by almost ten degrees, as if this black concrete redoubt existed within a climatic zone of its own.

Ogden paused by the staircase, listening for the sounds of any intruders. On the first afternoon, when he had snatched the children's blankets, flung together an emergency meal of bread, milk and salami, and raced back along the beach to the blockhouse, the German had relapsed into one of the intermittent comas into which he would sink without warning. Although still staring at the tide-line, right hand clasped around the trigger butt of the machine-gun, his face was so cold and pallid that Ogden at first thought he had died. But he revived at the sound of the milk pouring into his mess tin, sat up and allowed Ogden to drape the blankets around his shoulders. Unable to stay more than an hour for fear of alerting his wife, Ogden had spent the evening in a state of hyper-excitability, for some reason terrified that the local police and members of a German military mission might arrive at any moment.

By the next morning, after Ogden had taken the car to Sainte-Mère on the pretext of visiting the war cemeteries there, the German had visibly improved. Although barely aware of Ogden, he leaned more comfortably against the damp wall. He held the mess tin against his bandaged chest, picking at the remains of the sausage. His face had more colour, and the skin was less tightly stretched against the jaw and cheekbones.

The German was often irritated by Ogden's fumbling, and there was something strangely vulnerable about his extreme youth. Ogden visited him twice each day, bringing water, food and cigarettes, whatever he could smuggle out of the villa under the suspicious eyes of Mme Saunier. He would have liked to light a fire for the soldier, but the primus stove he had brought with him on this fourth morning would generate a little warmth. However, the German had survived in this cold —the thought of living through all those winters made Ogden shudder—and at least the summer was coming.

When he climbed the stairway to the barbette the German was sitting up, blankets around his shoulders, quietly cleaning the machine-gun. He nodded to Ogden, who sat panting on the cold floor, and continued to strip the breech, apparently uninterested in the primus stove. When Ogden handed over the pull-through the German glanced at him with a flicker of appreciation. He ate only when he had reassembled the weapon.

Ogden watched him approvingly, relieved to see the young soldier's total dedication to his defence of this lonely strongpoint. It was this kind of courage that Ogden most admired. Earlier he had feared that once the German had recovered his strength he might decide to leave, or fall back to a more defensible position. Clearly he had missed the actual landings on Utah Beach and had no idea that he alone was keeping the war going. Ogden had no intention of telling him the truth, and the German's resolve never wavered.

Despite his overall improvement, the German's legs still seemed useless, and he had not moved forward sufficiently to see the boathouse two hundred yards away. Each afternoon Angela and Richard Foster climbed the dunes to this wooden shack on its miniature wheels, and disappeared into it for an hour. At times, as he waited for them to emerge, Ogden was tempted to wrest the machine-gun from the wounded German and empty its ammunition belt through the flaking weatherboard. But the young soldier's aim was probably sharper and more steady. The flare-pistol lay on the fire-sill, the shell in its barrel. When the German had cleaned it they would be ready.

Two days later, soon after one o'clock in the afternoon, began the last military engagement to take place on Utah Beach.

At eleven o'clock that morning, as Angela sat at the breakfast table reading the local French newspaper, Richard Foster returned from the telephone in the hall.

"We'll have to leave this afternoon. The weather's closing in."

"What?" Ogden left his chess table and joined them in the dining-room. He pointed to the brilliant sunlight falling on the wet satin of the beach. "It doesn't look like it."

"I've just talked to the met. people at Cherbourg Airport. There's a front coming in from the Scillies. The barometer's going up like a lift."

Ogden clasped his hands, trying to control them. "Well, let's put it off for a day. The plane's fully instrumented."

"Not a chance. By this time tomorrow the Channel will be packed with cumulo-nimbus. It'll be like trying to fly through a maze of active volcanoes."

"Dick knows what he's doing," Angela confirmed. "I'll read the inventory with Mme Saunier after lunch. She can take the keys to the agents when we've gone." To Ogden, who was still staring uncertainly at Richard Foster, she said, "A day won't matter, David. You've done nothing all week but play about on the beach by yourself."

For the next half an hour Ogden tried to find some excuse for them to stay, pacing up and down the sitting room as suitcases were dragged around upstairs. He tried to shut the two women's voices out of his mind, realizing that his entire scheme was about to fall to pieces. Already he had made his morning visit to the blockhouse, taking coffee, soup and cigarettes. The young German had almost recovered, and had moved the machine-gun closer to the parapet. Now Ogden would have to leave him there. Within days he would realize that the war was over and hand himself in to the French authorities.

Behind him the front door closed. Ogden heard Foster's voice in the drive, Angela calling to him about something. He watched them from the window, in a flat way admiring their nerve. They were setting off for their last walk together, Foster holding Angela's elbow in one hand, the shot-gun in the other.

Still surprised by the blatant way in which they were advertising their affair—during the past two days they had done everything but get into Angela's bed together—Ogden pressed his hands against the window. A faint chance still remained. He remembered the almost provocative way in which Angela had watched him across the dining-table the previous evening, confident that he would do absolutely nothing. . . .

Fifteen minutes later Ogden had left the house and an exasperated Mme Saunier, and was running head down, shot-gun in hand, through the pools of water which the stiffening sea had swilled across Utah Beach.

"Langsamer! Zu schnell. Langsam. . . ."

Trying to calm Ogden, the young German raised a white hand and gestured him away from the parapet. He reached forward and shifted the bipod, swinging the machine-gun to take in the section of beach containing the boathouse, at which Ogden had been gesticulating since his arrival.

Ogden crouched against the wall, only too ready to let the German take command. The young soldier's recovery in the space of a few days had been remarkable. Though his hands and face retained their albino-like whiteness, he seemed almost to have put on weight. He moved easily around the fire-sill, in complete control of his heavy weapon. The bolt was cocked back, trigger set for automatic fire. A kind of wan smile, an ironic grimace, hung about his cold mouth, as if he too knew that his long wait was about to come to an end.

Ogden nodded encouragingly, holding his shot-gun in as military a grip as he could muster. Its fire-power was nothing by comparison with the German's machine-gun, but it was all he could offer. In some obscure way he felt obligated to this young soldier, and guilty at implicating him in what would in a sense be the last war crime committed during World War II.

"They're—Look!" Ogden ducked behind the parapet, gesturing frantically. The boathouse door had opened, a cracked glass pane throwing a blade of sunlight at them. Ogden lifted himself on to his knees, the flare-pistol in both hands. The German had come to life, moving with professional command, all trace of his injuries forgotten. He adjusted his rear sight, his bandaged shoulder traversing the heavy weapon. Angela and Richard Foster stepped through the door of the boathouse. They paused in the sunlight, Foster casually inspecting the near-by dunes. The shot-gun rested on his shoulder, trigger guard clasped around two fingers.

Unnerved for a moment by this aggressive stance, Ogden raised the flare-pistol, cocked the trigger and fired the fat shell into the air over Foster's head. The pilot looked up at its weak parabola, then ran forward, shouting to Angela as the shell lost height and fell like a dead bird into the calm sea.

"A dud . . . ! " Angry with himself, Ogden stood up in the embrasure, his head and chest exposed. Raising the shot-gun, he fired the left barrel at Foster, who was darting through the dunes little more than a hundred yards from the blockhouse. Beside Ogden the young German was taking aim. The long barrel of the machine-gun followed the running figure. At last he opened fire, the violent noise jarring the parapet. Ogden was standing in the embrasure, happily listening to the roar of the machine-gun, when Richard Foster stood up in the long grass ten yards from the blockhouse and shot him through the chest.

"Is he. . . .?"

Angela waited in the dim light by the stairway, the collar of her fur coat pressed against her cheeks. Avoiding the body on the floor of the barbette, she watched Foster rest his shot-gun against the wall and kneel on the floor.

"Stand back as far as you can." Foster waved her away. He examined the body, then touched the flare-pistol with a blood-stained shoe. He was still shaking, both from fear and from the exhaustion of the past week. By contrast, Angela was completely calm. He noticed that with characteristic thoroughness she had insisted on climbing the stairway.

"It's a damn lucky thing he fired that first, I might not have had time otherwise. . . . But where the hell did he find it? And all this other equipment?"

"Let's leave and call the police." Angela waited, but Foster was still searching the floor. "Dick! An hour from now I may not sound very convincing."

"Look at this gear—World War II webbing, machine-gun

ammunition, primus stove, German phrase-book and all these cans of soup. . . ."

"He was camping here. I told you it would take a lot to provoke him."

"Angela!" Foster stepped back and beckoned her towards him. "Look at him. . . . For God's sake, he's wearing a German uniform. Boots, tunic, the whole thing."

"Dick!"

As they made their way from the blockhouse, the alarmed figure of Mme Saunier was hurrying along the beach towards them. Foster held Angela's arm.

"Now. Are you all right?"

"Of course." With a grimace, Angela picked her way down the grimy concrete steps. "You know, he must have thought we were coming ashore. He was always talking about Utah Beach."

BRIAN W. ALDISS

▽▽▽▽▽▽▽▽▽▽▽▽▽▽▽▽▽▽▽▽▽▽▽▽▽▽▽▽▽▽▽

A Chinese Perspective

I

The tanks were of glass, a metre deep and almost as generous in their other dimensions. Each table contained eight tanks, and the laboratory contained ten tables. A constant temperature of 18·5 degrees Centigrade was maintained in every tank. And in every tank, oxygenators blew a chain of bubbles up their sides.

The water was of a different green in each of the tanks on a table, ranging from a pale stramineous yellow to a deep mid-viridian. The tanks were lit in such a way that watery reflections moved across the ceiling of the lab.

This perpetual underwater movement was lethargic. It lent the room a drowned and drowsy aspect in contrast with the dance taking place in all eighty tanks, where marine creatures of graded size underwent the capers of growth, performing such antics as their limited gene-patterns allowed.

Among this incarcerated activity went the Chinese girl who was known here as Felicity Amber Jones, neat in her orange lab coat, content because at present absorbed completely in her work.

The laboratory of which Felicity Amber Jones had charge was a part of the great institution of Fragrance Fish-Food Farms Amalgamated. The FFFFA, whose premises, buried deep into the plastic core of Fragrance II, produced one of the chief exports of the planetoid—a range of marine food-products famed all round the Zodiacal Planets. Those exports, packed in glass, plastic, or palloy, circulated in their various forms throughout the artificial worlds much as the free-swimming forms of oysters travelled through Felicity's ranged algae tanks on their way to maturity.

When it was time to go off duty, she registered the event on the computer-terminal in her office. Although she had plenty of other interests, Felicity always left this, her Main Job, with some regret. There was more peace here than at home in her cramped pile-apt. She switched off the overhead lights. The tanks, vats, and separators still glowed, spreading a languid jade reflection through the room.

At the changing-lockers, she removed her coat, standing naked for a moment before assuming a saffron overall, sokdals, and flesh mask. She called farewell to some passing colleagues as she made for the nearest exit.

Outside, someone had scrawled BANISH IMPERMAN-ENCE on the wall. Felicity made a moue at it and caught a petulent. In the moments of travel, she tried some astro-organic thought, but was too highly strung. It was almost time for her weekly assignation with Edward Maine, the great inventor.

II

In a homapt near the heart of Fragrance II, Fabrina Maine and her friend Anna Kavan stood before a small mock-fire. Its patterns cast themselves upon the legs of the two women in scarlet and gold, although they were over-shadowed by the gleaming wall-screen which Fabrina was now addressing.

Fabrina was a small plump lady whose wispy fair hair stood out unfashionably round her head; but she had a certain dignity. In an effort to improve that dignity, or otherwise express herself, she was currently studying Tease Structure, the psycho-dynamics of altered body-image. She adopted a vernal sacrifice position and said to the reporter on the screen, "Yes, of course I can provide referents of my brother Edward's behavioural drives—none better than I—but that may not be convenient. First, you should introduce yourself. Which zeepee are you from?"

The reporter, looming easily on the screen and dwarfing the apartment she shared with her brother, said, "My name's Sheikh Raschid el Gheleb, and I represent the *UAS Daily Modesty*. I've come up from Earth to investigate new tech-nophilosophical developments in the zeepees. So of course your brother ranks highly on the list of those people whom I hope to interview for my scatter."

She frowned. Edward's increasing success brought increasing interruptions to their snugly predictable lives.

"Your Main Job?" she asked the reporter.

"On Earth, we don't have that same concept, although the World State Employment Council is studying its possibilities. I'm just the *Modesty*'s technophilosophical correspondent—though I do also lecture in Predestination at Cairo University. I hope you don't feel xenophobic about me just because I'm from Earth; we're very interested in the zeepees, you know."

She sniffed. "We manage very well without outside interference. Edward will be back later. Ring another time. You'd better speak to him direct. In any case, he has an Internal booked as soon as he gets home."

She switched off and turned to Anna Kavan, leaning slightly towards the defile stance to show contrition. "Perhaps I shouldn't have been sharp with him, but I'm uneasy about the thought of the World State meddling in our affairs, and so is Edward."

"It's at least five years before the World State comes into being officially," Anna said, extending her hands to the fake flames. "Besides, the Chinese are very scrupulous."

"Why should I care about the World State or the state of the world when I have my little lin with me?" Fabrina asked. She turned and petted the animated ornament by her side. "Tell me something funny, Lin."

"We are all radioactive particles in the mind of God," said the lin. The women laughed.

"Now tell me a new story," Fabrina said.

And the lin said, "Here's one called 'High Courts'. There were high ideals in the courts upon the mountains. Photographers were scarce under the towering appletrees. No snails any longer laid their eggs among the eyes of the goats in the market. The Lady Cortara, that dinosaur of royal line, said, 'Life is like death by drowning: it feels good when you cease to struggle.' So worldly regiments failed to close the entanglement of minds."

"You'll be able to afford a better model lin now, Fabrina," Anna said. "Edward will be rich from now on."

"I happen to like mad old stories," said Fabrina. "And my little linikin's tales have the advantage of being original and sounding familiar."

III

In the boardroom of Smics Callibrastics, high in the Fragrance II urbstak, they were celebrating Maine's achievement. Wine flowed, as well as the more customary aphrocoza, mitrovits, pam-and-lime, and other good things. The prototype of Maine's prediction machine stood at one end of the chamber; Edward Maine stood meekly by it, allowing the press to photograph him, and his colleagues to congratulate him.

". . . and furthermore, I'd like to say, Edward, what a pleasure it has been to have you under our wing here at Smics for all these years," Marvin Stein-Presteign told him. Stein-Presteign was Managing Director, and built for the job, with plenty of meat separating him from the rest of the world, topped by a florid enough countenance to remind that world that blood pressure and work pressure often run in alliance. "Everyone enjoys working with you, Edward."

"You're very kind, sir," Maine said, smiling so energetically that his untidy fair hair, which stood out wispily all round his head, trembled in response. He was a small, plump man in his early thirties—clever but not very good at talking. Certainly not very good at talking to his meaty managing director.

Having shaken hands with Maine, Stein-Presteign moved away and said to Sheila Wu Tun, the Personnel Manager, "There's no cynicism about Edward—he surely is a thoroughly admirable little man."

"It's kind of funny the way everyone calls him Edward," Sheila said. "Never an Ed or a Ted or a Teddy. . . . It's a factor of his rather remote personality, I suppose."

"What's his private life like? Lives with his sister, doesn't he?"

"Yes. He's diffident with women, bless him. Although he has established a tentative relationship with a young woman who goes to his homapt once a week for an Internal."

"Well, we have your little treat in store for him. Perhaps we can step up his fun-level there."

"That's a thought—but Maine's entitled to be remote," Curmodgely from Statistics said. "After all, the man is undeniably a genius." He was rarely so bold with the Managing Director, but he disliked the patronizing way Stein-Presteign and Wu Tun spoke. He added with a note of apology, "I mean, his damned machine *works*. The future is now foreseeable, more or less. It's going to change the history of mankind."

Stein-Presteign said to Sheila, ignoring Curmodgely, "I'll see Edward in my office tomorrow." He moved on, leaving the lower echelons, who pressed admiringly if unavailingly round Sheila Wu Tun, to carry on the conversation.

Gryastairs of Kakobillis, who was heavy and eager, said, "Luckily it was our organization which employed Maine and not the opposition. I suppose you all know that Gondwana of Turpitude have a patent on a destimeter which gives reliable predictions for up to thirty-six hours ahead?"

"It won't work as efficiently as our PM, Mr Gryastairs," said a minor technician who had just joined the group. "Our chance theories are much more sophisticated than theirs, for a start. The destimeter uses only superficial biochemical and physiological manifestations. There's no hormonal print-out. It was Maine's genius that he accepted right from the start that alpha-wave intensity is the key to reliable prediction, and for that you need constantly updated information-flow regarding hormonal activity and related data such as glucose-breakdown. The destimeter doesn't even take account of blood sugar levels, which to my way of thinking—"

"Quite so, quite so," said Gryastairs heavily. "Given the Chinese proof that Predestination can be the basis of an exact science, obviously you are going to get a number of approaches to the problem. Machines follow theory, as I always say. My point is simply that it was Smics Callibrastics who had the good sense to employ Edward Maine when everyone else regarded him as a crank. Now, we should have a marketable PM at least two years before the opposition. There's no ceiling to our potential selling platform."

"I must talk to you about that," said little Hayes of Marketing. "It is going to be hellishly more difficult to promote and sell the product when the World State is established on Earth, and all their piddling new regulations and tariffs come into force—"

"Let's leave the World State out of the conversation just for tonight," Curmodgely said.

While his confrères were talking shop, Edward Maine shook all the extended hands and smiled his simple smile. Occasionally he brushed his hair from his face, which was pink from several glasses of wine. With all the compliments ringing in his ears, he was very much the picture of a successful inventor; a slightly complacent smile hovered round his lips, while his manner was a little abstracted, as if even now he was elaborating his theory of non-randomness which lay behind the prototype PM.

The prototype resembled one of de Chirico's metaphysical figures mated with a small battery car. Maine was gazing not at it but at an immense painting which hung on the wall behind it.

The painting was the sole ornament on the walls of the Smics boardroom. It showed a strange feast taking place in the market square in a terrestrial country which might be Mexico or South America or Spain. A drunken peasant girl lay sprawled on a crude wooden table among the dishes; several men were feeling her while they ate and drank. Other people, men and women, stood round the table, laughing as they fed. Some of the men wore old raincoats. A skeleton was present, dressed as a monk.

Maine was interested in this central tableau. He also liked the way in which the picture was crowded with barrels and bright costumes and pots. The cobbles of the market square were vividly depicted. At the corners were further perspectives, a white-walled lane leading downhill, a cobbled stair leading up. The houses had tiles on their roofs. Maine supposed that such places must still exist on Earth, or else why paint them? Real things were amazing enough without inventing any more.

Out of habit, he began visualizing all the possible parameters of action implicit in the situation depicted on the canvas.

The skeleton might signify that plague was about and that all present would soon die. Or further indignities might be heaped upon the drunken girl. Or the men might fight. Graphs of non-randomness flowed in his mind; where they intersected lay points of maximum possibility.

It would be wonderful to visit Earth again. . . .

He felt the scale of the sundial under his wrist-skin. Seventeen-thirty. Soon time to get home for his Internal. Oh, that lovely girl!—If only he knew her externally! Well, at least there was that to look forward to.

Sighing, he turned and shook another extended hand.

IV

The last hand had come and gone. Maine caught the mainline home as usual, changing on to a graft and so to his own particular warren, deep among the braces of Fragrance. He hardly thought about the celebratory party which had been held in honour of his research team; his mind was on the pleasures to come.

"How did it go, Edward?" Fabrina asked. "The party?"

"They were all very kind. It was a nice party. They are a pleasant firm to work with."

"Mr Marvin Stein-Presteign?"

"Oh, yes, even Mr Marvin was there. He had quite a conversation, as the PM forecast."

"Edward, did he—did he make you any kind of a *donation?*"

"Well, Fabrina, he made a speech. A eulogistic speech. Said that Western Civilization was not dead yet, and that we could still show China and the coming World State a thing or two . . . ." He broke off, using his sister's visitor as an excuse to evade his sister's interrogation. "Hello, Anna, how are you?"

"I'm just a radioactive particle in the mind of God," Anna Kavan said, smiling, as she came forward and kissed Edward's cheek. "At least, so your lin tells me. Why do you keep such an old-fashioned model, a man of your standing? You could afford some of the really intelligent ones, with up-to-date religious phobias and everything."

"Like Fabrina, I enjoy our old lin. It's our pet. Anything

too intelligent can't remain a pet. And the original idea of lins was to act as pet-substitutes, since live pets are not allowed in the zeepees."

"You're both very eccentric," Anna said. "And I am going back to Earth very soon, where I shall purchase a Persian cat."

"Some might think that was eccentric, Anna," said Edward mildly.

Putting on her sentient extra face, she moved to the door. "Edward, your innocence protects you from perceiving how eccentric I am. Stick to prediction and leave the squalor of human relationships to others."

She blew them a kiss and left.

"What exactly did she imply?" Edward asked his sister.

"It's fashionable to talk in epigrams nowadays," said Fabrina, who did not know either.

"Pretending she's about to go to Earth ... People are always saying that, and they never go. . . ."

Edward marched through into his own room, calling to the lin to follow him. The lin came in and stood itself against the wall until wanted, its plastic curlicues gleaming in the mock-firelight.

Among all the clutter of Edward Maine's hobby, which was also his Main Job, was his one extravagance. Most homapts, at least in the Superior group of zeepees, were equipped with funfaxes, for the reception of all media, including Internals. But Edward's was a two-way funfax. He could have his partner here with him.

Only in this vital respect had his shyness not entirely triumphed.

When the Intern-girl entered, shown in by Fabrina with proper courtesy and just a whiff of instinctive jealousy, she wore as usual a molycomp flesh mask, so that he had few visual clues to her real personality. She was dressed in a saffron tunic, with turn-up sokdals on her feet. There were white gloves on her hands. She bowed to him.

"You are well this week, Zenith?" he asked. Zenith was the code name they had agreed between them.

"Perfectly, thank you. As I hope you are."

"Yes. And you still find happiness in your Main Job? With what is it connected?"

"My happiness is connected with artificial seas, thank you."

Of course she assumed the Mandarin etiquette which was currently the rage on more progressive zeepees; so that she could only take her refusal to deliver a direct answer to a direct question—itself a breach of the Anonymous Internaliser contract—as far as a riddle. But the finesse she showed made him suspect that she was true Oriental.

As to her voice, it was low, but that meant nothing, for the molycomps often spread into pseudopods around the maxillae and sometimes down into the throat, altering the pitch of the voice in an attempt to baffle concealed voice-printers, just as her gloves baffled finger-printers.

"May I offer you an aphrohale before we go Internal?" he asked in a trembling voice. There she stood before him. He had but to reach out.

"It is better that we both defer to the terms of the contract binding us both, don't you think?"

"Of course, Zenith. As you wish. Apologies."

Formal as a sarabande, they stepped one to one side of the funfax, one to the other. Edward pressed his face to the viewer, checking that the controls were set for his stipulated ride and the automap clued to the contracted region of her anatomy. He scarcely felt the hypodermic sting his ear lobe, or the hallucinogen course to the pleasure-centres of his hypothalamus. He had paid for a full twelve-week course with Zenith; this was week eleven; he was to venture into unknown, unvisited sectors of the girl he so terribly thought he loved only twice more.

V

Her thorax was a complex geography moving towards Edward through a syrup of ultraviolet. A great epidermal plain travelled beneath his view, its pitted inclines seemingly bereft of life, although the plain itself shuddered and vibrated like a wheatfield in storm. Gleaming, it rose to take in the universe; but the universe was illusion—at point of impact, the vertiginous plain melted and folded, revealing blue craters through which Edward's viewpoint—Edward himself—penetrated.

As he sank through her internscape, both magnification and rate of progress accelerated. The subcutaneous constellations of her sweat glands and adipose tissues fell upwards, entangled in pathways of vein and nerve fibre. Beyond them, barely glimpsed, were colossal geodesic structures which he recognized from previous journeys as an edifice of costal cartilege and rib—structural supports of the energy jungle he now invaded.

The wavelength was decreasing. As if the distant superstructure was a radio telescope trained on the violence of a far nebula, he was conscious of varying densities and materials working round him. Much of this material was as hostile to him as any pulsar emitting gamma rays. Immune, he sank further down into her unknown galaxies, at once penetrator and penetrated.

He passed unaware into the races of her thoracic aorta. There was no sensation of travelling down a tube, so congested was it, so packed with racing amorphous things—and every object packed with semi-autonomous intent. The intense ultra-violet magnification enabled him to see through the walls to vivid pulsations of energy beyond. They were at once like lightning and spaghetti. Everywhere, the disturbed and anonymous life of energy. He was merging with it. As the depth, the drug, took hold, he was no more than a rhythm in this tide of rhythmic impulses.

The predestined course wafted him timeless through galaxies of pancreas, duodenum, kidney, where renal syphonings registered on his senses like ever-falling cascades of fire. From the boiling vat came a flood of grand spectral beings, lymphocytes and leucocytes, and the more meagre erythrocytes, pulsing yellow and mauve in colour, accompanying him down along the Amazon of the abdominal aorta and its deltaic offshoots.

Now the light was more subdued, the pace slower, the vanquishment of time and dimension more extensive. Now he was himself astro-organic—at once estranged from himself and co-extensive with all being. Inarticulate outpourings of truth and life bathed him and radiated from him.

Beside him among the mute arterial ways was another resence: Hers, and yet something much more enduring than

Her, a calm centre, which radiated back to him in dialogue the comforts he was involuntarily pouring out. It assured him of something for which his ordinary state of being had no vocabulary—something to the effect that this microcosm of body had no more to do with the whole human being than had the macrocosm of the starry universe, yet that both microcosm and macrocosm were intimately, intricately, non-randomly, related to the human ... and there was a word there like psyche or soul ... a non-existent word which possibly implied "conundrum".

And the Anima which teased him in a way that seemed lucid at the time—that Anima was as much of him as of her, a common spirit which perhaps, in similar circumstances, he might equally well have found in a leopard or a reindeer, a spirit born of all the mindless energy, yet itself calm, mindful.

It led him to one of the cable-like branches of the nervous system, where obscure messages rattled past him like lighted express-trains at night, carrying news of who-knows-what to who-knows-where. In the hypogastric system, lights were as jarring as sound, until he slipped away into a less frenetic area, resting in a rococo region of ligament and ramus patterned like a feather. The impetus of his voyage was dying. He floated there in stasis, knowing that soon tides over which he had no control would bear him back again to whatever condition he had relinquished.

At that, a sense of desolation seized him, but he threw it off in wonder at the splendid pelvic landscape surrounding him. The solemn structures among which he moved, bathed in low X-ray, had no macrocosmic equivalent, being at once gaseous formations, jungle growths, architecture. He became enclosed in a cathedral-like galactic lagoon, where nerve fibres stood out to meet him like roots of mangroves, welcoming him to the infinite confines of her vesico-uterine fold. There he stayed while a state much brighter than darkness fell, brooding like God over the measureless waters.

VI

When Edward found himself back to ordinary consciousness again, he was touched with disappointment. It was under the cloak of such characteristic melancholy that the girls who hired themselves out for Internals generally managed to vanish away, avoiding meeting their clients face to face.

As he sank into a chair, soaked and exhausted, Edward saw that his hired Zenith was going.

"One week more," he said. He held his face with trembling hands.

"I will return next week."

"Zenith—whatever your name is—stay a moment until I recover. Touch me!"

"You know the Contract."

He looked at her desperately, and his gaze lit on the lin, standing silent against the wall.

"For courtesy's sake—for kindness—let my lin amuse you with a short tale! Lin, tell Zenith one of your stories."

Before Zenith could say anything, the lin spoke.

"This story is called 'Pacific Squalor'. New taxation caused squalor in a Pacific town. 'Weaving mills require a pretty sponsor,' cried the citizens atrabiliously. But an airport was built and a sparkling bucolic comedy performed. All denied attempting to pervert justice. 'Let fate no longer lead to loneliness,' whispered the oldest lady. So patterned windows were built."

"You have an old-fashioned lin," said Zenith.

Edward wiped the damp hair from his forehead. "You must know more about me than I about you. I am not rich."

"I apologize for implied criticism. The story your lin has told pleases me."

Every time, he had coaxed a little conversation from her. In pleasure now, he said eagerly, "It really amused you?"

She stood before him, the molycomp mask smiling but expressionless.

"Didn't Anton Chekhov say that stories should not be about life as it is or as it ought to be but as it appears in dreams? Your lin's story is of that kind."

"You know Chekhov's writings?"

"I make a close and interested study of European writing . . . I mean, that is one of my Side Jobs . . . Now please excuse me —I have over-stayed my time."

In her tunic, her robe, her gloves, her mask, she went. Edward sat on his chair.

"Would you like a story or a joke?" asked the lin.

"No."

She had made a slip there, definitely a slip. "European writing" ... that was not a phrase anyone of American or European stock would use about a Russian writer. Despite his French influences, Chekhov would be regarded as a European writer only by someone completely outside the European community. An Asiatic, for instance. He was more certain than ever that Zenith was Chinese. And after next week, he would never see her again. Contracts were non-renewable. The damage that Internals did to anyone submitting to them— damage that could ultimately result in death—shrouded the transactions in mystery and restriction. The Japanese, Edward recalled, had invented this ritual, investing it with all the formality of a tea-drinking ceremony.

Much as he might dislike that formality, he saw its point. The intimacy of a person-to-person Internal was such that it had to be guarded by formula. Otherwise he, at least, would have been too shy to face the confrontation.

"The Contract!" he said aloud. Always, he was bound by contracts, written or unwritten, whether to his firm or his sister, his landlord or his Internal-girl. With a flash of insight, Edward perceived that all men were similarly bound, whether they recogized it or not. Otherwise, his predestination machine would have no hope of working. The illusion of free will was simply a lubricant to keep the machine working smoothly.

He couldn't face it. Getting up, he staggered over to the aphrocoza bottle.

VII

The computer controlling the gyroscopes at the heart of Fragrance II kept the planetoid riding precisely in its orbit. That orbit was elliptical, with the planet Earth at one of its nodes, set at an angle of 83.45 degrees to the plane of the ecliptic, so that the sun's energy washed ceaselessly like an ocean about the speeding body.

In its eternal morning, Edward Maine woke to another

manmade morning, accepted coffee from Fabrina (who offered it in the classical auspices stance), and staggered over to do his daily horoscope seated at the PM.

The analytics went into action, reading his basic physiological functions, such as pulse rate, hormone level, encephalic activity, tension index, and so on, and immediately the transmitter began a print-out.

The very first symbol on the paper caught Edward's attention. It showed that this was to be a day of prime magnitude. He had never received that signal before, except once—on the day they had been expecting it at Callibrastics, when the breakthrough came with the application of chance laws to personal data banks.

For a second time the analytics went into action, feeding Edward's response level into the computer, where it would be matched against all the background data plus the new data on all local events arriving during the artificial night of Fragrance. This double-check on response levels ensured that, by gauging Edward's current reaction to challenge, the day's reading of event-flow would be as accurate as possible.

The event-flow began to appear. The further ahead in the day, the less reliable the prediction. Possibility percentages were attached to each nodal event. All items were listed in likeliest chronological order, related in the PM's usual cryptic style.

** Key day. Surprise gift from corp mixed with contempt	95
View provides revelation on which future hinges	89
Do not attach too much importance to self	
HL (Hormone Level) indicates sudden mind-change	91
Unsettling news. Fogginess. Presumption leads to quarrel with sister	85·5
Concealed beauty leads to religious argument	78
Lack of lobster recognition interests	77
Make simpler daily the beating of man's heart	
Priestly contact aids welfare approach	69
Search yields nil result	79

Summary: day of interest, many new possibilities

Edward sat looking at the print-out for a long while. Every line seemed to pose a fresh mystery, although that was the way with the PM prototype, even on a quiet day. The problem was often a simple semantic one: that to predict an event accurately, the terms had to be imprecise; conversely, when the terms were precise, the accuracy quota was forced down. Heisenberg's uncertainty principle ruled.

All the same, some of the factors were mildly staggering. "Quarrel with sister". Precise enough, but he never quarrelled with Fabrina. Then, "Do not attach too much importance to self". This contrasted with the machine's favourite homily, which was that Edward should attach more importance to himself. Advice instead of straight prediction generally indicated fuzzy set thinking, where the computer was unable to make any either-or evaluation, or else concealed a surprise factor determined by event-currents (in the jargon of Callibrastics) on which the computer had insufficient data. The final line sounded horribly downbeat, whereas the summary held ambiguous promise.

One thing at least was clear. He had a challenging day ahead. He took a timid shot of aphrocoza before heading for the elevator.

VIII

Edward spent the first hour of the morning with a calculator, trying to work out applicable Laplace formulations for human action. Once they developed a suitable tool for handling the equilibrium and motion of human life-flow, they would have a convenient way of making the PM smaller and more marketable. Edward believed that in a non-intermeshing event world, perturbations of behaviour would be periodic rather than cumulative; if Callibrastics could achieve a field-equation to cover this reaction, an all-applicable calculus of chance would do away with most of the tedious process of physiological function-reading which at present inaugurated every day's prediction.

Edward was deep in the work, and enjoying it, when Sheila Wu Tun poked her elegant face up on his screen and said, "Edward, dear, would you mind going to see Mr Marvin Stein-Presteign, please?"

A—F

"Of course, Sheila." He jumped up. Making sure that none of his assistants had their eye on him, he licked his hands and tried to straighten out his untidy hair. He adjusted his collar as he made his way to managerial level.

Surprise gift from company. Surely that could only be good.

Stein-Presteign was all smiles. He was a genial green colour. His office, as befitted the managing director of Smics Callibrastics, was set on the outside of the Fragrance Light Industrial pyramid. His window looked out over the edge of Fragrance before it fell away in sheer cliff, and the sun, blazing through the planetoid's dome, was toned down by chlorophylter shutters, whose output went to feed the riotous blooms of Stein-Presteign's indoor garden.

For a world that practised the formalities, Stein-Presteign was remarkably informal. He bowed as deeply as his solid bulk would allow and motioned his visitor to a chair.

Awed as ever in the presence of his boss, Edward sat meekly down to listen to a general preamble.

"The scatters are always telling us that we are through creatively," Stein-Presteign said. "The argument goes that the Renaissance was the period when Western man set his targets towards the next few hundred years. In Italy in the fifteenth century, rich middle-class families in Milan, Venice and Florence and such cities suddenly came out with dynamic ideas of humanism, individualism, and speculation about the material world. You could say that the Borgias and the rest of them were the early founders of those goals that led us to space travel.

"Then the movement spread outwards through Europe and so, eventually, to the Americas. Particularly to North America, although Brazil is now having her turn. But the general impression seems to have gotten around that, with the rise of China to world dominance and the dwindling of mineral and fossil oil deposits, the spirit of the Renaissance is dead."

He put his fist down heavily on the desk, leaning forward and looking hard at Edward. "I do not believe that the Renaissance is dead, Edward. I have never believed it. We have in you and your team here in Callibrastics proof positive that the old inventive enquiring spirit of Leonardo and the other guys lives on. The scatter-pundits fail to see that the general retreat of the brains of much of the western world to the zeepees in search of free energy has caused a revolutionary regrouping. My firm belief is—I have stated this before and shall state it again, in defiance of defeatist thinking—that the zeepees duplicate in many essential ways the conditions of the Italian Renaissance cities. My belief is that Fragrance and the In-gratitudes—even Turpitude, for God's sake—are so many little Florences and Milans. . . . Of course, the Italians didn't have the goddamned Chinese to deal with. . . ."

The managing director followed up this last remark with a moody silence. Feeling something was required of him, Edward said, "Of course, an argument by analogy—" but Stein-Presteign swept the puny sentence away with a new flood of talk.

"Well, I've been reviewing things in that light since I returned home from the party last night. Among the matters I reviewed was your pay structure, Edward, and it did occur to me that for a man as distinguished in his way as Leonardo da Vinci, you have not been treated entirely with the generosity for which Smics Callibrastics is rightly renowned, right? That is to say, not on a scale commensurate with the generosity of the merchant princes towards the painters, architects, and scientists they patronized. So I determined to make a gesture—a grand gesture that will perhaps fire you to greater things."

"Really, sir, you're very kind, but—"

"Edward, the company is going to send you on vacation to Earth for a whole month. You need a vacation, and travel will broaden the mind. You have no damned personal life here worth speaking of. Well, we're going to send you down there —" he gestured eloquently towards the window "—to relax and refresh the springs of your mind, work up some more psychic energy. We pick up all the tabs, O.K.?"

Edward hesitated, and Stein-Presteign added, "What's more, the vacation, including the space travel involved, is for two. So you can take that sister of yours along for company."

Confused though he was, Edward registered the note of contempt in the director's voice. Unable to sit still, he got up and went to the window to hide the workings of his face. Taken at face value, the offer was terribly generous; but could he take it at face value? Stein-Presteign despised him. Were they trying to sack him?

Between elation and dismay, he stared out at the panorama of urbstaks marching towards the edge of Fragrance's disc. Maybe the planetoid was too small for him, although that was also one of its attractions; yet how wonderful to see the oceans again, as he had when a boy.

From where he stood he could see the far-ranging boxes of the administration of FFFFA, whose industrial levels went down into the core of Fragrance. Most of the planetoid's food was produced there—whereas on Earth he would be able to eat natural food again. A phrase floated to his mind: "My happiness lies in artificial oceans. . . ."

He turned about.

"I accept your kind offer. I'd love to be Earthside and stand on a shoreline watching the ocean again. I'll go."

Pulling a solemn face, Stein-Presteign came round the desk and shook Edward's hand without speaking, looming over him as he did so. He laid a hand on his employee's shoulder and said, "There's one point to take into consideration, Edward. We—you, I, Callibrastics, the whole of Fragrance—stand to get very rich from our PMs. We can sell 'em by the thousand among the zeepees and break even very comfortably, as I suppose you realize.

"But our real target must be Earth. We must be able to sell PMs on Earth. That's where the real market lies."

"That shouldn't be hard," Edward said. "The Chinese have long believed in predestination—"

"You're being politically naïve, Edward." He took a step forward, almost as if determined to crush Edward under his great prow. "What the Chinese believe on that score is neither here nor there. What they do believe in is selling their own wares—just as we do, come to that. They're getting this World State into constitutional order, and there's no doubt they can set up destructive tariffs against us out here. Many of my friends believe that is one of the chief objects of World State. I don't myself. My belief is—I have stated this before and shall state it again—that the Chinese are good horse-traders. And that's where you come in."

"I hardly know what a horse looks like," said Edward, aghast.

"Holy gravities!" Stein-Presteign exclaimed, clutching his forehead. "I'm speaking metaphorically, son, metaphorically! Does the name Li Kwang See mean anything to you?"

"Apart from the fact that it's a Chinese name, no."

"Li Kwang See is a very distinguished bureaucrat. He's served his time in the Peking government and now he's just been appointed Minister for External Trade, a post he takes up when the World State becomes reality. He has the usual prejudice of his kind against Western science. When you're on holiday, Edward, the company wants you to go round and call on Mr Li Kwang, and persuade him to like our PM."

"You want me to—?" He was overcome by excitement.

"Callibrastics *trusts* you, Eddy." Again the hand on the shoulder. "*I* couldn't be trusted to chat up Li Kwang. I'd be too heavy-handed. But your nice quiet little way of going about things . . ."

"All right. Of course I'll go and see him," Edward said, breaking free of what threatened to be an embrace. "I believe in the virtues of the PM probably even more than you do, sir. I certainly know more about its working. Some of these Chinese statesmen are very civilized men. If I can't sell it, nobody can, sister or no sister."

He blushed, seeing himself in the diplomatic role. "People were good enough to say last night what a pleasure it was to work with me—well, I will impress Mr Li Kwang favourably. We can get in before Gondwana and our other rivals. I can get him to order some machines. He'll know someone in the Internal Trade department—I'll come back with a big order, rely on me."

"Of course, I have always admired your enthusiasm, Edward." Stein-Presteign retired round the desk and gestured curtly to Edward's chair. "It is best that we all know our capabilities and limitations. Frankly, you alarm me. You must understand that all we want you to do is to establish a friendly contact with Li Kwang, nothing more. When the time comes to sell, believe me, Edward, Callibrastics will send out its prime sales force on the job. Professionals, not amateurs. We certainly shall not rely on anyone in Research for such a delicate task. . . ."

Seeing that he had been too crushing, he added, "But yours will be the perfect touch to convince the Minister that our slice of Western science is fully in accord with Chinese principles, non-exploitive, non-imperialist, and so on. You're so obviously a non-imperialist character that you are our first choice for such a mission, right? O.K., get Sheila Wu Tun to assist you with any little problems. She has been briefed."

Edward rose. "You're extremely—I'm extremely—" He held out his hand, then he scratched his head with it. Then he left.

IX

He went back and stared at the flowers growing under the falsie in his office so much less prolifically than the flowers below the managing director's real window. He decided that he was trembling too much to do any creative work and might as well go home for the day.

Pleasant odours wafted through the carriage on the way home —someone had slipped their card in the Perfume slot—but he was restless and curiously upset. On the one hand, the corporation had been generous; on the other hand, they had tied a condition to the vacation and had been insulting. Of course, he deserved all he got, both the good and the bad. *You're too damned self-effacing for your own good*, he told himself. *And at the same time you think too much about yourself.*

He attached too much importance to self—at a time when predestination brought the whole nature of self into question. That was something they'd never had to bother about in ancient Venice or wherever it was.

To his relief, the homapt was empty when he returned. At this time, Fabrina was at her job at the Fire Department. The lin was activated by his presence; it unplugged itself from its charge socket and came to him. Its simulated wrought-iron framework gleamed. It had dusted itself this morning.

"Your pleasure levels are low, Edward. Would you care for a story?"

"No."

He tramped past it into his room and poured himself a large aphrocoza. The mixture of liquid and heavy gas rolled into his beaker like a slow wave. He poured it into mouth and nostrils, quaffing it back till all was gone. Then he felt slightly better.

The lin was standing meekly beside him.

"All right, all right!" Edward said. "For g's sake, do your thing!"

"Here's a story called 'Volcano Obliteration'. Lorna put her hands conversationally round an old grey falcon," the lin said. "In the town, a silver band played, but she had heard too many promises. She cried, 'I must return with honour to my father.' But a volcano obliterated the valley. Now she lives with incredible leopards while a harlot plays 'Flower Patterns' in her head. She attempts to mind the animals courteously."

"Good, now go and plug yourself in again."

"You have tired of my stories."

"Emotional blackmail is something you weren't programmed for."

Edward sat silent and glum, pouring more aphrocoza into himself and finally falling asleep in his chair, to undergo curious waking dreams which were dispelled when Fabrina entered the homapt.

He went through and said to her, "I've just dreamed up the final proof of why God can't exist. Everything is predetermined; our more fortunate ancestors were able to believe in free will only because they did not understand that random factors are themselves governed by immutable laws."

"You're home early, Edward. I've bought us a halibut steak for supper."

"Everything was always predetermined. How could anyone big-minded enough to be God enjoy sitting back for countless aeons of years and watching what was to him a foregone-conclusion working itself out? . . . Of course, I suppose what seems such an incredibly long time to us may be just a flash to him. Maybe he has a lot of pin-ball machine universes like ours all spinning at once."

"You've been at the aphrocoza, Edward. It always gets you on to ontology."

"Maybe we could develop a computer which would prove conclusively whether or not God exists. No, that would hardly be possible—just as Karl Popper proved that no computer can predict the future that includes itself, although it can predict personal futures. Perhaps there are personal gods. Or maybe fully developed PMs will turn into personal gods. . . ."

"Father used to say that God was much more dirty-minded than was generally allowed for."

"There are limits to the possible. There must be a formula for those limits. It might be possible to compute those limits. But then, again, if we knew what the limits were, and how near we were to them, that would make the universe even more boring than it is now. Think how tired I am of my *own* limitations. I'm just a souped-up version of lin."

She settled into a bending reed position and said dismissively, "You know you like Lin's stories when you're sober."

"Ah, ah, ha—" He waved a finger at her. "But why do I like them? I enjoy their limitations. I enjoy the sense of being able to determine the limits of Lin's brain, of being able to encompass easily the farthest distance its story-patterns can reach. You don't mean to tell me God is as petty-minded as to enjoy our little patterns of circumstance in a similar way?"

"Has something happened to upset you?"

"There are those who might say that 'orbitally-perturbed' was a better phrase than 'upset', my dear, but—in a word, yes. I was up before Wine Stain this morning, and he has given me a month's vacation on Earth, to go wherever fancy takes me, to wander in the Rockies, to march to the sea . . . Thalassa! Thalassa!" There it was out!

Fabrina's pose collapsed. "You shouldn't say such things, whether you're high or not. I try never to think or speak about Earth. . . ."

He was startled at this. "You don't hate Earth? Just because we hear how much it's changing!"

She looked up at him and then covered her eyes. "Hate? I never said anything about hate. It's just that we've been on Fragrance for so long that I've ceased . . . I've ceased to believe anywhere else really exists. Fields, ordinary skies, irregular ground, wide horizons, trees—I can't imagine them any more. There's just these walls and the fake view out of the falsies, and the caverns and trafficways. Anything else is like—a Greek myth, I guess. I can't even believe in Death any more, Edward, you know that? I think we're doomed to go on here forever, unchanging."

Edward went rigid, defending himself against what she was saying. "Time goes too fast. . . ."

"You only add to the imprisonment, Edward. Father always said you lacked humanity. . . . You spend your life trying to drag in the future to be more like the past, to make everything all the damned same. . . ."

He moved over to her, leant over her, only to find himself unable to touch her, to do more than stare at her carefully turned shoulder.

"Fabrina, why are you talking this nonsense? What's the matter with you? Things are changing all the time! Are you really afraid of change? Didn't you hear what I just said?— Callibrastics has given me a vacation for two on Earth. That's good! You act like it was something awful."

She looked up at him. He took a step back.

"You're not just fogged with aphrocoza? It's true? Oh, Edward, a whole month on Earth for the two of us!" She jumped up and threw her arms round him. "I just thought you were lying, and I couldn't bear it. It reminded me how I hate this place. When do we go?"

"You don't hate this place. You have your friends here, every comfort."

She laughed bitterly. "O.K., you like it so much, you stay and I'll go. I'll take Anna—she's dying to get back!"

"Listen, Fabrina, you aren't invited yet."

"I'm coming with you—you said so."

Suddenly he was furious. His hair came quivering down about his eyes; he dashed it away. "All I said was it was a vacation for two. I didn't say who I was taking with me. Why should it be you? Why do I have to have you round my neck all the time? If I want a holiday, then I'll take someone else. You're only my damned sister, not my wife, you know!"

They stood facing each other, slightly crouched, their hands rigid and not quite clenched, as if they were about to attack each other.

"I know I'm not your wife. I'm more like your servant. All these years I've looked after you! If you're going to Earth then you'll take me and nobody else."

"I'll take whom I please." But he weakened, recalling Stein-Presteign's contemptuous assumption that he would go with his sister because he had nobody else. Assumptions such as Stein-Presteign's and his sister's carried terrible power.

"You'll have to take me, Edward. What would people think if you didn't?"

This unexpected feebleness on her part strengthened him. "I don't care what people think—this is something I've earned and I'm going to enjoy it. I'm going to take a woman with me, I'm going to enjoy myself. Just for once, I'm going to live. That's something you've never thought of."

"What woman would have you? They'd laugh!"

"Little you know about women! Father always said you should have been a boy."

"Don't bring that up! Let's not go into the past. The things our parents did to us are all over and done with. Father *wanted* me to be a boy, didn't he, because you were so flaming inadequate in the role, but that's not my fault. You were always his little pet, weren't you, and what went on between the pair of you was none of my business."

"You tried to make it your business, just as you still try to interfere in all my relationships now. Besides, who was mother's little pet, eh?"

"Well, come on then, give—who was mother's little pet? It wasn't me, that's for sure. It was Alice, wasn't it, your favourite sister!"

"Leave Alice out of this, you bitch. She's dead too, and we both know what killed her."

She hit him across the face.

He stepped back, raising his hand to his cheek, resting his knuckle on his lip and glaring at her across the edge of his palm.

"You're still lousy with guilt," he said. "It shows in everything you do. It settles like a blight on everything you touch."

"If you're trying to blame your blighted life on me, think again. You may recall that it was you who persuaded me to come and live up on this miserable pseudoplanet."

"More fool me!"

"Right, more fool you! You always were a fool."

"I'm going out," he said. "I can't take any more of you!"

"And you're a coward, too!"

"Relax, I know you'd love to have me strike you and pummel you into a pulp. That's really what you want, isn't it? Not just from me, from any man!"

"You talk so big to me. You creep to all the real men in your precious Callibrastics, don't you?"

He went through into his room and sat on a chair to pull his sokdals on. As he came back through the main room to reach the outer door, she said, "Don't forget Anna will be here at five."

He left without answering. Unfortunately it was impossible to slam their airtight door.

X

Fragrance Fish-Food Farms Amalgamated presented a clear profile only when their administrative levels rose above mean city-level. Below that, successive storeys down mingled with the surrounding establishments and were interpenetrated by the mainlines and tunnels of the public transport system, so that they merged into the complex web of the city capsule. Most storeys nevertheless had a formal entrance as well as many functional ones, perhaps as a fossil of ancient two-dimensional approaches to urban planning, and it was at one of these formal entrances that Edward Maine presented himself.

Edward had a Brazilian friend in FFFFA called José Manuela do Ferraro, who worked in the Genetic Research department of the giant corporation. A neat little Japanese assistant came to meet Edward and escorted him to José's floor. She led among huge vats milling with young prawns and deposited him at the door of José's office.

The Brazilian was a big man, who jumped up and shook Edward's hand, clapping him on the back and smiling broadly.

"You're very successful nowadays, Edward—I saw a report

of your celebratory party on the scatter. It makes you too busy to attend Tui-either-nor meetings, I guess?"

"Afraid so. Are you still a priest in your Side Job?"

"Can't afford to give up Main Job—besides, it fascinates me so. Come and see what we are doing in the Homarus division."

"That's very kind, José, but—"

"Come on, we can talk as we go. I miss our arguments at Tui meetings, Edward. You were so good—you sharpened my wits. Now I suppose you work too much with computers to have any religious feelings."

Edward had other matters than religion on his mind, so all he said, reluctantly, was, "We need computers."

"Agreed, we need computers at this stage of man's progress," José said, opening a swing door for his friend. "But progress should be towards the sciences of self-knowledge not towards technology-slanted sciences. That's a deadend. Even I have to work with computers in Main Job, while denouncing them in Side Job. We must think in fuzzy sets, not the old either-or pattern so basic to Western ideology."

"I know, I know," Edward muttered. "But either-orness has brought us a long way."

"Now we are being defeated by alien Chinese ways of thought. You must believe in my sub-thought. Sub-thought exists and is measurable—we are getting proof. Sub-t is much more random and instinctive than ordinary logical thought; it must not be structured like thought. Sub-t is related to will, and will, as we know, can modify neural patterns in the brain. If we believe in Freud, then we have Freudian dreams, and so on. If we believe in computer-human analogies, then we will come to think and sub-t like our machines. So we will be totally dominated by either-orness. Then all creativity will be lost."

"Creativity always breaks out anew, every generation."

"Yes, but unpredictably—even in your worlds of predestination, old friend! With Tui-either-nor, we can nourish it, make barren logic subject to creativity, rather than the other way round as at present."

"That's putting it too strongly," Edward said, with a feeble smile.

"No, it's not, not while the western world is in recession generally. Tui is the old Mandarin symbol for water—a lake, for instance, signifying pleasure and fluidity. That's what we need, fluidity. Among all the religions of the zeepees, Tui is the only fructifying one, the only one that genuinely offers redemption—the redemption not just of one's self but of others!"

"I must try and get round to meetings again," Edward said. "Do you still make those ringing priestly addresses to God about Tui?"

"Of course."

"And does God answer?"

José laughed good-naturedly. "When you speak to God, that's just prayer. When he starts speaking to you—that's just schizophrenia."

They were walking among gigantic three-layered tanks in which large lobsters sprawled. The tanks were dimly lit, while the laboratory itself remained unlit. Yet it looked as if many of the lobsters could see the men, so quickly did they turn to the glass walls of their prisons and signal with antennae and claws, as if asking to be released.

"We are just beginning to realize how many kinds of thinking there are," José said. "Predestination works only for those who believe in it. . . ."

"I feel bound to challenge that statement!" Edward exclaimed. "After all—"

"Don't challenge it, remember it. Feel it fertilize you. I will show you how a little Tui thinking worked for us here." They had come to a fresh series of tanks in which more lobsters sat. José changed the subject as smoothly as if he imagined he was still talking about the same thing. "These lobsters that you see here are not much different from the ancestral lobster, *homarus vulgaris*. You can see they're a sort of dull reddy-yellow, spotted with little bluish-black patches. The only difference is that these chaps are bigger; they weigh up to six kilos. We have to breed 'em big, which we do in the traditional way of mixing inbred lines with crossbreeds for hybrid vigour. By using ideal temperatures, we can persuade them to grow to mature market size in two years rather than three."

"Do you import sea water from Earth?" Edward asked.

"Genes, no—far too expensive, *and* sea water is not pure enough for our purposes. This is all artificial sea water—in fact, synthetic water in the first place, hydrolized out of hydrocarbons and oxides floating in space."

He rapped against the glass. "But you see the trouble with ordinary lobsters. They're nasty pugnacious creatures, so aggressive that they have to live in solitary confinement throughout life, or they'd eat each other. Which puts up *per capita* costs greatly, when you consider that on Fragrance alone some twenty-three million kilos of lobster meat are consumed per annum—which means a lot of lobsters, and a lot of tanks."

"I mustn't take up any more of your time," Edward commented.

José took his elbow and led him back along the way they had come, where the rows of tanks were more brightly lit. Here, lobsters jostled together in apparent *bonhomie*, armour notwithstanding.

"These certainly are highly-coloured," Edward said. "I didn't recognize them as lobsters at first."

"They don't recognize *each other* as lobsters," José said. He beamed, and made embracing gestures at the crustacea. The latter were certainly a remarkable sight, being in all cases bicoloured, the two colours contrasted and arranged in stripes and jagged lines, rather like the camouflaged dreadnoughts of World War I. There were many colours in the tanks: lobsters yellow and black, lobsters white and cerise, lobsters scarlet and orange, lobsters viridian and grey, lobsters sky blue and sienna brown, lobsters carmine and paint-box purple. There were scarcely two lobsters of the same pattern.

"What we have done is simple," said José, rapping on the plate glass with one creative knuckle. "Firstly, we have altered their genetic coding so as to transform their original vague coloration until we hit on strains which are the eccentric hues you see now. Then we bred them true, using cloning methods. Next, taking a clue from the coloration, we made use of research into orientation anistropy in acuity."

"Whatever's orientation anistrophy in acuity?"

"Not anistrophy. Anistropy. It's an anomaly of vision.

Permit nothing but horizontal lines in the environment of an infant mammal, and ever after it will have no neural detectors for vertical ones, becoming completely orientated on the horizontals. We found that the immature visual cortex of the lobster responds in the same way. See what I mean? The effect is on the brain, not the vision, but what happens is that, after the treatment we give the larvae in their visual environment, no striped lobster can see another striped lobster. Although they basically have the same nasty pugnacious natures as their terrestrial ancestors, they live together peacefully. For them as for us, it all depends how you look at things."

"Very interesting," said Edward politely. Then he added, "Yes, that really is very interesting. . . ."

"You get the implications for human conduct, eh?" said José. "You see where my Tui thought came in? I believe that the culture matrix of our civilization—of any civilization—imprints us from birth so that we can only see horizontal lines or, in other words, only think along channels deemed correct by long-established custom."

Genuinely interested now, Edward said as they walked back to José do Ferraro's office, "I wonder if all the slightly differing environments of the zeepees will eventually give rise to a generation who are oriented to verticals or—to an entirely new way of thought."

"My guess would be that we're seeing some such phenomenon already. It would account for all the cults springing up daily. I believe that Tui is one of the true new directions."

They settled down in the office and José got them two pam-and-limes from the machine. As they were sucking, he said, "So, what can I do for you, my lapsed friend?"

"Don't call me that, José. I still believe, but I've been so busy."

"Ha, you're killing your spiritual life with work—you'll become a robot. The sad thing is, you know what you're doing. . . . Well, how can I help you?"

Now that his moment had come, Edward was embarrassed. "It's about a girl, José."

"Good. I didn't think you were interested. Women are full of Tui-either-norness. Do I know her?"

"You may do. I believe she works here in FFFFA."

"But you aren't sure?"

"It's an Internal girl, José. She comes personally to my place, but in disguise, of course. She has dropped clues about her real identity. For instance, once she said to me, 'My happiness lies in artificial oceans'. I made nothing of it at the time. This morning, it suddenly hit me that it could be the remark of a girl who worked in FFFFA. A reference to your sea-water tanks. Then again, a remark she made about Chekhov convinced me she must be Asiatic."

"Who's Chekhov?"

"How pleased you make me that I know some things you don't! He's a writer. Never mind him. You have a lot of Chinese staff here, haven't you?"

"You probably know that Four F A's fifty-five per cent Chinese-owned. Eighty per cent or more of the work staff are Chinese or North Korean. If your girl's here, she's one of probably two thousand. You'd have no way of identifying her, not if you've never seen her externally."

Edward paused, then he said, "Yes, I have a means. I think I have. I think I could identify her internally."

"How can you do that? I've never heard of such a thing!"

"Nobody has. It's my own idea. And it's not unlike your variable lobster idea. José, I've studied my Internal-girl through the eyes of the electron microscope plus the eyes of love. I've been down into her with magnifications in the millions, and I've seen something in her which no other human being has—her print, as individual as—no, far more individual than any lobster."

"You mean—you don't mean a disease?"

"No, no, I mean her histocompatibility antigens."

"Oh, the substances that set up immune reactions in tissue transplants."

"Exactly. They insure that we are all immunologically foreign to each other, unless we happen to have an identical twin. They're sort of chemical badges of personal identity. There's a sufficient diversity of them to insure that everyone's antigen kit is different. It's the most basic form of identification there is."

"And you know what your girl's kit looks like?"

"I have stills of her antigens. They're beautiful. I know them by heart. What's the matter? You're wearing your priest face!"

José do Ferraro was looking at him with a peculiar creased face, its expression seeming to alternate between mockery and affection.

"Oh, Edward, 'Make simpler daily the beating of Man's heart . . .' Every day love reveals itself in a new form, as fluid and vigorous as Tui itself. Here you stand, enraptured by the girl with the beautiful antigens. . . ."

Edward was touched by this speech, since he had not thought of himself as capable of rapture. "You don't believe I'm being silly?"

"I didn't say that, did I?"

Edward laughed. "O.K. Do an idiot a favour. Your welfare department must have records of all the girls employed here. Can we run their medical data through a scanner? Under suitable magnifications, I know I could identify my Zenith."

"Such records exist, of course. But it's illegal for anyone but the qualified Welfare staff to see them. So we'd better go and see Dr. Shang Tsae, who works in Welfare—happily, his Side Job is acolyte to Priest Ferraro. . . ."

XI

"I was worried about you. Wherever have you been?" Fabrina asked. No sign of the quarrel.

"Oh, engaged in a little private research of my own," Maine said. "I'm exhausted. Let me rest." He walked over to the mirror and tried to pat his hair into order.

"Of course, my dear. Lin, come over here and tell your master a story. Make it a nice restful one."

"All my stories are adapted to the mood of the moment," said the lin, humbly yet smugly. "This one is called 'Dinosaur Inspector'. 'Taste the squalor of old obliterated airports,' cried the dinosaur inspector. The people and incredible harlots were lusty upon the mountains. The dunes knew no spring. No animal eggs slept among the entanglements. But one strong man changed everything. Now bucolic perverts no longer lead the market. Falcons fly and magnesium bands play atrabiliously."

"Not very cheerful," Fabrina complained.

"I'm going to take a shower," Maine said.

José do Ferraro had secured Edward access to the medical files of F F F F A, thanks to the illegal aid of Dr. Shang Tsae. Then Edward had had to attempt his task of antigen identification without the aid of computer—something for which he had scarcely bargained. He allowed himself twenty-five seconds to flip up each internscape in turn and scrutinize it. Even so, it was going to take him fourteen hours to get through the whole batch of two thousand, and sometimes he had to shuffle through several internscapes of one woman to get a clear view of the antigens. He tried to speed up his viewing; then fatigue slowed him again. The day had been fruitless, as predicted by his PM. He told the sober little Chinese doctor that he would return the next day.

XII

Early on the following morning, Edward Maine heaved himself from bed and padded over to the PM, letting it gather all his physiological data while he was still half-asleep. On depressing the read-out bar, he became fully awake.

** Key day. Persistence needed at start. Do not yield to impatience	
Antigen quest rewarded	96
Oysters yield great beauty	94·5
Increased heart-rate leads to precipitate action	94
Visit to the ever-punctual fly	79·5
Conversation delights	87
More initiative needed	
Outburst of invective can be avoided	77·5

Summary: happy day, partly enjoyed in attractive company

The second key day running. His life was certainly changing. One of the constant troubles he had had while developing the PM was that nothing ever happened in his life, so that in consequence the machine had nothing to predict; which made it difficult to tell whether it was working or not.

Now it seemed to be working full blast.

Just for a moment, as he dressed, Edward wondered how much the PM really told him. He could have guessed without its aid that this would be a key day. From the line "Antigen quest rewarded" onwards, it looked as if he would trace his longed-for Zenith; but that also was expected. On the other hand, it was difficult to tell from the read-outs where the unexpected lay. There were displeasing implications in that last line, "Invective can be avoided". With whom? The machine could not tell him, or Heisenberg's uncertainty principle would be violated; it predicted the unexpected in such a way that it remained unexpected.

As soon as he could, he returned to the file-room of the FFFFA.

It was over half-way through the morning before he thought he had what he wanted. Before him glowed a remarkably clear shot of antigens in body tissue; they resembled strange deep-ocean sponges, and were brightly coloured. His heart beat at an increased rate. He felt his mouth go dry. In colour, in shape, they matched with Zenith's. He forgot that he was regarding a complex defence system designed to protect the human body from invasion by cells from another body; instead, he was gazing at a part of a world with its own perspectives, atmosphere, and laws which had no exact counterpart anywhere in the cosmos—an alien territory of beauty and proportion almost completely overlooked by man in his quest for new environments. By a paradox, this most personal view of his love was totally impersonal.

He turned to the file and read the name there: Felicity Amber Jones. Main Job: Marine Larvologist; speciality, Bivalves.

Felicity Amber Jones. Beautiful name. Of course, it was probably not her real name. The fashion was to adopt a name on arrival at the zeepees.

Whatever her name, it was Felicity Amber Jones herself he wanted. . . .

An information board told him that Bivalves were in Level Yellow Two.

At Level Yellow Two, a preoccupied lady at a console told him that he would find Felicity Amber Jones along to his right.

Edward could hardly walk, so weak did his legs feel. His popliteal muscles trembled. He made his way along, clutching at a bench for support, face close to a range of tanks in which little agitated blobs of life flitted. Each successive tank contained water of a slightly different hue from the previous one. And in each, the blobs became larger and less agitated. In the last tank of the series, the blobs had come to rest on plastic trays inserted vertically into the water, and were recognizable as minute oysters. There stood a young Chinese girl in an orange lab coat, doing complicated things at a trolley involving small oysters and full beakers. She looked up at his approach and smiled questioningly.

He had never been in love before—not properly. "Are you Felicity Amber Jones?" he asked.

She was in her twenties, a neat little figure with a slender neck on which was balanced one of the most elegantly modelled heads Edward had ever seen. The lines of this exquisite head were emphasized by a short crop of hair which curled round the back of the skull to end provokingly as two upturning horns. These seductive dark locks pointed to two dimples nestling under slanting cheekbones. Her eyes, slightly set back in her eye-sockets, were round and moist, being sheltered by dark eyelashes.

Didn't those pupils widen involuntarily, despite lack of any other sign of recognition, as she answered, "Yes, I am Miss Jones."

"Look, I'm Edward Maine." He stammered his address.

"Oh, I see. Are you interested in our oyster-breeding? From pinhead to adult, it takes only fifteen months under our accelerated growth scheme. Here you see the algae tanks, each with a different algae table for different stages of larval growth, with temperature—"

"Miss Jones, you recognize me, don't you?"

She put a finger—the smallest finger of her right hand—curling it like a little prawn—into her mouth—receiving it between dainty white teeth—which were embedded in the clearest of pink gums—and said, "Have we met before, Mr Maine?"

"Oh, yes," he said. "You're the girl with the most beautiful antigens in the world. I knew them instantly. You're the—well, you come to visit me at home once a week. . . ."

Her gaze evaded him. Turning one shoulder—the gesture itself poetry—the shoulder itself a miracle—she made a little fluttering noise.

Standing on tiptoe in order to see her cheek over her shoulder, he said in a rush, "Look, please—I know it's a terrible breach of etiquette—I know I shouldn't be here—but I've got a vacation on Earth—a whole month, courtesy of my corporation—and I can take along anyone I like—please, will *you* come with me?—I mean, it has to be you—you can name your own terms, of course—but please don't tell me I am mistaken—because you're too beautiful to be anyone but—Zenith!"

She turned back. With an effort, she raised her head—despair of any sculptor—and looked into his eyes—beauty of a Medusa—and said, "Well, I may as well say it. You're right, I am Zenith. They'll sack me from the Internscan Union for admitting it."

To his extreme pleasure and embarrassment, he found that he was clasping her hands. Even worse, lit by artificial sea water, he was kissing her on the mouth.

Felicity Amber Jones proved to have just the shape and flavour of mouth of which he had always dreamed.

"I should be more formal," she said, drawing back. "Internal girls are not meant to behave so freely. Please do not try to kiss me again!"

"I'll do my best," he said. He was not on oath. "I feel I know you so well, Miss Jones, Felicity—Miss Jones. Now we must get to know each other in more traditional ways. You—you are so delightful on the microscopic level that I long to discover all the other ways in which you are delightful."

"Please speak more formally to me during my Main Job."

"Are you afraid the oysters will overhear?"

She laughed. "Your average oyster is a very unreliable creature. It can't be trusted to keep its trap shut."

"Then we must go elsewhere to talk."

He was not sure exactly what to do with the girl when he had found her; her presence added to his usual confusion. But she was pliant and docile and readily agreed to any suggestion he made.

Despite which, it happened to be at her instigation rather than his that they found themselves in the Inarguable Paradise, the biggest of Fragrance's three fun-centres. The Inarguable Paradise had, as one of its chief attractions, The Ever-Punctual Fly. This Fly was a small satellite which orbited the planetoid once every fifty minutes. Unlike its parent body it had no artificial gravity; one of its chief attractions was the free-fall restaurant, in which delectable dishes were enjoyed while watching agorophobic views in absurd postures.

There were some other Chinese-Western couples here; such liaisons were common enough—at least on this zeepee—not to excite comment; but Felicity Amber Jones declared that this was the first time she had been out informally with a westerner.

"We call you 'foreign devils'," she told Edward. "The Chinese are at least as conscious of race and nationality as you Americans are."

He found her mixture of directness and modesty both exciting and paradoxical. She was so perfect, her outline, her every contour, so clearly placed, that he was in awe of her. He wondered what her real name was—it was the custom with many people to take up a new name on arrival in the zeepees. His own terrestrial name had been Oscar Pythagoras Rix.

"Will you really come to Earth with me? I won't ask anything of you but your company."

"Oh, that's quite all right."

It was not exactly the answer that he had expected; yet he wondered if its seeming complaisance was more than he had hoped for. A premature gratitude flowed into the lagoons of his being.

He pressed her hand—opportunely, as it happened, for at that moment a quartet of Voivodina gipsies, specially imported from Earth, began a passionate lament to love, springtime, swordplay, Smederevo, the tide, innocence, moonlit nights, deserted churches, and a pair of forgotten lace gloves.

Edward did not tell Felicity Amber Jones that he had a commission to carry out on Earth. That might, he considered, make her less keen to join him. Instead, he concentrated on the pleasure aspect, unwilling to believe she could wish to come along for his company alone.

"What would you most like to see when we reach Earth? The glaciers of Alaska? Smederevo?" The wild music was still provoking his blood.

"Oh, I would love to see the reindeer herds of the Chinese Arctic, grazing by the East Siberian Sea. I have never seen a reindeer, and they're so guilty and luxurious."

"I've never seen a penguin. How about a trip to the Ross Ice Shelf in the Antarctic, to see the Adele penguins? You know they reproduce in sub-zero temperatures?"

"We mustn't concentrate only on cold regions. What about the warm regions? How marvellous to see Kilimanjaro rising from the zebra-trampled veldt and floating in the crumpled air."

"How marvellous to swim in the Red Sea and wave to passing dahabeeyahs!"

"To take a trip to the Iguazu Falls, where Brazil, Uruguay and Argentina meet."

"To jump into the chain of volcanoes along the spine of Sumatra."

"To dive down to the new underwater city off Ceylon."

"To surf off Honolulu."

"Do you really know how to surf?" she asked.

"No. But I've seen guys do it on the scatter. . . ."

XIII

When he returned home, the twenty-hour Fragrancian day was almost spent and a new one only half an hour away. Edward had held her hand on parting. They smiled at each other and promised to meet another day.

Now, like any callow youth, he cursed himself for not showing more initiative and kissing Felicity Amber Jones good-night. Surely she would have allowed—wanted—it after such a splendid evening.

Fabrina was home with Anna Kavan. They were practising

altered body images together, and becoming rather entangled. Fabrina stood up, blowing her hair from her eyes.

"We wondered what had happened to you. That reporter from Cairo is trying to get in touch with you again."

"Only good things happened," Edward replied, moving with nonchalance towards his room.

"So you are going to Earth, Edward," Anna said. "Aren't you fiendishly fortunate? You wouldn't like to take me with you, I suppose? I hear you have a spare ticket."

He turned and confronted them both, drawing in his stomach and standing his full height.

"Not any more! You might both like to know that I'm taking a girl friend to Earth with me. It's all fixed, and I don't want any arguments."

Fabrina threw herself at him. "You fool, Edward, you fool! I can guess who it is—it's that little Internal-girl of yours, isn't it? You know nothing about her. She'll make your life a misery, you see."

"Hope what you like," he said, and escaped into his room. As the PM said, outbursts of invective could be avoided.

XIV

Next morning, relationships between Edward Maine and his sister were strained.

"What will you do while I'm on holiday, my dear?" he asked.

"I'd rather not talk about it. I'm too hurt. You don't care a bit about me."

That killed that conversation.

The lin said, "Neither of you is very happy. Let me tell you a story."

"I'm perfectly happy, and I do not want a story," Fabrina said, sniffing into a tissue.

"This one's called 'Floating Airports'," said the machine, temptingly.

"No."

"It is full of atmosphere and there is action on a metaphysical level. Also it features a strong tax inspector, together with some animals such as you like."

"Oh, for god's sake, let him tell his story!" Edward said.

"Thank you. 'Floating Airports'. All over the old grey oceans airports floated. The towering sponsors walked drowning under deserted windows. And the tax inspector claimed, 'Now all can sleep who cease to guard the leopards'. So the strong officer went to the weak ruler and applied modesty. 'Large export markets lead to decayed temples,' one stated. So the animals laid eggs among the worldly."

"Very nice," said Edward politely. His sister did not speak. The lin bowed and retreated to stand itself against a wall.

For Edward, it was a busy morning, and one on which he embarked with some apprehension, since the PM's read-out forecast two embarrassing encounters. He went to Smics Callibrastics to sort out unfinished work, and was besieged by callers from other departments, among whom the most persistent were Sheila Wu Tun from Personnel and Greg Gryastairs from Kakobillis, who wanted errands run or messages delivered when he was on Earth. Edward was glad to escape at noon and go down to the travel agency, On the Scent, at Main Plaza East, to make his arrangements for the flight.

On the Scent were very helpful. He was booked aboard the *Ether Breather* in two days' time. The manager was somewhat awed by meek little Edward Maine, for the firm had given him a very generous luggage allowance. Kilo-costs for freight were so much steeper for the Fragrance-Earth run than for interzeepee trips, that anyone who travelled to Earth with more than two kilos of personal baggage was marked out as someone special; Maine, with his massive allowance, was a being apart.

The being apart was not content with his corporation's generosity, however. As usual, it had an ulterior motive. Callibrastics had prevailed upon him to take the prototype PM along, in order to do a field test in the more random conditions which prevailed upon the mother planet.

Slightly dazed by a pile of documents and brochures, Edward made his way from the travel agency to the nearest aphrohale parlour and got gassed on a nitojoy-pip.

As the heavy fumes poured into his nostrils, he heard the sound of musical instruments. A small religious parade was approaching, charmed on by pipe and drum.

It was a cheerful sight, bright even in the Plaza, which had been decorated for striking colour effects. Most of the people in the parade wore brightly coloured dominoes, complete with cloak and half-hood, and many of the hoods mimicked animal heads. Edward recognized the style. These were followers of Tui-either-nor and, if he had continued with one of his Side Jobs he would now be among them, complete with mouse-mask and a lust to convert.

Feeling guilty, he slipped back to a table at the rear of the parlour; which was a simple matter, since most of the patrons had moved forward to see what was going on. Religious belief was a participator sport in the Zodiacal Planets.

When the procession stopped near the parlour, one of its number, a well-built man in giraffe-mask and priest's insignia, began to speak.

"Friends, would-be friends, wouldn't-be friends, greetings all! Let me tell you what you're thinking right now. To some extent, you are aware of this procession. But you'll soon dismiss it: your mind's on trivial personal matters. It will be no part of you. Why not make it a part of you? You'll be richer. We're here to make you and Fragrance and the world a richer place." The haughty giraffe face surveyed the denizens of the square.

"Do you know what sub-t or sub-thought is? It's a random pattern of thought which we all possess. It exists and is a measurable quantity. It has been denied in western thought because it has no logic to it. That is why we have sunk into materialism. Sub-t can give you a rich spiritual life, with all alternatives open. This little procession can be your procession towards Tui-either-nor, the full thinking and spiritual existence. Espouse alternatives, or you will find yourself in one of life's cul-de-sacs.

"Only yesterday, my friends, I had an old acquaintance come to me in my Main Job—yes, like you I have to work for my living—I'm not a fake priest—and this old friend was in search of something. Once he was a member of this movement, but he reneged. He hadn't the persistence, the initiative required to follow what he believed in his heart. He had become a hollow man."

Edward began to look about him, feeling warmth creep round his cheeks and ears. Eyes of frog, cat, leopard, hippo, marmoset, he sensed were on him.

"Yet that old acquaintance, my friend," said the giraffe remorselessly, "deluded as he was, he was in search of love, and love in a new form. He knew without knowing—he knew by sub-t—that his own spiritual life was dead, and he was driven to exercise fantastic ingenuity to look for a means whereby that dead life might be made alive again. There was a force in him greater than himself. You and I might think him a poor shrivelled creature, but all the while his life was being lived secretly for him.

"My word to you is—"

Putting two F-tallies on the table, Edward crept blushingly away without waiting for the word. He felt indeed a poor shrivelled creature as he hurried towards the nearest trafficway. As he scrambled into the first carriage, his attention was caught by a message scrawled on the nearest wall: AMBIGUITY CLARIFIES.

Suddenly, he hated Tui. Life was difficult enough without emphasizing its difficulties. He was inadequate enough without anyone emphasizing his inadequacies. He could see why an earlier generation had turned away from religion and the spiritual life. It was too much for them.

What they really needed were fixed co-ordinates.

A predictable path through life.

No nasty surprises from sub-t or the collective unconscious or the endocrine system.

Just the dark glasses and white stick of certainty.

His immediate impulse was to go home, but he could not face his sister. Feelings still ruffled, he headed for Felicity Amber Jones's conapt, right in the heart of the urbstak.

Section Coty was a crowded place. Lower rates went with higher densities. He remembered that Felicity had said he should not come to her home. He pressed her signal all the same, and in a moment she appeared at the door, wearing a knee-length gown of cerulean blue chased with an embroidered electric design in silver. She wore a matching blue ribbon in her hair, which gave her an incongruously childish look.

Smiling, he waved the wad of documents at her.

"I've got our tickets! We catch a flight the day after to-morrow, Felicity. Can you be ready in time?"

She looked anguished. "I live in a poor way here, Edward. You will despise me when you see how dreadfully I exist."

"I'm not a bloated capitalist. Why should I despise you for being poor?"

"You know I had to take to being an Internal-girl. That's to support my brother, Shi Tok, who is an artist. He's here now. He lives with me."

"I'll be glad to meet him. You didn't tell me that you live with your brother, as I live with my sister."

She let him in reluctantly. "He is very prejudiced against Americans, worse luck."

Sharply, he said, "Have you told him we are going to Earth together?"

Felicity covered her nose and mouth with a narrow hand and bowed her head. As she did so, a man appeared from an inner room, wearing a paint-stained shirt and smoking an absurdly small pipe. His hair was cut square, his face painted in stripes.

"What do you want?" he asked.

"This man is my friend, Shi Tok. His name is Edward. Edward this is my brother, Shi Tok. He is a great artist."

"You probably don't care much for art, do you?" Shi Tok asked.

"Why, yes, I have a great respect for works of art—and for artists."

"I see. The usual crappy worthless lip service. Why don't you get honest and say that you hate and fear art and artists?"

"Because he does not wish to be as rude as you," Felicity said. "Give Edward a pam-and-lime or something."

"No, I'd better be going, Zenith. I can see I'm not welcome here."

"Why's he calling you Zenith, Felicity? Say, Edward, while you're here, why don't you come and see what I'm currently working on? With all that enthusiasm for art, you might get a buzz."

Despite himself, Edward found himself being pushed into a small room where the three of them formed a crowd—perhaps because of the way in which brother and sister jostled and gestured, continually getting in each other's way—she trying to produce beverages, he to produce art-works.

The table was piled with boxes full of plaques. Another plaque stood in a vice attached to the edge of the table. Shi Tok spun the vice open and held the plaque out to Edward, who accepted it reluctantly. The plaque was a rectangle about the size of an envelope and not much thicker. It was cream in colour.

"I haven't finished that one yet. Know what it is?"

"Is it ivory?"

Shi Tok laughed harshly. "I didn't mean what is it made of. I mean what does it represent. But no, of course it is not ivory. It's just a block of garsh, one of the new palloys. Ivory! Stars above! Don't you know that all the tariffs and duties stacked against the zodiacal planets by Earth make it almost prohibitive to import ivory to Fragrance? Not that I could afford ivory even at Mother Earth prices. I'm a poor artist, Edward, a creator, not a civil servant, or whatever secure dull little job you hold down—no, don't tell me. That sort of information makes me feel bad, puts me off my work. . . . This is only a block of garsh, manufactured just a light-second away on one of the Ingratitudes. You know what it is?"

Since there seemed to be no answer to this question, Edward took the glass which Felicity offered with some gratitude and said, "I'm not against art, although it's true I have a secure job. I'm a sort of artist myself, in a way—although perhaps not in a way you might recognize. What form does your art take?"

Felicity's brother looked upwards at the low ceiling and made grunting noises of despair. "This is my art-form." He waved the garsh under Edward's nose. "And these boxes are stacked with more of them, masterpieces every one. Look!"

He stirred up the boxes, pulling out rectangular plaques at random. Each block had a band incised and painted across it. The bands varied slightly in width, colour and positioning, but there was never more than one band to a plaque.

"They're all named on the back, and signed by me," Shi Tok explained. "Here you are: *A Clutch of Underground Cathedrals, The Last Bite of an Unseen Shrapnel, Legs Trapped in an*

Embroidered Sea, Suntans of an Inoffensive Moon, The Spirit of the Male Climacteric Regards Narcissus, Friction Between Skull and Prisoner Brain. . . . Take your pick."

"Um . . . do you sell these?" Edward asked.

"Of course I sell them . . . when I can. . . . They go to rich dolts in your country or mine with more cash than brains. I rook 'em for what I can get. Like you, they hate and fear art, but they think it impresses other people, so I turn out this real junk for the pleasure of making fools of them."

Edward sipped his pam and looked at the floor. "Is it pleasurable to make fools of people?"

"They were fools long before I got to them. Why give them the real thing when they can't appreciate it? Art's as dead in China as it is in America. The artists helped kill it—they don't know what the hell they're doing either. The stupid oafs worked themselves into a dead end."

Edward gnawed his lip and scratched his leg.

Felicity said, "Edward is going to visit Earth soon," and was ignored.

"Well," Shi Tok said, throwing the plaques back in the box, "why don't you say something? Don't you like my works of art?"

"It's not for me to say," Edward muttered.

"Why not? I'm asking you, aren't I? You did come here uninvited, didn't you? What do you think of them, you a sort of artist and all that?"

Edward looked at him and felt a blush steal round his ears and cheeks. "I think nothing of them, if you want the truth. Which appears to be exactly what you think of them. I'm sorry that you can claim to be an artist and yet know that what you produce is worthless, however much you get paid for it. You must be aware of the contradiction there. Perhaps it's that which makes you so angry all the time."

The stripes rippled on Shi Tok's face. He raised a clenched fist, as much for emphasis as attack. "I sell these for what I can get. No one respects the real artist these days. Even the lousy critics—"

"I'd better be going, Felicity," Edward said, setting his glass down on the table close to the vice. "Thank you both for the drink."

"It's all very well for you to be superior, you don't suffer—"

She followed Edward to the door, despite the roaring of her brother. At the door, she stood on tiptoe and kissed him on the cheek.

"You're just wonderful," she said. "A real man."

XV

Despite all the efforts to glamorize it, getting to Earth was just hell.

It started being hell at Fragport, where passengers for Earth had to go through long examinations in Customs, Medical, Expatriation, and Ecology, as well as the space line's Check In —where great exception was taken to Edward's PM, although he had all the requisite documents, and some small exception to his lin, which was only allowed through because it was an obsolete model (and he had only brought it to spite his sister).

Several people had come to interview Edward before he left Fragrance.

He was cornered by a plump shiny young man with a sharp-bladed nose, who shook Edward's hand and said he was proud to meet him.

"My name is Sheikh Raschid el Gheleb, and I lecture in Predestination at Cairo University. That's Cairo, Earth, of course. I've been trying to catch up with you for some while. Of course I am personally interested in your attempts to build a Predestination Machine."

"Kind of successful attempts," Edward said.

"So I understand. Spare me a moment of talk, please. What interests me is that Predestination is a pretty new thing in the West. Perhaps it is merely because I am Arab that I equate the outgoing capitalism of the West over the last few centuries with a firm belief in free will. The religion of the West, Christianity, lays heavy emphasis on choice."

"Ah, the either-orness of Heaven and Hell," Edward murmured, remembering the teaching of his Tui-either-norness phase.

"Now that Christianity is dying out and the West, faced with Chinese supremacy and the World State, has fewer alternatives, the peoples of the West—in the United States in particular—are turning more and more to predestination. This seems to me interesting, because the Chinese, in a sense, have always believed in predestination. So both sides of the world are becoming philosophically more ready for union. Do you see it that way?"

Edward hesitated. He liked discussions; they made him feel important; but he also wanted to board the *Ether Breather* and be alone with Felicity. "No, Sheikh, I don't quite see it that way. The impetus that moves the West towards predestination is mainly scientific and technological. It's the running down of ready sources of energy which has given the average man fewer alternatives. Better scientific knowledge of the workings of the brain and the genetic system has simply ruled out the old notion of free will. We really are programmed—it is that knowledge makes a PM possible."

"I see, a diametrically opposed approach to the Chinese, in a way. I wonder if the Chinese will object to your turning what they have regarded as a philosophical outlook into a mechanistic one. May I ask you if your PM takes coincidences into account?"

"We are still in the prototype stage, you understand. But of course predictions can be thrown badly wrong by coincidence until such time as we fully understand the working of chance; there will then be no random factors, and coincidence will cease to exist, just like free will."

"Do you personally believe in coincidence, Mr Maine?"

"Not in its old sense of a freak and rather unsettling concurrence of events, no. It is only under an Aristotelian system of logic that coincidences appear unaccountable."

"Mr Maine, thank you. May we ask which ship you are taking to Earth?"

"We shall be on the *Ether Breather*. If you will excuse me."

"I see—a real-life case of ether-or eh? . . ."

XVI

The *Ether Breather* had come in from the Tolerances, and was already crowded. Edward and Felicity found adjacent couches in the Soft Class lounge and strapped themselves in.

There was a fifty-minute wait till blast-off; no foggers or sniffers were permitted.

"Shall I tell you a story?" asked the lin, ever-solicitous, from under Edward's couch. "I have one called 'Familiar Struggle'."

"At least the title sounds appropriate at the moment." Felicity said.

" 'Familiar Struggle'. Bishop Cortara stood on heavy stone. 'Struggle is as sure as death or spring: so be leopards while the high valleys flower.' But the squalid photographers had heard too many promises. Musical weaving-mills burned. Pacific courts decayed. The pretty regiments came. He put his arms round a returning falcon and floated above the familiar windows of the Pacific."

Edward fell asleep. When he woke, they were nosing out of the hangar in a mild cuddle of acceleration.

Passengers had the option of listening to music or of using the small screen-table before them either to watch a current film, generally Chinese or Japanese, or to view the panorama beyond the ship as seen from the captain's monitor. Most people opted for the film—*Confessions of the Love Computer*—but Edward and Felicity switched over to the spectacle of space.

Flying among the Zodiacal Planets provided a superb visual experience. The planetoids glittered all about, like a galaxy built of poker chips, their palloy hulls and domes giving them a high albedo. They circled Earth like a swarm of floodlit mosquitoes. There were hundreds of them, given life by the thermonuclear ardours of the sun.

Most of them had been constructed three and four decades earlier, in ambitious response to the Great Power Crisis. Energy was here for the taking—but energy always at a price. Many of the zeepees had been built under private enterprise, by large corporations of all kinds. At first, when enthusiasm was high and expertise rare, the failure rate was formidable. There were romantic tales of half-finished zeepees, of ruined zeepees, of zeepees unregistered at Lloyd's, of zeepees filled with water or poisonous gases, in which renegades and pirates lived; such things were the standard fare of scatter shows. Eventually, governments had stepped in when death tolls grew high enough to rouse public opinion. Later, groups of zeepees had formed alliances, often slightly altering their orbit to do so, and now governed themselves like so many city states.

Independent zeepees still existed; but they were mainly the poorer ones. Even the alliances fell increasingly into the hands of terrestrial nations as tariffs nibbled away their profitability. All came more and more under the Chinese hegemony. The Chinese owned—if only at second- or third-hand—the essential space routes and most of the space lines. Chinese artefacts and fashions ruled increasingly on even the most strenuously independent zeepees.

There were pessimists who claimed that the great days of the Zodiacal Planets were already over. Optimists claimed that the great days had hardly begun, and that the time would come when zeepees equipped themselves with their own fleets —a nucleus existed already—and towed themselves to new orbits round Venus, away from terrestrial interference. Nonsense, said the pessimists (who as usual in these cases called themselves realists); in a cytherean orbit, solar emissions would prove lethal and, in any case, the zeepees were only economically viable as it was because they were not too far from Earth. We don't need Earth any more, cried the optimists. The day will come, said the realists, when all our beautiful new worlds will float silent and deserted about the mother planet, stripped of their luxury and machineries—and that in our lifetime. Never, said the optimists, upping their insurance.

"We're lucky to be the generation that enjoys all this beauty," Edward said. "But I'm looking forward to the sight of an Earth landscape again. To gazing at distant horizons. Myopia has become such a fashionable zeepee complaint. Of course, much will have altered since I was there last, because of the energy shortage. It's fifteen years in my case."

"Only five in mine, but things will have changed," Felicity said. "Do you know what they have now? Sailing ships again! Big ones!"

"So I heard."

"They are so short of horsepower. One horsepower will

shift only one kilo in the air or nine kilos on land, but over five thousand kilos by water. So now all cargoes go by the oceans, just as in earlier centuries. In Shanghai and Canton, the ship-yards have built huge windjammers with five masts which travel at seventeen knots—as fast as the old mammoth tankers."

"They must need huge crews. The profession of sailor has returned."

"No, it hasn't, Edward. These windjammers are quite solitary, with no crew aboard except just one technician. The constant sail-changing is now fully automated and controlled by computer in response to weather-readings taken on-ship and from weathersats. Isn't that romantic—those great white ships sailing the oceans all alone, each managing its own lonely course?"

"Marvellous!" he said. "Like albatrosses. . . ." He sat relishing the picture she conjured up in his mind, thinking how much of life he had missed by his concentration on work for Callibrastics. And he thought too of a model yacht he had had as a boy. He launched it on a pond near home and it sailed to the far bank, with a brave wooden sailor standing by its mast.

"I'd really like to see one of those ships," he said. Oh, the early days of life, before the machineries of the brain took charge. The dragon-haunted seas of Earth and youth. . . . A wave of poignance cut through him, so that he could have wept. In his early teens, he had once loved a girl whose father was a seaman in the navy. She had written him a mad twelve-page letter describing Montevideo, exorcism, the secret parts of her body, and many other interesting things, and then had disappeared from his life. The oceans of the world were beyond all prediction.

Finally, he turned to Felicity, fragile in her couch, and gazed into her deep, dark eyes.

"We know such different things about each other. I know about you internally, but nothing about your circumstances, although I had the pleasure of meeting your brother—"

She burst into laughter, hiding her pleasant mouth with a hand.

"You hated my brother, just as he hated you! Why are you always so polite?"

"I was taught that one should be polite to Chinese girls."
He smiled.

She clutched his hand, giggling. "Don't be polite much longer, Edward."

He thought he caught her meaning. Turning to her hungrily, he said, "Tell me more about yourself, where you've come from, what you want from life, what you think about, what happened to you when you were surrounded by real seas, not artificial ones!"

Felicity told him of a life lived mainly in the Province of Chekiang, of their holidays by the sea, of camping in the mountains, of her father's rise in the civil service, and of his promotion to Peking. She was most happy in Peking when she joined a girls' Whole Diet Circle, which was established in a small rural township that was wholly self-supporting; there she had learnt fish-farming and other ecological arts. During those happy days, catastrophe overtook the family. Their mother became increasingly difficult, family quarrels an everyday occurrence. A favourite younger daughter was run over through the mother's neglect. The family polarized, Shi Tok siding with his mother, Felicity with her father. They felt scandal close about them. The father was given a post in the city of Hangchow but, in a fit of rage, he sent Shi Tok off to the zeepees to work for his living.

"And it was all predictable," Felicity said. "My mother was suffering from a brain tumour, as we should have diagnosed. She died suddenly, only a few weeks after Shi Tok had left home. My father became a very sad man, particularly when Shi Tok would not communicate with him, believing that mother's death came through his neglect. I volunteered to go and see Shi Tok, but it is expensive to travel in space and, with having to support Shi Tok, I might never have saved enough money to return if you had not come along. . . ."

He tried to hold her story in mind, but his sense of injury won.

"You only came with me because you wanted to get back to your father!"

"That is not so, and I am very grateful to you. You know that; I have shown you."

He remained uneasy.

Ether Breather was not designed for high stress. Its structure was built from various of the metal-plastic alloys. To get down to Earth, at the bottom of its steep gravity well, passengers had to change into a much stouter ferry.

Accordingly, they disembarked when they were 5,700 kilometres from Earth, alighting for a couple of hours at a duty-free way-station called Roche's Limit.

As they stood at one of the great windows of the way-station, looking out on the tremendous bowl of Earth below them, Edward said suddenly, "I will take you to China. We'll go together. First, I must visit Cleveland, Ohio, to see my only surviving relations. You can come with me, and then we will visit your country. I have an errand for the corporation, after which we shall be free to do what we like."

"Lovely, Edward! I will show you the ocean, and you shall watch the new breed of clipper ships sailing the China Seas!"

He clutched her and she did not draw away. "That will be marvellous. First, I have to talk to a Minister in Peking, a man called Li Kwang See. It is important to get his approval of the PM unofficially."

She gave a little squeak in the region of his right shoulder and buried her face in his chest.

"Do you know the minister's name?" he asked.

Felicity covered her mouth and nose with a narrow hand, shaking her head. "Go on," she said indistinctly. "Why do you need Chinese approval?"

"We must secure Earth markets for full expansion. The World State will be in operation soon. Everything is getting very Chinese these days. . . ."

"Only American things! Meanwhile, Chinese things are getting westernized."

Her voice was strained; he attributed it to the fantastic view before them.

"Even my little old lin is Chinese in origin."

"I know—the very name Lin is Mandarin, meaning a fabulous creature like a unicorn, whose voice coincides with all the notes of music—melodious, you'd say!"

"My lin isn't much like a unicorn."

"Maybe not. But it is symmetrical and beautifully proportioned, *and* it only appears when benevolent kings are on the throne. And those are legendary characteristics of our unicorns."

"Aha! Then I like my lin a great deal, and will never part with it."

They crowded into the ferry when it came, together with a flock of other passengers, happy that theirs was not a longer wait—unlike the zeepees, Roche's Limit worked by the twenty-four-hour terrestrial clock, and there were only four ferries a terrestrial day to and from Earth.

The nightmare of sinking down to the planetary surface. The choking moment of landing. The nausea of full gravity. The rank smell of natural atmosphere, full of millions of years of impurities. The horror of finding that they had arrived during that antiquated and inconvenient hiatus, night. The boredom of getting through Check Out, with its interminable examinations. The contempt at the antique forms of transport. The excitement of being together in this irrational, random world. . . .

XVII

A week in Cleveland, Ohio, was like a cycle of Cathay. They left after only five days. It was true that Edward's old uncle was kind to them, and took them pedal-boating on the Cayahoga River. "You'd never believe that this waterway was once notorious," he told them. "It was the first body of water ever to be insured as a fire-hazard. Now you catch big fish in it, and the duck-shooting's great, in season."

But Cleveland itself was a relic when it was not entirely a slum. Its industries had died for lack of nourishment. Like most of the great industrial cities of the West, its inhabitants were villagers again, painfully feeling their way back to a rooted way of life.

There was no private transport. They caught an infrequent coach to the West Coast, waiting in San Francisco until they could get a passage to one of the distant Chinese ports. Eventually, they boarded a steam-assisted schooner, *The Caliph*, bound for Hangchow.

Edward Maine was anxious. A veil had come between him

and Felicity. He did not understand, and feared that he had somehow offended her, so maladroit was he with women.

They had a fair-sized cabin opening on the promenade deck. After long arguments with their steward, Maine managed to get both the PM and the lin brought up from the hold and installed in the cabin. The familiar objects brought with them a sense of security.

"That makes it more like home," he said. "Lin, can you tell us a cheerful story?"

"America is disappearing," said the lin, which was perfectly true. Already land was a mere blue line on the horizon. "I have a story called 'Deserted Dunes'."

"Would you like to hear it, Felicity?"

"I suppose so."

"Leopards burned atrabiliously among the magnesium fountains. Musical girls walked among sand dunes because heavy increases in taxation were demanded. One old man said, 'The ocean will return next year.' Spring brought rain. Stone decayed. And again bells sounded along the deserted temples."

She forced a laugh. "Very cheering. 'The ocean will return next year. . . .' I wonder what exactly that means!" She looked a little green, as if the pitching of the schooner was having its effect.

With an effort, he went over to her and took her in his arms. "I know Cleveland wasn't too successful. This is the first time we have been alone together since Fragrance. The world distracts us. . . . What the lin says means nothing—and nothing will return unless we seize it now. Oh, dear Felicity, I don't know what you really think of me—I know you really only came along for the ride—you really want to be with your father and never go back to Fragrance, isn't that it?—but I care greatly for you, and I want to know what you feel about me. Please, please, speak out to me!"

She gave him a look of—he took it for despair and something more. Then she broke from him and ran from the cabin. He followed, watching her run along the deck, her coat flapping in the breeze, a vivid figure against the tumbled drama of ocean. Then he went back into the cabin and shut the door.

For a long while, he sat on the edge of his bunk. Then with

an effort, he rose again, beginning to unpack the parts of the PM and assemble them. *The Caliph* had its own wind-assisted generators, and passenger electricity was on at this hour of day. When the machine was assembled, he plugged it in at the power point and switched on.

The PM was not programmed with supplementary terrestrial data as yet. Edward realized more clearly than ever how far ahead lay the first generation of portable PMs. Nevertheless, the prototype should still be reliable as far as his and Felicity's personal situation was concerned. He was determined that they must disentangle that situation as soon as possible; the sudden lapse in their easy relationship was more than he could bear.

As the machine began to read him, he became aware of a queasiness in the stomach, a light film of perspiration on his forehead, the symptoms of incipient *mal de mer*. He tried to relax as the PM absorbed the levels of his physiological functions.

He set the machine to print out for the next twelve hours only. It began to deliver, its print finger moving with an irascible, jerky action common to machines and tyrannosauri.

Persist in your mission
Anxiety precipitates crisis   76
Fragrance faces imminent destruction   99
Shock endangers love   47
Maintain contact with girl
Further study of chance laws needed   99·5

Summary: multiple crisis in attractive company

Edward switched the machine off, pulled the plug from the power socket, and began to dismantle the machine, making a long face as he did so.

The PM was programmed for the confined world of Fragrance II. It had been fed no routine data since leaving the zeepee. Its prediction of catastrophe was a phantom, based purely on his current physiological state which, on Fragrance, would indeed have presaged some phenomenal disaster: here it presaged only possible sea-sickness.

"Maintain contact with the girl" was another plain nonsense, since on shipboard it was impossible to do anything else.

Unless—the thought came like a shot—Felicity fell overboard.

But it was a miserable little read-out, with crazy probabilities. And the "Further study of chance laws needed" was irrelevant, since he had stressed such needs at every stage of research. The PM could not be expected to work in transposed environments without elaborate preparation.

He ought to dismiss the read-out, knowing how out-of-touch with reality it was. He was listening to a blind oracle, he told himself. Then he remembered that oracles were traditionally blind.

Searching the ship for Felicity in a state of anxiety, he found her eventually in the stern, leaning against a covered winch, staring at the horizon below which the last of America had disappeared.

"Don't stand here, my dear Felicity. It's too cold. Come into the cabin."

The sails drummed above them. He put an arm tightly round her waist, taken again by her beauty, for all her present pallor.

She gave him a tortured look, then followed meekly. He kept one hand on her arm and the other on the rail. Noise was all about them, in sails and boat and sea, while his lungs rejoiced in the wild air. He was not going to be sea sick. There were minor victories of which no one knew. . . .

Even in the cabin, with the door closed, they could still hear the gallant sound of sails and rigging. Felicity stood looking so helpless that he became angry.

"You've fooled me, haven't you? You came with me simply to get to Earth. I was mad to expect anything else. You don't want anything further to do with me, do you?" He ran his hands through his wild hair.

"Don't try to drive me away, Edward. What you say is not true."

"Then tell me, for god's sake. Something's the matter. What is it?" He was shaking her angrily.

"All right, all right, you bastard! I'm not afraid of telling you—I'm afraid of your being unable to understand. . . . You are going to visit Li Kwang See, is that so?" Her face was set. She scowled at him.

"I told you it was so."

"Edward, Li Kwang See is my respected father."

"Your father?" They stared at each other meaninglessly. "Your father?" He did not know what to say. He went and gazed out of the small window at the hammering waves until he regained his voice.

"The minister is your father? Are you a member of the Chinese secret police, the Khang?" He turned to examine her. "You were put on to me when my holiday on Earth was first on the cards. Your agents probably heard about it before I did. I was *tricked* into choosing you."

"Edward, no, please don't think that. I'm nothing to do with the Khang, of course I'm not!"

"No? Wait—I know. It was that sneering thing Stein-Presteign said, moving me subtly towards you. This was all engineered by Callibrastics, so that someone would come along with me and see how I performed. Typical of them! You're paid by Callibrastics, aren't you?"

"No, Edward. I don't know anyone connected with your firm. It's just coincidence, nothing more. When you mentioned my father's name on the ferry to Earth, I could have died with astonishment. Literally, I could have died!"

"Yes? Then why didn't you say something then?" The tears in her eyes only made him more savage.

"I was just so amazed . . . I couldn't speak. I had to have time to think it over. But it really is just a coincidence. I cannot come to terms with it myself."

He shook his head. "You ask me to believe that? How many Chinese are there? Eight hundred million? And I pick on *you* by accident? I'd be mad ever to believe that."

"You must believe it. I have to believe it. Or else I have to believe that you sought me out just because you thought I would help you speak to my father and win his favour."

"Nonsense, I hired you by accident, through the Intern Agency! I didn't even ask for a Chinese girl."

"Well, then, and you came to seek me out by devious means

at FFFFA. *I* didn't seek *you* out. The advantage is with you, not me, and for me it's just as much of a coincidence as for you."

"An eight hundred million to one coincidence? It's a trick." Another thought struck him. "You're lying, aren't you? Li Kwang See *can't* be your father."

"He is, he is! Why are you so horrid? Your little scientific world's turned upside down."

They continued to argue. They ate no meal that evening. Finally they fell into their separate bunks exhausted, and slept. The morning made no difference. Still they argued.

For a whole sea-week they argued. Sea-sickness never touched them, so busy were they with the problem.

"This is ridiculous," Edward said at last. "After all, I know a great deal more about the laws of probability than you do, Felicity. I cannot believe that this is a coincidence; the odds are just too long against it. It runs counter to everything in my theory of non-randomness—I'd be mad to believe it."

"I'm fed up with your stupid little mathematical arguments,' she said wearily. She was pale and fatigued, huddled in the cabin's only armchair. "You're mad to let a coincidence, however big, get in the way of our love."

So exhausted were they that for a moment neither of them seemed to realize what she said. Then he looked at her again.

He began to smile. A great burden fell from him. She smiled back, concealing her nose and mouth with one small hand.

"Felicity, Zenith . . ." he said. He took her into his embrace, feeling her arms move about his neck as he kissed her, feeling her lips open and her slender body press against his.

"Oh, Felicity . . ." he whispered. They scrambled into the lower bunk, weeping and laughing and kissing.

XVIII

Edward never accepted the coincidence. By the end of the voyage, when they were adepts at love, he had come to live with it. But his mind still rejected it whenever the thought of it arose. It was as if he opened a familiar door and found that it led, not into the kitchen, but to the summit of Everest. It would always be there. He could not assimilate it.

Felicity adjusted more easily. As she explained, her view of life was in any case more random than Edward's. She positively skipped on to the Chinese shore at Hangchow.

The stinks and perfumes of the place amazed Edward, as well as its bustling life—private lives lived much more publicly than he was used to. He viewed it all with fascination and a little dread, realizing again how much of his urge to create a working PM stemmed from his own timidity, his suspicion of the new, the exotic. But with Felicity for guide, he felt entirely safe.

They spent that night in a small hotel overlooking the Grand Canal and next morning boarded a train for Peking. The train was pulled by an enormous steam engine and was spotlessly clean. As they waited in Hangchow station, little old ladies with faces wrinkled like contour maps of the Pyrenees sprang out of the ground and rubbed down windows and brass-work until everything gleamed. Then the express set off again through the great tamed tawny countryside.

To Edward Maine's eyes, Peking looked formidable, grim, and bleak, even in the fresh spring sunshine. At first it seemed like one more big monolithic capital, with its enormous squares, factories, and barracklike buildings. As they crossed Chang-an Square in a blue trolley-car, the wide spaces made him feel dizzy; but Felicity effected a partial cure by showing him slogans set in coloured tiles into the series of grey paving stones. She translated for him, squeezing his hand.

"You young people, full of vigour and vitality, are in the bloom of life, like the sun at eight or nine in the morning. The world belongs to you. China's future belongs to you. Mao Tse-Tung."

He liked the sentiment. It was still only nine-thirty, he thought.

The trolley-car took them past one of the great grey old watchtowers which had overlooked the city for a thousand years, to an older part of the town.

Felicity guided them to a small hotel in a side street where tourists rarely went, where the human scale was more to their taste.

"Oh, you will grow to love Peking, Edward. You see it was

never a motor-car city, like the big cities of America and even Europe; so now that the motor car has gone, the city remains as it always was, without malformations. Wait till you get used to it!"

"I don't want to get used to it. I like it all as it is now—novel in every stone."

It proved difficult to visit Li Kwang See officially. The Ministry for External Trade and Exotic Invisible Earnings was a gaunt grey building near the Tou Na Ting Park, its flanks patched by large-letter posters. It was eight storeys high and lacked elevators. Edward, clutching his letter of introduction from Stein-Presteign of Smics Callibrastics, took a whole day to work through junior officials on the ground floor up to senior officials on the top floor. The officials, dressed in grey or blue, were always smiling. One of them, greatly courteous—this was on the fifth floor, when Edward showed signs of impatience—said, "Naturally, we realize that Smics Callibrastics is very important, both to you and to the planetoid Fragrance II. Unfortunately, in our ignorance, we fail to have heard of the company, and so must remedy that error by applying to a better-informed department. You must try to excuse the delay."

He smiled back. The whole exercise, he thought, was beautifully designed to make him see matters in perspective. A Chinese perspective. He admired it, admired both the courtesy and the slight mystery—just as he admired those qualities in Felicity.

During his second day in the waiting-rooms and staircases of the Ministry of External Trade, it was revealed to him that the Minister himself was at present negotiating a trading agreement elsewhere, and that consequently the Ministry was unable to help him this week. They hoped that he would enjoy the simple pleasures of Peking, and that they might be able to assist him on another occasion. They presented him with a free ticket to a concert in the Park of Workers, Farmers and Soldiers.

"Oh, my father is so elusive!" Felicity exclaimed, when all this was reported to her. To relieve her feelings, she tore up the free ticket and scattered the pieces equably about the room.

"All these bureaucrats are the same. While you were languish-ing in that horrible building, I was speaking to some relations who live near here. They will try to trace my father. Mean-while, tonight they invite us both to a feast."

The feast was a glory in itself and successful as a social occasion. Among the multitudinous courses, many a toast was drunk to matters of mutual esteem, such as good health, lon-gevity, wisdom, freedom from indigestion, prosperity, and the success of trading enterprises. Edward blundered home after-wards, holding Felicity's hand down narrow lanes, sharing his new knowledge of China with her.

"You see, this part of the world is better off than anywhere else on Earth. This is China's century, as one of your uncles said. I suppose the same claim could be made back in history. But now China has come out from behind her wall. She's been well-organized and peaceful for millennia—that excellent Shantung wine must have helped in that respect. Even during the purges in Mao's time, there was a tradition of forgiving and even welcoming back those who confessed the error of their ways. And no other country got by without mechanization on China's scale—India is a rubbish-tip by comparison. So now that fossil fuels and metals are as rare as rubies, China is not faced with the massive need to adjust which confronts the West. Why, take that gorgeous roast sucking pig we had—it never needed an internal combustion machine! That lobster in prawn and ginger sauce—it had never been near a nuclear fusion plant! You can't tell me that that stuffed goat's udder ever drew up at a filling station and found it closed for lack of gasoline! . . ."

They climbed laughing into their hard broad bed. He fell asleep with his head on her soft narrow breast.

XIX

A smiling, reserved uncle on a bicycle brought them word that Brother See was in committee at No. 35 Flowering Vegetable Lane.

Edward went there. The lane managed to look almost as rustic as its name, although new concrete houses had been slotted in an ugly way behind the walls which sheltered tra-ditional homes of artisans.

It was evidently still necessary for him to get global matters into proper perspective. He sat out another session of waiting in a small upstairs room, looking out over concrete, grey-tiled eaves, dangling cables, a wooden house where two children played with a wooden doll, and a pigsty which contained five small porkers and a flowering cherry. He liked it.

His read-out that morning had told him he would sight his quarry today; but he remained sceptical of anything the PM said until he could feed it up-to-date programming. However, at three-thirty, a small procession of men in pallid business suits walked in dignity through the waiting-room. One of them had a face like a squeezed lemon and looked at Edward with a marked gaze as he passed; that would be the minister, Felicity's father.

My father-in-law? he asked himself. That would depend on how the interview went, among other things.

Mindful of his manners, he followed respectfully down the stairs. An old car like a hearse waited outside on the cobbles. A lackey sprang to open doors and the company climbed in. The hearse drove off.

As Edward stood watching it go, preparing to be at least a little angry, the lackey came up and offered him a small yellow envelope. He tore it open. Inside was a square of card. On it, printed, the legend: Minister for External Trade and Exotic Invisible Earnings. Beneath it in a perfect script were the words, "Happy prognostications show that we shall meet soon in more harmonious surroundings".

"He must have a better PM than I have, then," Edward said, stuffing the envelope into his pocket. But the message pleased him, nevertheless.

When he showed the card to Felicity, she chewed the edge of it and puckered her brow in thought. To please Edward, she had gone out and bought a cheongsam, although she protested that the garment was wildly old-fashioned and, in any case, not true Chinese but invented in Manchester, England, for the benefit of the cotton trade. In this garment, as she lounged in a cane chair, she looked perfectly provocative. He went over and stroked her thigh.

"My father is a wily old fox," she said. "This is what I

think. He did not expect that you would grasp all the implications of this message. But he guessed that you would bring it to me, and that I would understand it. The message shows that he is inharmonious here, therefore he wishes to get away for a while. You see, he prefers philosophy to trade. So he will go to our coastal house in Chin Hsiang, in the Chekiang Province. He has learned from the pedalling uncle whom you met that we are together, so he expects us both to join him informally."

"It *must* have been more than coincidence that we came together. Otherwise how should I manage?"

"If you are grateful, then never, tell my honoured father that I was once Internal-girl and had men peering at the inside of my magnified private organs!"

"Shall I ever see those delicious organs again?"

"You will have to make do with your pornographic still photographs of them. So, let's pack up and go to Chin Hsiang."

"It should be good there at this time of year. How far is it?"

"Only two and a half thousand kilometres by rail. A full day's journey on the train. Lin, you are very idle while in China, so you may tell us a story while we pack up."

"I have a story called 'Justice Performed'," said the lin.

"It sounds like a good omen for Edward. Let us have it in an alto voice this time. Proceed." She gave the machine a mock-formal bow.

"Flight was impossible where perverted justice ruled. 'Let us return with honour to the volcano,' cried the lusty silver band of oldest harlots. 'Let us build the weaving mills among the mountains.' Next year, musical patterns led to familiarity. Falcons brought spring. Towering photographers performed before the strong ruler. Sleep came."

"That's very sweet," Felicity said. "You know, Edward, it would be both politic and polite if you give a present to my father when you meet. Why don't you donate this antiquated lin to him?"

"It's worth nothing. I'd be ashamed to present him with something so limited."

She smiled and said, "Of the lin as of humans, the attraction lies in the limitations and in the maximum that can be achieved within those limitations. I hate my brother's toy paintings because he cowers within his limitations, but this lin is bold and imaginative within *his*, and my father would surely appreciate such a gift."

Edward clapped his hands together. "Then it shall be done. Lin, you are to have a more appreciative master."

"We are all in the fiery hands of God," said the lin.

XX

Chin Hsiang was a quiet agricultural town, built where two canals met. There were inviting hills to the south, their lower slopes sculpted into paddy terraces which flowed like living contour lines. The town itself was set partly on a hill. The modest house of the Li Kwang family was half-way up this rising ground, its wooden gate opening on a square. Blossom trees were flowering everywhere. Lying to the east, and tiny in the distance, was a bay of the sea.

"It's one of the loveliest places I've ever seen," Edward exclaimed. He went and walked in the square under the midday sun. There were a few stalls in the centre of the square, tended by stalwart peasant women, who offered gay paper toys, picture books, chillis and blue-shelled eggs and toads in baskets, pallid lettuce and withered tomatoes, huge radishes, bright green peppers, and little fish speared on reeds. Beside them were barrels and pots and colourful animals dangling on strings.

The whole picture pleased him. An ochre-walled lane led down from the square, a cobbled stair led up. The houses had tiled roofs. It reminded him of something, but of precisely what he could not recollect. He felt at home there.

That afternoon, they went to meet Felicity's father, the Minister. His bungalow overlooked a secluded courtyard shared by the main house. Felicity led Maine to a bare room at the rear of the bungalow, where a small fire burned. The fire was of sticks and peat; real flames played there, real ash fell. Maine, long accustomed to the mock-fire in his homapt on Fragrance II, gazed at it with astonishment; he had lived too much of his life between fireproof doors.

The delicate noises of the fire emphasized the quiet of the

room. There was one window, which looked out at the courtyard without admitting much light. Beneath the window was
a large desk of polished wood. Behind the desk stood a small
man dressed in an old-fashioned grey suit. He made a small
bow as Maine stepped forward. It was the official Maine had
seen in the ministry in Peking, his face wrinkled like a lemon,
his eyes guilty and gentle like a reindeer's.

When the ceremony of greeting was over, Felicity brought
them some wine and the men sat down facing one another.

"There is something eternal about China," Edward said,
embarking with verve upon a flattering speech. "I am very
pleased to be here. Of all civilizations, yours weathers the ages
best. You have accepted time as a natural element. In the West,
time is a challenge. We've treated it that way ever since the
Renaissance. The Renaissance has provided our great fund
of ideas over the past few centuries. I mean the dynamic ideas
of humanism, individualism, and speculations about the external world. You could say that the impulse which sprang
from the prosperous families of Italy in the fifteenth century
led us eventually to space travel, and so to the Zodiacal Planets,
which are like little city states.

"But we're in trouble now that that questing spirit has
brought about the exhaustion of fossil oil and mineral deposits.
Some say that America and the West are played out. I don't
believe so. But I do believe the times are temporarily against
us, and that we are having to weather a storm of our own cre-
ating. Whereas China sails grandly on as if time does not exist."

He paused several times during this speech, inserting gaps
and "ums", as he tried to remember what he wanted to say.
He was not good at big theories, and had to recall what the
eloquent Stein-Presteign would have said in similar circumstances.

"You are generous in your comments," Li Kwang See
replied. "The strength of China lies in her land, and in the
peasants that work it. There is nothing else. Possibly in the
West you have been too arrogant with your land, and have not
understood its meaning and importance. The big businessman
has possibly been more revered than the small farmer, if I may
so comment. However, as to time, let me relate to you an

amusing incident which illustrates that time can stand still even in your ever-moving country.

"Whenever I am in Houston, Texas, I visit the elegant museum there to look at one thing and one thing only. That object is an eighth-century vase of the T'ang dynasty. When I regard that vase, the material and the spiritual come together and I am restored. The last time I was there, standing by the vase, a guide came along with a bunch of tourists, and he said to them, 'This beautiful vase is thirteen hundred years old.' Now, when I was there fifteen years earlier, that same guide announced to another bunch of tourists, 'This beautiful vase is thirteen hundred years old.' So, you see, time has been standing absolutely still in the Houston Museum for at least fifteen years."

Edward wondered if he cared for the humour of foreigners, but professed to enjoy the story. He then produced the lin with due formality.

Li Kwang admired the curlicues of its plasticwork and Edward asked the machine if it had a suitable story for its new master.

"New master, I have an exciting story for you," said the lin. "It is called 'Old Regiments'. The regiments with goat eyes came among the valleys. Lonely old officers cried among the royal courts because taxation returned. 'The export market is a dinosaur; it increases the flight from towering ideals,' one said. But the magnesium airports changed towns. Volcanoes were built. Promises were obliterated. Girls put their arms demandingly round old fathers."

"Very pretty—although we hope that exports are not necessarily in conflict with towering ideals," said Li Kwang, smiling politely and hiding his mouth behind his hand.

"At least we can make part of the story come true," said Felicity, going over to hug her parent. "You see, girls put their arms demandingly round old fathers. Daddy, you must listen to what Edward has to say about his invention, the prediction machine, because it is very important for him that you approve of it. Tell him, Edward."

So Edward embarked on an explanation of the principles of the PM. He described how the prototype worked. He put it frankly that the PM represented a large financial investment, and that his corporation would be greatly assisted if they knew in advance that they would be able to export and sell the machine on Earth as well as among the zeepees—a matter on which he understood Li Kwang's word to be all-important.

For most of this speech, Li Kwang listened while gazing out at the courtyard, where a shower of rain was falling.

When Edward had finished, he gestured to his daughter to pour more wine.

"My word is a poor thing," he said. "You must not set too much store by it. Your invention sets great store by words. We are all aware of the power of words and must bow to them, but we should seek escape from their demands when we can. It is mistaken to fall even more into their power. Words must be staunched with silence."

"Daddy, let us talk philosophy later. First, you must say yes to Edward."

He smiled at her reproof, his face wrinkling into an even closer resemblance to a lemon, a humorous lemon. "It is precisely because this is a philosophical matter that I am not able to say yes to our guest, vexing though that is for me." He leaned forward and said to Edward, "Mr Maine, you probably know that in China we already have a method of guidance for every day of the year. I will not call it prediction, but prediction is possibly a misnomer also for your prototype, seeing that it interpolates advice among its percentages. Our method of divination is based on one of the sacred books of the Orient, the *I Ching*—or *Book of Changes*, as it is known in the West. The *I Ching* is almost four thousand years old and still regularly consulted. It is a permanent source of wisdom, as well as a daily guide."

"Oh, I know about the *I Ching*, sir, and I assure you we wouldn't want to put it out of business," said Edward hastily.

"That is kind of you. Most considerate. However, the problem lies elsewhere. You see, your invention dramatically embodies a basic conflict between East and West, whether you realize it or not."

Taking alarm at this, Edward said, "I certainly do not realize it, sir. With the ability to see ahead a little, men should be less in conflict."

"Allow me to make myself clear. Your machine is very elaborate in itself. It has complex diagnostic elements, and of course it relies on a power input. Then, it is not really effective unless its data is kept current by daily bulletins from a computer system, thus encouraging centralism. All told, it is most ingenious and will for that reason always be expensive and cumbersome; ever more pertinently, it will merely intensify the self-generating nature of Western technology—technology demands more technology."

"But—"

"On the other hand, here is my modest divination machine."

Li Kwang rose, turned to the north-facing wall behind him, and lifted a black package from a shelf set at shoulder height. He set this on his desk. From the same shelf, he took a container of carved cherry-wood, and placed it beside the package.

He opened the package, which was a book wrapped in a square of black silk. "This is my copy of the *I Ching*," he said.

He opened the container. A number of polished sticks lay inside. "These are fifty twigs of the common yarrow, which I gathered myself in a Chin Hsiang hedgerow. They and the book constitute the world's best-tried method of divination.

"I need only these. Oh, I also need a little time and thought, and maybe a little interpretation from Confucius. But that's all."

Maine laughed. "Without wishing to sound scornful, Minister, when our PM is perfected, it will cause you to wrap your book up and put it back on its shelf for good. A four-thousand-year-old book can't take much account of today's hormone levels, can it now?"

"Nor will your machine ever be advanced enough to enable us to grasp something of the sensuous cycles and rhythms of nature which shape our inner being, or help us to live in harmony with our surroundings, as does the *I Ching*."

As he said this, Li Kwang slowly folded up the book and closed the box of yarrow sticks. He replaced them on their appointed shelf.

Maine told himself that this was merely a discussion, and

he must not grow angry. He glanced at Felicity, but she had moved tactfully to the window and was staring out at the rain.

"Maybe our PM is a bit more accurate than your yarrow sticks," he said. "At least it works on a scientific principle. It's rational, it doesn't grow in hedgerows. Once we fully grasp the laws of chance and can predict coincidences, then we'll be almost one hundred per cent accurate."

"And of course you see that as important. Yet in part you work on something called the Uncertainty Principle! Now that is very much how the *I Ching* works. The uncertainty is essential, forcing us to learn; otherwise we would all be robots, utterly predictable in a universe where every event is as foreseeable as a railway line."

"You are making excuses for the inaccuracy of the *I Ching* by saying that. We do not excuse our inaccuracy; we aim to eradicate it. We want accuracy—and we're getting it. What's more, we have only been working on this project for a decade, whereas you've had four thousand years!"

"Frankly, accuracy is one of the most destructive targets of the West. Also, you must realize that to work with devotion on something for four thousand years is very instructive, whether it is a rice field or an item of philosophical debate."

"Yes, but if the concept is all wrong . . . I mean, I don't want to knock the *I Ching*, but I do know that the Chinese have claimed that it has predicted all the great Western inventions, like electricity and nuclear energy. That seems nonsense to me."

"Forgive me, but it seems to me nonsense to say that the West invented electricity and nuclear energy. Both natural forces have always been around, and were around even four thousand years ago."

"A slip of the tongue. I meant that we harnessed them. What I was going to say was, if you believe that the *I Ching* is true, that it functions effectively, then you should not mind the PM being sold on Earth, because it will not supersede your system. We maintain that millions of people who will live under the World State will be unable to use or believe in the *I Ching*, and so will turn to the PM for guidance. Besides, we are not in competition. If we make a little money, you do not lose it, because nobody makes any money from *I Ching*, as you yourself admit."

"That is one great attraction of our ancient system. It is diffusive and not profit-cumulative."

Maine gave up for a moment, and took a deep swig of the wine.

"May I ask if you got a prediction on our little meeting and how it turned out, Mr Maine?" Li Kwang asked.

"Well, you know this prototype is rather cumbersome; we didn't want to bring it on the train, so we've left it in Peking for the time being. Eventually, we hope to get the production model down to the size of a small radio. But I'm sure it would have said, 'Persistence needed, do not yield to impatience.' "

Both men laughed.

"In the circumstances, I consulted the sticks to see how I ought to conduct our discussion," said Li Kwang. "My six sticks which I drew gave me the two trigrams of the Khien hexagram. Let me show you with match sticks."

He drew a box of matches from his gown and from it extracted six purple matches with yellow heads. He lined them up neatly together, parallel and not touching.

"There you are, the Khien hexagram. Six long sticks. No need to break a single match."

"What does it mean?"

"It symbolizes a lot of things. This undivided stick being lowest represents a dragon hidden. That is to say, it is not a time for activity. Maybe that signifies my coming to Chin Hsiang for a bit of a rest."

"Go on."

"I should also say that the whole hexagram represents some great originating power from heaven. That surely indicates that *you* are being considered, having arrived from space. Dragons also represent great men, and this second line shows there is an advantage in our meeting. The third line is difficult and vague. It could indicate that much talk goes on over the day and that by evening apprehension remains. Taken in conjunction with what follows, it indicates that I should avoid what is error in my eyes. And so on. . . . The dragon goes beyond the proper limits."

"Is that dragon you or me?"

"It could be me. If I behave properly in respect to the demands made on me, then a proper state of equipoise and fortune will be reached. That is a reference to your request to sell your machine here, of course."

Maine clenched his fists together. He longed to sweep the feeble little sticks away. But at that moment, a servant entered the room and announced that a light meal was served.

Li Kwang would talk only on general topics during the meal. He was smiling and polite, and received without emotion the toned-down version Felicity gave him of Shi Tok's behaviour on Fragrance.

"He sent you one of his paintings, father," Felicity said. She produced it. It was one of the oblongs of garsh; a band of an intermediate brown had been painted across it. "Shi Tok says it is called *The Benefits of a Fast-Paced Sleep*."

For a long moment, Li Kwang studied the plaque. "I shall look at it later and derive benefit from it," he said. Then he went on placidly eating his rice.

When they reassembled after lunch, Maine was feeling desperate.

"May I say, sir, that I was asked to come and speak to you because naturally my corporation wants to know the size of their market before investing their capital. I was not happy to represent them in such a matter. My strong feeling is that we should now shelve this discussion, because it is premature. If you will permit, I should like to come back in, say, a couple of years, when we have a PM model which will impress you more than anything I can say."

"Since you are frank with me, I will be frank with you. I will speak as your friend and as Felicity's father. It is not your machine to which there is a fundamental objection, but to the thinking behind it."

"But you do not yet know how reliable it can be, whereas— forgive my saying this—you demonstrated the vagueness of the *I Ching* just before lunch."

Li Kwang bowed his head. "My daughter will excuse me if I make a philosophical point. Ultimately, it does not matter whether or not the *Book of Changes* is 'true' in any empirical sense. Those who consult it value the way the book speaks to the older, less logical areas of the mind. It is a map to behaviour, not behaviour itself. Whereas you are producing, or trying to, a behaviour substitute. Further, it does not matter whether our map is 'truthful' or not since, if all accept the co-ordinates, then the map becomes reliable through general concurrence."

"Are you saying that if the map is inaccurate and leads you to fall into a ditch, you will all pretend there is no ditch?"

"No. I am saying that if all agree to believe in a certain god, then his power over men's minds is the same whether he exists or not. We do not believe in a god, but we have a belief in belief itself. That remains comfortably constant. Whereas you would be perpetually altering your procedures, adding new scraps of knowledge, new theories of chance. . . ."

"Sir, that's not a valid objection. It simply means that new models would be needed from time to time—to the benefit of our clients, our shareholders, and the corporation. I hope your fundamental objection is not that we shall make money?"

"That is part of my objection, yes. All over America, to this very day, you still come on piles of old scrap automobiles or washing machines. And the useless motorways, mile after mile. All obsolete technology that exploited people in various ways to benefit corporations. In the World State, we plan to live in poverty, as China has always done. There will be no room for extravagant gadgets."

Clutching his head, Maine groaned. "You mean you're actually legislating for poverty! You'll have a world full of peasants in one generation. . . ."

"Ah, but in the second generation, we can build from a position of equality."

"You'll drive out all the initiative to the zeepees. There will be nobody to build for you."

"I'm sure you know the answer to that, Mr Maine. We shall build for ourselves. Nobody has ever helped us, and nobody has to help us now. Western know-how will be very welcome—but it will have to concentrate on the things that are real, and not on illusions."

"You are looking at all this from a very Chinese point of view."

"In case you think I am indulging in an idle East-West

hassle, let me say that you could easily come to appreciate that point of view yourself. You admit that your attitude to life is not your firm's. One understands that you personally are not exploitive or aggressive, if I may say so—although you are a unit of an exploitive and aggressive society. I read in you characteristics of humility and endurance which would find ready welcome here. You should not waste them on a corporation which battens on your talents while secretly despising you."

Maine stood up. "Sir, I have taken up too much of your time. I can see that you are dead set against my invention and the capitalist society. I will report what you say to my managing director when I get home."

"As you will. Can the lin tell you a pleasant story before we part?"

"Thanks, but no thanks." He turned and left the room, marched out of the front door, through the yard, and into the road. The rain had stopped and the late afternoon sun shone brightly. He walked briskly to the square. As he went, he heard running steps behind him. Presently, Felicity caught up with him and took his arm.

"Oh, Edward, father has made you angry! I'm so sorry! He didn't say a definite No. You should have discussed longer with him and reached an accommodation."

"I'm sorry, Felicity, I don't want to talk about it. Of all the stubborn and difficult old—oh, I know it wasn't up to him personally. He was just speaking as a Minister. Jees, how hidebound can you get? This is just too difficult to believe, Felicity. I mean even fifty years ago I might have expected to meet up with such awful anti-Western nonsense . . ., and all that old crap about the mystique of China . . . China! What's so special about China? How's it any different from America?"

"Some say that the Americans raped their continent, whereas we have always had to serve or be raped by ours."

"Whose side are you on?" he asked, and then broke into angry laughter. "Let's get away for a while. My head's bursting. Let's go and look at the sea."

"It's farther than you think. It may be dark before we get there."

"Stop talking in that defeatist Chinese fashion. Let's go."

They took the ochre-walled lane down from the square, and came along by one of the canals. Then the track took them away among the fields. They climbed a hill where slack-eyed peasant women walked home pushing babies and wood on the handlebars of their bicycles. Where merging tracks joined, an aged man sat by a small locker on wheels, a paper umbrella above his head. Felicity bought two ice creams from him, but Edward was nervous of his and threw it away.

As they climbed the slope, planting their feet firmly on the well-trodden ochre soil, Edward said, "You know what will happen? I can predict quite easily. In a way, your father's view makes sense; I have to admit it. His is basically the view of conservative people everywhere. But, pushed to its logical conclusion, such a view stifles initiative. The World State will kill initiative."

"End of Renaissance?"

"Very definitely. China never had a renaissance, I gather?"

"We had a revolution."

"Maybe your renaissance is to come. . . . What is going to happen is that more and more positive-thinking people will migrate to the zeepees. And from there they will be driven outwards, to look for new fields to explore."

There was a small silence. Then she said, "My father is not a fool. He knows that what you call positive-thinking people always move outwards. He relies on that."

"He has a funny way of showing it."

"He has the only way of showing it. Men have dreamed of a World State for centuries. Now it is coming. It must have time to settle down, to get into working order. For a while, it needs stasis rather than progress. How can you achieve that without smothering the progressives? Why, by driving them out. They'll survive and profit by isolation."

"Like little city states," he said. Irreconcilable points of view existed and were necessary: maybe what was unnecessary was that either side should lose by the conflict.

Their way was downhill now, and the sea glittered through spring foliage. As they trotted forward, they lost the sun behind the shoulder of the hill to their rear. The track took them round a copse of flowering tung trees, and the ocean stretched ahead.

On it were three sailing ships, their sails still tinged with sunset pink, although the water was grey.

"Oh, that looks so wonderful!" Felicity cried. "That's what we came to Earth for!"

"Better than your artificial oceans?" He took her slender arm.

"Yes, and those are the automated windjammers I told you about."

He counted the masts. Five masts apiece, most of the canvas out to catch the evening breeze.

"Heading for Shanghai or the ports of the Yellow Sea," she said.

They stood and looked at each other as the dark came on.

"Do you think your father understands as much as you claim he does—that Western ideas are vitally necessary to mankind?"

"I'm sure he read it in his Khien hexagram. It is a fundamental truth that most wise people have always realized: East and West are necessary to each other, like yin and yang."

"Now you are speaking metaphorically."

She shook her head. "No, I was speaking personally, if you must know."

They lay down together on the edge of the cliff, and dark came on.

Out to sea, the sailing ships faded away, heading for unknown harbours. Overhead, as the sky darkened, the stars began to spread. Venus stood out sharply, and then the familiar constellations. But far eclipsing them was a great halo going clear into distance, comprising hundreds of brilliant points of light. The darker the sky grew, the more brightly the Zodiacal Planets shone, ringing in the Earth.

The World State would come into being. Every night, the eyes of its citizens would be directed upwards, above the hayricks and the sullen chimney-tops.

733961

733961

823.0876

Anticipations / edited by Christopher
   Priest. New York : Scribner, c1978.
   214 p. ; 21 cm.
   CONTENTS.--Watson, I. The very slow
time machine.--Sheckley, R. Is that
what people do?--Shaw, B. Amphitheatre.
--Priest, C. The negation.--Harrison,
H. The greening of the green.--Disch,
T. M. Mutability.--Ballard, J. G. One
afternoon at Utah Beach.--Aldiss, B. W.
A Chinese perspective.

   1. Science fiction, English.
2. Science fiction, American.
I. Priest, Christopher.

GA   30 JAN 79   4269023   GAPApc   78-52223